WAR ANGEL CONTINGENT

THE EVERLASTING FIRE SERIES
BOOK1

BY
INTERNATIONAL
BESTSELLING AUTHOR

S.J. WEST

CONTENTS

COPYRIGHTS

ISBN-13: 978-1548445478

Cover Design: Paper & Sage Design, all rights reserved.
Interior Design & Formatting: Stephany Wallace, all rights reserved.
Proof Reader: Allisyn Ma.

Published by Watchers Publishing July, 2017.

www.Sjwest.com

BOOKS IN THE WATCHERS SERIES

The Watchers Trilogy

Cursed

Blessed

Forgiven

The Watcher Chronicles

Broken

Kindred

Oblivion

Ascension

Caylin's Story

Timeless

Devoted

Aiden's Story

The Alternate Earth Series

Cataclysm

Uprising

Judgment

The Redemption Series

Malcolm

Anna

LIST OF BOOKS IN THE WATCHER SERIES

Lucifer
Redemption

The Dominion Series

Awakening
Reckoning
Enduring

The Everlasting Fire Series

War Angel Contingent

OTHER BOOKS BY S.J. WEST

The Harvester of Light Trilogy

Harvester

Hope

Dawn

The Vankara Saga

Vankara

Dragon Alliance

War of Atonement

Vampire Conclave Series

Moonshade

Sentinel

ACKNOWLEDGMENTS

I would like to express my gratitude to the many people who were with me throughout this creative process; to all those who provided support, talked things over, read, wrote, offered comments, allowed me to quote their remarks and assisted in the editing, proofreading and design.

I would like to thank Lisa Fejeran, Liana Arus, Karen Healy-Friday, Misti Monen, and Erica Croyle, my beta readers for helping me in the process with invaluable feedback.

Thanks to Allisyn Ma, my proofreader for helping me find typos, correct commas and tweak the little details that have help this book become my perfect vision. Thank you to Stephany Wallace for creating the Interior Design of the books and formatting them.

Last and not least: I want to thank my family, who supported and encouraged me in this journey.

I apologize to those who have been with me over the course of the years and whose names I have failed to mention.

CHAPTER 1

"I thought you said she was here, Enis."

"That's what I was told, Evelyn," Enis replies with a heavy sigh of disappointment. "The guard watching the cabin's security camera footage said he saw Jules in here raiding the liquor cabinet."

"Grab all the bottles out of the cabinet and take them back to Grace House," Evelyn instructs him, sounding irritated. "We don't need to indulge her need for self-destruction. You would think after five years she would have gotten over what happened to Timothy."

"How does anyone get over someone they love dying like that?" he questions her. "Especially someone like Jules."

Evelyn sighs. "I don't know, but drowning herself in alcohol isn't going to magically make all of her pain go away. I'm just not sure when she'll realize that fact."

"Jules is strong," Enis says confidently. "She'll come around in time."

"Well, until that miracle occurs, I refuse to encourage her drinking habit. Grab what you can and meet me back home."

Evelyn phases out of the room while Enis walks over to the liquor cabinet against the far wall of the living room. He bends down and opens the doors to peer inside. After seeing more than twenty bottles of alcohol, he whistles in amazement and shakes his head. He closes the doors, stands to his full height, and places his hands on top of the cabinet before phasing, presumably deciding it's the easiest way to take the large number of bottles back with him.

I lean away from the edge of the picture window and prop my back up against the wood planks on the outside of the cabin, exhaling a sigh of relief. I didn't want to face my mom or Uncle Enis. Especially not tonight of all nights. I lift up the bottle of vodka in my right hand and take a long swig, both loving and despising the burning sensation the liquid makes as it clears a path from my mouth straight to my stomach. After drinking my fill, I walk over to the edge of the back porch and sit down heavily on the top step of the stairs that lead down to the backyard. I faintly take note of the axe jutting out from the stump of a felled tree. I don't remember putting it there and can only assume it was something the previous occupants of my abandoned home left behind. I wanted to sell this cabin, but my mom talked me out of it. She reminded me that not all of my memories associated with this house were bad ones. Once upon a time, it was a happy home, filled with love and possibilities for a bright future.

I take another swig of vodka to blur a frequent unwanted visitor of mine: guilt.

"Does that help?" a strange woman's voice asks unexpectedly.

I look up and see the woman standing beside the axe and tree trunk I just noticed. Her long blonde hair hangs straight past her shoulders. She's wearing a black empire waist dress with short, beaded sleeves and a long flowing skirt. Her right hand is resting on the knob of the axe handle, and I vaguely wonder if she intends to pull it out and kill me with it. I know exactly who she is because I was counting on her to eventually come back here one day.

"Hello, Helena," I say with a slight slur. "Fancy meeting you here."

Helena tilts her head to the left as she scrutinizes my disheveled appearance. It occurs to me that I haven't bathed in three days and probably look and smell as horrible as I feel. Whatever. My puny existence may be snuffed out in the next few seconds anyway, so it doesn't really matter. As a reflex, I use my free hand to brush some wayward strands of hair hanging over my face to the side. As I watch Helena continuing to observe me, I find myself wishing my hair was the same color blonde as hers. Even in just the light given off by the moon, it glistens with an otherworldly luster. That combined with the glow of her flawless pale skin and sparkling blue eyes gives the misguided impression she's an angel sent straight from Heaven, instead of being Hell itself personified in human form.

"I've seen you before," she says, narrowing her eyes on me. "In Evelyn Grace's nightclub. You're her daughter, right? This cabin used to belong to you and your late husband."

"Score two points for the little lady," I reply sarcastically. "She's right on both counts."

Helena straightens her head and tilts it down slightly as her stare becomes more sinister. "I wouldn't be impertinent with me if I were you. Since you know my name, I assume you realize what I can do to you."

"Kill me?" I scoff. "Bring it on, sister. At least it would save me the trouble of figuring out how to do it myself. This stuff," I say, holding up the vodka bottle, "is the coward's way out. It's probably the slowest suicide of all time, but it has to work its magic eventually, right?"

Helena narrows her eyes at me but not angrily. What I've said seems to have piqued her curiosity. Honestly, I'm not sure if that's even more dangerous than her wrath.

"And what tiny human problem has caused you to feel so apathetic about your mortality?" she asks.

"One that you can probably sympathize with," I reply cautiously, watching for her reaction to my next words. "I killed the man I loved."

Helena remains deathly still, not giving away any emotional response to my confession. She continues to stare at me as she asks, "Well, since it's obvious you know my story, I think it's only fair that you tell me yours. How exactly did you kill your mate?"

To buy myself some time to contemplate whether or not I want to answer her question, I bring the lip of my vodka bottle up to my mouth and drink what's left until it's completely dry. By that time, my mind is so fuzzy I actually forget what it was we were talking about.

Since the bottle in my hand is useless to me now, I let it slip from my fingers and roll down the wooden steps to the ground.

"Well?" Helena asks rather aggressively. "How did you kill him?"

When I look up at her again, I find three Helenas staring at me now. I have to squint to squeeze them all together into one figure.

"What's it to you?" I ask her belligerently, throwing caution to the wind with my tone. "Why do you want to know so badly?"

Helena shrugs a delicate shoulder. "I'm curious to know whether or not your soul will be mine one day," she states simply.

I lean to my left and rest my head and shoulder against the wooden post of the porch railing before closing my eyes so I don't have to look at Helena's expectant face.

"Maybe it will," I answer. "Maybe it won't. I'm not sure what side of the fence my soul is on to tell you the truth."

"Why don't you tell me what you did and let me judge your fate," she suggests.

"And ruin the surprise?" I try to joke as I force myself to open my eyes again and look at her. "Now why would I want to do that? There are so few surprises in life. I don't think I want to ruin the last one I'll ever have."

"You *do* realize who I am, don't you?" she asks threateningly. "I can make you tell me the story by force, but trust me when I say that you'll wish you were dead afterwards."

"That type of threat doesn't really work on me," I tell her wearily, closing my eyes again. "Whatever you do to me, I deserve it for what I did to Timothy. In fact, do your worst. I've earned it."

Seconds pass. Then minutes. Helena remains silent, and I assume she's probably phased away. When I open my eyes again, I'm surprised to find her standing at the foot of the stairs, studying me as though I'm an insect she's considering stepping on.

"Do it," I dare her, half hoping she'll take me up on my offer.

Unexpectedly, Helena smiles. "Although I would love nothing better than to torture you, I get the feeling *not* torturing you will hurt even more. You're too eager to die, and I'm afraid that takes all the fun out of it for me."

In what seems like an unconscious move, I watch as she rests her hands on the prominent baby bulge jutting out from her otherwise slim figure.

"They're looking for you, you know," I tell her. "Those War Angels from Earth. They seem pretty desperate to take your baby away from you."

"I'm aware of their idiotic quest," Helena says as if the subject bores her. "They've been using my Nexus to search for me, as if I can't sense what they're doing there."

"I assume you phased outside the cabin because you know they have cameras set up on the inside."

"Exactly."

"What I don't understand is why you came back here at all. He isn't here, you know. He's dead, and he's never coming back."

Helena's smile slips as her expression returns to a reserved one.

"I'm fully aware of that fact," she informs me tersely. "And why, pray tell, are you here? I was told you abandoned this cabin after your husband died."

I shrug. "I guess I keep hoping I'll find something that will trigger a memory about our lives together that I've forgotten about. It would be like being given one last gift of time from him."

"It doesn't sound like you're deserving of a gift considering you're somehow responsible for his death."

"If he's forgiven me for what I did, I will."

Helena begins to laugh, and I inwardly cringe at the sound it makes. Her laughter resonates like the cries of thousands of tortured souls. I don't know if that's actually how it sounds or if my own guilt is causing me to filter it that way.

"Would you like to share what you find so funny?" I ask her angrily. I don't know why I told Helena, of all people, why I keep coming back to the cabin. Not even my mom or Uncle Enis know the real reason.

"I just deem it amusing that you think the dead can tell you anything beyond the grave, much less leave you a loving keepsake that will absolve your soul of its guilt. Thank you for sharing your delusion with me. I was in desperate need of a good laugh."

"I guess it takes a rare talent to make the queen bitch of Hell laugh. Should I take it as a compliment?"

"I wouldn't."

"Oh well, I guess a girl can't have everything."

"No one person can have everything."

"Not even someone as powerful as you?"

Helena is silent for a few seconds before replying, "Least of all me."

I watch as her gaze drifts up to the second floor of the cabin.

"I see you had the window I broke repaired," she comments dryly.

"My mother had it fixed."

"Did she also replace the piano I shoved through it?"

"No. I told her not to bother."

Helena looks at me quizzically before asking, "Was there a reason why you didn't want a new one?"

"It was my husband's piano. I don't play. So there was no reason to replace it."

"One less thing of his for you to dispose of, I suppose."

"Yeah. I guess."

I notice Helena grimace slightly, as if she just experienced an unexpected pain. She rubs the front of her belly up and down as if to soothe an ache.

"Baby kicking?" I ask out of politeness.

"Yes. He kicks quite often now. I believe he's ready to be born."

"Yeah. That's what I figured. The War Angels have tripled the bounty for you in the last few days. Whenever someone does that, it means they're running out of time to find the person they're looking for."

"I can't believe they put a bounty out on me," Helena says with a contemptuous roll of her eyes. "It makes me sound like I'm a common criminal."

"Maybe that's the way they see you. You did kill one of their own kind."

"But not on purpose," Helena is quick to clarify.

"Either way you look at it, Cade is dead and you're the one who killed him, whether you meant to or not. In their eyes, I don't think it really matters. All I know is that there's a lot of money to be made off bringing you in before that baby is born, and I intend to take the Empress of Cirrus' cash one day."

"That's laughable," Helena scoffs. "A drunkard like *you* bringing *me* in. How exactly do you intend to do that?"

"Oh, I didn't say I would be the one to bring you in, just cash in on the bounty."

"Same question: How do you intend to work that miracle?"

"I wouldn't be much of a bounty hunter if I told you all of my trade secrets."

Helena winces again, but this time her breathing pattern changes and she acts like she can't take in a deep breath. I stand from my seat and hold onto the railing as I make my way down the four steps to her. She's bent over slightly at the waist as she tries to compose herself.

"Do you need a doctor?" I ask her, lightly cupping her bent elbow with one hand to help steady her.

Helena shakes her head vigorously. "No. I don't need a doctor."

"Have you even been to a doctor since you found out you were pregnant?"

"No," she says with finality, as if it's a closed subject.

"If this is an abnormal pain, you need to go see a doctor," I advise her.

"Nothing about this pregnancy has been natural," she assures me. "I don't need a doctor to tell me something I already know."

It only takes me a second to figure out why Helena is refusing medical attention.

"Are you scared of what they'll tell you about the baby?" I ask her. "I overheard some of the War Angels placing bets on whether it will come out looking human or like something else."

"And I will make them regret placing wagers on my child's well-being," Helena says vehemently between labored breaths.

"I don't think they meant any disrespect to the baby," I reply, "just to you."

"I could care less what those half-wits think about me," Helena declares. "And you can tell them that they're fools if they believe I'll willingly hand over my son to them."

"How do you know it's a boy?" I ask in surprise. "I thought you said you hadn't been to a doctor yet. Did you do a ultrasound on yourself or something to find out?"

"I don't need to look at him," she tells me, wrenching her elbow out of my grasp. "I just know."

Helena phases to points unknown by me, because I'm not an angel, but I do know a couple who can follow the phase trail she left behind. As quickly as my alcohol-numbed legs will take me, I head back into the cabin's interior. As soon as I step inside through the backdoor, I wave at the camera stationed on the opposite wall, knowing the guard on duty ordered to keep watch will see me and get word to either Uncle Enis or my mother that the prodigal daughter has returned.

I lean against the door opening to wait for someone to show up. Less than a minute passes before the dynamic duo make their appearance.

Of course my mother shows up impeccably dressed. She's wearing a well-tailored white pantsuit that would look silly on any other woman her age. Her long blonde hair is styled loosely in waves that cascade past her shoulders. The look of disapproval on her face is the only thing marring her beauty.

"Oh, Jules," my mother says disappointedly as she takes in my drunken state, "when will you stop torturing yourself like this?"

"No time soon," I answer, because it's the truth. I'm not in the mood to discuss my lack of virtues with my mother yet again, so I quickly change the subject. "Helena was just here."

"Where?" Uncle Enis is quick to ask, taking a step forward as he readies himself to go where I direct.

Sweet, loyal Uncle Enis. If he wasn't my "uncle," I could have easily fallen in love with him. Sure, he is handsome with his chiseled looks and curly brown hair, but it is his soul I love. It's almost impossible for me to believe he used to work with Lucifer when that particular devil was earthbound. In fact, he and mom only recently left Lucifer's employ, as it were. After Lucifer returned to Heaven, he left the rest of the rebellion angels to fend for themselves. From what I understand, that certainly caused a ruckus among the angels he left behind. Most of them felt abandoned and decided to try and make Lucifer's daughter, Anna (the empress of the cloud city of Cirrus on Earth), pay for his rejection of them. My mom said God pretty much put the kibosh on the rebellion angels' plans for revenge, and the leader of the rebels, Hale, is still trying to figure out a way to exact his vengeance on Anna. I don't see that happening anytime soon, though. He lost over half his supporters after God's interference. I figure he's going to need some time to lick his wounds and reorganize before he tries anything else.

"She was out back at the foot of the steps," I tell him.

He immediately phases. I turn around to look back outside and ask him, "Can you still see her phase trail?"

"Yes," he answers, but I notice he doesn't phase to wherever Helena has scampered off to.

My mother walks up behind me to peer out into the backyard over my shoulder.

"She's in Hell," my mother informs me, obviously being able to see Helena's phase trail from where she stands. "She must have known you would contact us and went to the one place she knew we couldn't follow her to."

"And why is that exactly?" I ask. "You used to go back and forth to that place all the time. Why can't you go there now?"

"Hell is Helena's domain. If she wants to be left alone, that's where she goes because she can block anyone else from entering. I've told you this before, Jules. More than once in fact."

The condescension in my mother's voice grates on my nerves. I don't know why she expects me to remember every little detail about angels. It's hard enough these days for me to remember how to walk in a straight line, much less keep up with her kind's peculiarities.

"It doesn't matter," I say, feeling the full effects of the alcohol in my body kick in as my eyelids become too heavy to keep open any longer. "She'll have to come up for air eventually, and when she does, I'll be able to find her."

"Tough talk coming from a drunkard," my mother replies, but not unkindly. Her voice is simply filled with the usual disdain for my current state. I feel her place her hands on my arms and pull my body back against her, because she knows I'll be passing out soon and will most likely end up flat on my face if left unattended. There's only so many times you can break your nose without it making your face look odd. "How exactly do you plan to work such a miracle, Jules?"

My mom might be a thorn in my side most of the time, but she's one of the few people in my life I know I can count on and trust.

"I put a tracer on her," I say right before sleep has a chance to claim my conscious mind, providing me a small respite from the real world. "You better get in touch with those War Angels and let them know so they can be ready to pony up the dough they'll owe me when I find her."

"Good girl," I hear my mom whisper in my ear as she accepts my full weight against her.

I know she'll take care of me. She's done it more times over the last five years than I care to think about. One day, I hope I can break away from my self-indulgent pity fest, but today isn't that day. No amount of alcohol can make me forget what I came home to on this night five years ago, and I fear it might take an act of God to change the path of self-destruction I'm heading down now. Miracles might happen on Earth on a regular basis, but in my world, they've been few and far between.

CHAPTER 2

"I say we wake her up and find out what she knows."

"Evelyn said Jules was pretty drunk when she found her. For all we know, she might have just hallucinated seeing Helena at the cabin."

"I may have been drunk," I say to the men talking about me, still keeping my eyes closed as I continue to wake up, "but I didn't hallucinate her, Roan."

Cautiously, I open one eye to check where it is my mother laid me this time to sleep off my drunken stupor. I quickly close it again because bright sunshine is not what my already aching head needs at the moment.

"Can one of you close the curtains in here, please?" I request as I begin to rub the ache out of my temples with the tips of my fingers. "I can't think straight when my head hurts like this."

"Close the curtains for her," I hear Roan say to his companion. "I'll be right back."

I know there are four windows in my mother's living room, so I wait until I hear the man who stayed behind slide the curtains across all four rods before cautiously opening my eyes again. I slowly sit up on the white suede couch I'm on and find a cup of piping hot black coffee sitting on the glass and steel table in front of me. I reach out and grab the white porcelain mug, bringing it to my lips and taking a sip of the nectar for faster sobriety.

I hear the man who closed the curtains walk around the couch as he comes to stand across the coffee table from me. I take another sip of the hazelnut flavored coffee before looking up into his disapproving face.

"Gideon, isn't it?" I ask the War Angel. How do I know he's one of the War Angels from Earth? He's wearing one of their signature black leather uniforms with the "WA" insignia embroidered over his heart on the jacket. He's handsome in a rugged sort of way with his high forehead and sharp cheekbones. He has dark brown hair that he wears parted to the side, and the muscles beneath his jacket are so large they make the leather of his uniform ripple when he moves.

"Yes," he replies, crossing his arms over his chest in a defensive stance without saying anything else.

I've met a few of Empress Anna Devereaux's War Angel contingent, but the only one who comes to see my mother on a regular basis is Roan. From what I've been told, he's the War Angels' second in command. An angel by the name of Ethan Knight is first in command, but I've never met him. I guess our insignificant planet of Sierra isn't high on his list of priorities. He and his men have been searching for Helena for months now. I'm just not sure why she's been letting them.

"Helena knows you're using the Nexus in Hell to search for her," I inform him.

"We figured as much," Gideon says, not looking at all surprised by my announcement. "I don't suppose she told you why she's been letting us use it."

"I only talked to her for a few minutes. We didn't exactly become besties within that amount of time. I'm good at making people tell me things they wouldn't normally tell others, but even I need more time than that to trick the embodiment of Hell into spilling all of her secrets to me."

Gideon chortles at my remark. "Good luck getting her to tell you much, if you ever even see her again."

"Oh, I'll see her again," I say confidently. "It's only a matter of time before she comes back to this planet."

Gideon looks confused. "Why are you so sure she'll come back?"

"She's been back to the cabin at least twice that we know of, right? Her memories of Cade are drawing her back there. She can't help herself from going to the one place she was happy. She might be the most evil creature in the universe, but she felt the joy love can bring. It's something she'll always yearn to experience again, even if it's only through a distant memory."

Roan phases back into the room. He immediately walks over to me, raising his right hand, which has a small silver rod in it.

When he raises his hand to my forehead, I pull back slightly and ask, "What the hell is that thing, and what are you planning to do with it?"

"You said you can't think straight when your head is hurting. This," he says, holding out the silver rod in his hand, "will take the pain away if you'll let me use it on you. It's a healing wand they use back on Earth."

"Healing wand?" I ask, eyeing the device warily. "Sounds a little too good to be true."

"It's technology well beyond what your planet has at the moment. You're a few centuries away from figuring out how to make something this sophisticated."

"I guess you can use it on me," I say hesitantly. Although it's always been my practice to run away from people who offer miracles, I know I can trust Roan.

My mother has already told me that Sierra's technology is primitive compared to what Earth has. Although from what she said, Earth had a war to end all wars about five hundred years ago. Apparently the people with the most wealth built cloud cities to live in while the people left on the surface ended up almost destroying each other. Once the war was over, those in the cloud cities basically enslaved the survivors and posted people they called "overlords" to watch over their productivity. My mom said Empress Anna is trying to change the way cloud cities treat those who live within their territories and that she's having great success now that Helena is otherwise occupied with the arrival of her first child. Right now, there are only two cloud cities still trying to maintain absolute control over their down-worlders: Nimbo and Virga. The only reason those cities are still trying to keep the down-worlders in their place is because each of them is still being ruled by a prince of Hell.

A prince named Levi stole the body of Nimbo's emperor, Zuri Solarin, on Helena's orders. She was then presented to the world as Zuri's new wife, granting her the title of empress. From what I understand, she publicly argued against Anna's desire to help the down-worlders gain cloud city technology to make their lives easier, and she was also instrumental in nearly costing Anna her position as empress. However, almost all of Anna's problems were resolved with a favorable outcome with help from an unexpected source: Helena. Once she discovered she could love someone else besides herself, Helena decided to end her campaign to ruin Anna and rode off with Cade into the happily-ever-after sunset. Unfortunately, Helena's plans fell through a crack she didn't see coming. In an ironic twist of fate and startling tragedy, it was the strength of Helena's love for Cade that ultimately ended his life on Earth, forever damning Helena to live an eternity without him by her side.

After Roan waves the healing wand across my forehead, the ache inside my skull quickly dissipates, leaving my mind clearer than it has been in ages.

"I don't suppose you would be willing to let me buy that thing off of you," I say to Roan as he takes a step back from me, tucking the healing wand into one of his back pockets.

"Sorry," he says with a smile. "That would be against the rules of accelerating a world's technology before its time. Now that you can think straight, can you tell us exactly what happened last night between you and Helena?"

I go on to tell the men what was said—at least what I can remember of the conversation anyway. I don't mention that I might be forgetting a few details. I honestly don't know if I am or not. The whole night is a little on the fuzzy side, but I'm pretty sure most of what I'm saying is true.

"Enis said her phase trail led straight to Hell," Gideon says after my retelling of the previous night's events. "Did she happen to mention where she's been hiding out all this time? A planet name or even a solar system?"

I shake my head, finding it strange not to feel any pain associated with the action. I can't even remember the last time I was able to do it without getting a little dizzy afterwards.

"She didn't tell me where she's been or what she's been doing," I tell them, seeing the immediate disappointment on both of their faces. You would have thought I just kicked their favorite dog or something considering their expressions. "But I assume my mom told you that I was able to put a tracer on Helena."

"How did you get away with that anyway?" Gideon asks, sounding skeptical that I could pull something like that off without getting caught in the act.

"I was lucky enough to have an unexpected distraction help me out. The baby started kicking and she doubled over in pain," I say. "When I went to help her, I grabbed her arm by the elbow and was able to leave a skin-colored tracer there."

"And she didn't feel you do that?" Roan asks cynically.

"It's the size of a freckle," I explain. "No one ever feels it, and it doesn't wash off. It has to be scraped off. So unless she has itchy elbows, odds are she won't find it."

"But she has to come back to this planet before you can track her, correct?" Roan asks.

"Yes. Sorry, but I don't think there's a tracker on this planet that can comb the known universe."

Roan considers this for a moment. "What if you were on a different planet? Would you be able to still track her if she was on it too?"

"I should be able to," I say hesitantly. "What are you going to do? Phase me to every known world in the universe?"

I meant it as a joke, but from the serious way both Roan and Gideon are looking at me now, I can tell my witty suggestion is exactly what they want to do.

"Would you be willing to do that?" Roan asks.

A large golden dollar sign suddenly flashes in my mind.

"For a price," I reply, trying to keep my tone cool. I don't want to act too eager. The more of a hassle I make this little adventure of theirs sound, the more money they should be willing to give me for my time. "I'll do it, but you may not want to pay my fee."

"And exactly how much is your time worth?" Roan questions cautiously.

"I want half of what you're offering for her capture, whether we find her or not. If we do find her, then you can give me the rest of the bounty."

"Are you insane?" Gideon thunders angrily. "You want fifty gold bars just for a *maybe?*"

Calmly, I place the coffee cup back on the table, raise my legs, and rest my feet on it as I lounge back on the couch with my arms crossed over my chest.

"You got a better lead on Helena available?" I ask them, knowing if they did, they wouldn't be standing in front of me now. "You should also know that Helena told me she thought the baby was going to be born soon. So the longer you wait, the closer she gets to popping out the miracle child. From what I saw, she seems awfully attached to the little tike already, and it's not even born yet. My mom said you were afraid she might love it to death like she did Cade. If that's the case, I'm not sure why you're wasting time haggling about this with me. We could be out searching for her now instead of talking about it."

"I don't know if I respect you or despise you," Gideon says, looking properly confused by me.

I shrug. "I can be an acquired taste," I admit, but I'm certainly not apologizing for my business sense. "If you want my opinion, I suggest you guys make a decision quickly. If you're not willing to pay me, I need to start working on another bounty. I don't have a rich empress of some fancy cloud city backing my every move. Us ordinary folk have to actually go out and earn a living to survive."

Roan stares at me for a long time. I'm not sure if he's trying to intimidate me or what, but my only response is a loud yawn.

"Look, fellas," I say, putting my feet back on the floor and standing up. "I have a job I need to get back to, so either give me an answer within the next ten seconds or I'm out of here."

"Could you make that ten minutes instead?" Roan asks. "I can't authorize such a large payment myself. I need to speak with someone who has more authority than I do before I can make such a promise."

"Sure," I say graciously. "I was just about to go down and get some breakfast anyway. You have until I'm finished eating to tell me what the verdict is."

Roan inclines his head in my direction. "We'll be back as soon as possible with the decision."

Both he and Gideon phase away. I turn toward the door in the living room and walk out of it to descend a flight of stairs that takes me directly down to my mother's nightclub. I place my hand on the black steel door at the bottom of the steps and wait for it to read my palm print. A faint blue glow appears underneath my hand just before the door slides open, allowing me entry into Grace House.

After my human mother died and my rebellion angel mom took over her body to masquerade as Evelyn Grace, she built Grace House as a way to provide us with a healthy income. She and Uncle Enis are partners in the everyday running of things for the nightclub, and they co-parented me, which was a job unto itself most days while I was growing up. I may not have had the most conventional upbringing, but I always knew I was loved. I still do.

I walk through the nightclub's interior to the swinging door that leads to the kitchen area. At this time of day, the club is empty and eerily silent. The only sound I hear is the banging of pans in the kitchen where I know I'll find Uncle Enis cooking my breakfast. As soon as I walk through the door, my nasal passages are filled with the aroma of a cheese and ham omelet and a side of bacon. The omelet is his signature breakfast dish, and the three slices of bacon are a must-have for me every morning. In my line of work, I need my energy reserves at full capacity so I can run after criminals regular cops can't seem to catch. Most days I only have time to eat one meal, and everyone keeps telling me that breakfast is the most important meal, so I try to make sure I eat a large one.

"I thought those two would probably end up waking you up," Uncle Enis says as he slides my folded omelet onto a white plate.

"I suppose I have you to thank for the cup of coffee," I say knowingly.

"I figured you would need it after last night. Do you want some aspirin this morning for your head?"

"No. Roan brought some sort of magic wand back from Earth that took my headache away."

"Ah, yes. A healing wand."

"You know about those things?" I ask in surprise. "Why haven't you ever stolen one and brought it here for us to use? That thing could save me from ever having a hangover again."

"You know what else can do that for you?" he asks. "Not drinking so much alcohol that you pass out from it. Seriously, Jules, you have to stop drinking so much. You're going to ruin your liver."

"Considering what I do for a living, I probably won't live long enough to contract cirrhosis."

"Don't talk like that," Uncle Enis admonishes me. "If your mother and I have anything to say about it, you'll live a long long time."

I don't make a reply. I just sit down heavily on my regular steel stool at the counter across from the stove. My uncle reaches over and hands me the plate with my breakfast on it. I bring the plate up to my nose and inhale deeply.

"If this isn't heaven on a plate, I don't know what is," I declare before setting the offering of food down in front of me and grabbing my fork to make the first cut into the omelet.

"So where are Roan and Gideon?" he asks.

"Went back to Cirrus, I think," I say before stuffing my mouth full of egg, ham, and melted cheese. After I swallow, I continue. "They want me to traipse around the universe with them to find Helena with my tracker. Personally, I think it's a waste of time, but if they're willing to pay me to do it, I'm game."

"I realize the odds of finding her that way are low, but why do you think it's a waste of time?"

"If we just bide our time, I'm sure she'll come back here eventually. I'm probably one of the few people who can understand her emotional state right now. At some point, she'll return to the cabin because it's the one place that still has untainted memories of Cade attached to it."

"Yes, but like you told us, it looks like she's close to having the child. They want to get to her before she does."

"Has Roan told you how they plan on forcing Helena to give the baby to them?"

"Do you honestly think they would divulge that type of information to me?"

I shake my head. "No. But I thought you might have overheard them say something when they thought you weren't listening."

"The only one who lets anything slip is Xander, and that's only when he gets drunk."

"Yeah, I've seen him and his brother here before. What's the brother's name?"

"Zane," Uncle Enis answers. "He's basically Xander's keeper from what I understand. Whenever Xander has a night off, he likes to come here and get wasted."

"I thought angels couldn't get drunk."

"We can if we drink more than our metabolism can keep up with. He probably drinks in one night what you do in a whole year."

I have to whistle in amazement at that as I pick up a slice of bacon and nibble on it.

While I chew on the crispy deliciousness, Uncle Enis says, "I think Xander is trying to break the habit, though. Zane told me his brother has been attempting to wean himself off the stuff, but that he's become addicted to it."

"I didn't realize angels could become addicted to anything either," I admit, finding these War Angels more and more interesting.

"Why did they have to go back to Cirrus to get the okay to hire you?"

"Roan said he couldn't approve the amount I was asking for himself and had to talk to someone with more authority."

Uncle Enis raises both of his eyebrows, looking both concerned and surprised.

"How much did you ask them for?"

"Half the bounty upfront that I get to keep whether we find her or not. Then, after we find her, I get the rest of it."

"You asked them for fifty gold bars?" Uncle Enis exclaims. "Do you realize how much money that is on this planet?"

"I know exactly how much it's worth: twenty-five million credits."

"Well, I hope they give it to you. Then you can stop being a bounty hunter."

"Who said I would stop working?" I ask, feeling slightly offended. "What else would I do with my time? Lay around all day and let servants answer my every beck and call? Do you really think that's the type of life I want to live?"

"Then what are you going to do with all that money?"

"I'll keep a good chunk of it in the bank for a retirement nest egg, in case I live that long. The rest I figured I would anonymously give away to some worthwhile charity."

"And if you actually do help them find Helena and earn the rest of the bounty, what are you going to do with the other twenty-five million credits?"

"I don't know. If you and mom want it, you're welcome to have it."

"We don't need money. We have plenty."

"Then I'll just give it to some more charities."

Uncle Enis leans back on the counter behind him and stares at me hard.

"What?" I ask cautiously. It's obvious he wants to ask me something.

"Evelyn and I thought you would quit work if you earned this bounty on Helena. At least, that was our hope. It seemed like a logical assumption considering how often you've been making yourself visit the cabin the past few months. We both know how hard it is for you to go there."

"Which is why I kept the place stocked with alcohol," I confess. "I don't suppose you would be willing to take the liquor cabinet back up there for me, would you?"

"And face the wrath of your mother?" he scoffs. "What do you think my answer is?"

I slice another section of my omelet with my fork and stuff it into my mouth. Uncle Enis' question is a rhetorical one that doesn't require a response. We both know he will never go against my mom's wishes, no matter what.

After I swallow what's in my mouth, I ask, "So where is Mom this morning?"

"She had a meeting with our alcohol supplier. He was trying to raise the prices on us, but I'm sure your mom will be able to make him see reason."

"You know, if the two of you would just let me give you money from the bounty I'm going to collect, you wouldn't have to keep running this joint. The two of you are going to have to go somewhere else soon anyway. Mom can't keep having plastic surgery to look older, and your ageless beauty is already raising some eyebrows."

"Some men age better than others."

"That excuse is getting pretty thin, Uncle Enis. You know it as well as I do."

Uncle Enis drops his gaze from mine as if he wants to broach a subject with me but isn't sure if he should or not.

"What are you hiding from me?" I ask, suspicious of his behavior.

He raises his eyes to meet mine again and says, "Evelyn and I have talked about moving to Cirrus on Earth, but we're not going to go unless you come too."

"Why do you want to live there, and why haven't either of you mentioned this idea to me before now?" I ask, finding it strange that the two of them want to change their lives so drastically.

"We want to go back there and help protect Lucifer's daughter. We both feel like it's something that we should do."

"To earn your redemption from God?" I ask.

"Basically, yes. We would feel more worthy of asking Him for forgiveness if we helped her deal with the remaining rebellion angels who want to harm her and her children. I don't know how long that will take though. It could be years before Hale and the others make a move against her. There's just no way of knowing."

"Then why don't the two of you go there now?"

"Do you really have to ask that question?" Uncle Enis tilts his head as if I should know better.

"I am an adult," I respond. "I can take care of myself."

"Your mother and I will never leave while you still need us. You should know that by now."

Secretly, I'm happy to hear him say what he just did. I rely on my mom and uncle to keep me from going off the deep end. Yet, a part of me hates being so selfish. What if this is their one and only chance to do something worthy enough to save their souls? Unlike most people in the universe, I've always known that God was a real entity. When you're raised by two fallen angels, it's hard not to believe in the Almighty. Strangely enough, neither of them tried to make me resent the God they felt betrayed them. They never pushed their beliefs onto me and always urged me to use my mind and follow my heart where He was concerned.

While Uncle Enis washes the dishes he dirtied while preparing my breakfast, I quickly finish eating my meal. I assume Roan will be back shortly to tell me whether or not my bargain has been accepted. Either way, I have work to do today. His answer just decides whether or not I'll be spending my day searching for Helena or tracking down a wife beater who skipped out on his bail.

Just as I'm eating the last slice of bacon on my plate, Roan walks into the kitchen.

I turn around on my stool to watch him as he approaches.

"Have my answer?" I ask him.

"Not exactly," he says hesitantly, looking unsure about how I will react to what he has to say next. "There was some debate on whether or not your help is worth what you're asking for. My commander would like to speak with you in person, if that's agreeable to you."

"Sure," I say, hopping off my stool. "Where is he?"

"I was asked to bring you to Cirrus."

"Why can't he come here?"

"He needed to tend to something back home first, but he said to bring you to the palace now, so that you're there when he gets through."

"Sounds like a flimsy excuse to me," I say. "I think he just wants me unbalanced while we're on his home turf."

Roan remains silent, but his nonresponse speaks volumes and lets me know that my assumption is correct.

"Do you want me to go with you?" Uncle Enis says from behind me.

I don't look back at my uncle. I keep my eyes on Roan as I say, "No. I can handle this negotiation. That's what it is, right? Your commander will try to work his charms on me and renegotiate the terms I've set."

"You would have to talk to him about that," Roan replies, refusing to acknowledge that my take on the situation is the correct one.

"Fine," I relent. "Let's go."

"If you're not back soon, I'm going to come and look for you," Uncle Enis tells me.

I look over my shoulder and wink at him. "I've got this. Don't worry."

Roan phases to right beside me and takes ahold of my arm.

"Are you ready?" he asks.

I nod my head and Roan phases us to Cirrus.

I'm soon standing on a large veranda. My breath catches in my throat at the sight of the city laid out in all its splendor before me. In my twenty-eight years of life, I've never seen a sight to match its beauty. I look up and notice a slight shimmer to the sky. I know what it is. It's the forcefield that encapsulates all cloud cities and keeps them safe from the turbulence they would otherwise have to deal with at this altitude.

Roan lets go of my arm and says, "Stay here."

He phases again, leaving me alone to take in the spectacle of the castle the veranda I'm standing on is a part of. It looks like something out of a fairy tale where the beautiful queen and her dashing king live out their lives in tranquility. Considering the trials and tribulations I know Empress Anna has had to endure, any peace she might be able to find in her life now has been well earned.

As I let my gaze travel around the veranda, I notice a set of large glass doors that lead into the interior of the palace. I walk to them and try to turn the knob on one door but find it locked. When I peer inside, I see that it's a grand ballroom.

"I guess they want to make sure the riffraff don't just walk in and steal all their gold," I grumble to myself.

At least I think I'm talking to myself, until I hear a man behind me say, "It seems to me that the only people we need to worry about stealing our gold are greedy bounty hunters."

I quickly spin around to look at the man who just spoke to me and find him standing by the veranda's stone railing.

Unexpectedly, I feel the earth beneath my feet tremble.

CHAPTER 3

I literally have to bend my right leg at the knee slightly and take a small step forward to brace myself, in order to keep from falling onto the stone beneath my feet, as I feel the building lurch to the right.

"What was that?" I ask the man standing in front of me, still feeling startled by the strange movement. "And who exactly are you?"

"That was the propulsion system beginning to move Cirrus through the sky to its new location," he answers. "And I am Ethan Knight."

I had already assumed the man was the War Angels' commander, but it's never a good idea to take things for granted until they're confirmed. Ethan is tall, but to be honest, I haven't ever actually met a short angel. I know from my mother that the War Angels were able to design the bodies they came to Earth in, just like the Watchers who came before them did. I can't say I've seen one yet that isn't handsome, but Ethan seems to be in a different category from the others. When someone, man or woman, takes on the responsibility of leading others, they always tend to observe things with an air of caution. I suppose if you've been given the task of safeguarding lives, you can never be too vigilant.

Ethan's hair is dark brown and just long enough for it to brush the tops of his shoulders. The front isn't quite as long as the back. It causes a framing effect around his face, which is, if I'm being honest, gorgeous. I can't honestly say I've ever seen a man as handsome as him in my life. Perhaps it's the hint of vulnerability I see within the depths of his chocolate brown eyes that makes him attractive to me. He may be the commander of two thousand War Angels here on Earth, but there's a part of him that's exposed, which touches a sympathetic part of my soul that I wasn't even sure still existed until this moment.

He's dressed in his War Angel uniform, which tells me that he's on duty. Although I get the impression from Ethan that he's probably always on duty and rarely takes time off to enjoy the pleasures of an earthly life.

"I'm Julia Evelyn Grace," I say, feeling the need to tell him my entire name for some odd reason. I almost never do such a thing, but with Ethan, I feel like I should. "Most people just call me Jules though."

Ethan doesn't say anything right away. He simply stares at me without uttering a word or giving away anything on his face to let me know what's going through his mind as he continues to study me.

After a while, I become self-conscious and begin to wonder if he's attempting to use some sort of angelic power I've never heard about on me. Is he trying to read my mind? Good Lord, I hope not, because some of my thoughts right now are anything but pure. The odd thing is, I don't know why I'm imagining Ethan and myself in rather compromising positions. I haven't taken a man into my bed since Timothy died. I simply haven't been interested in sex, but right now, my body is definitely urging me to reconsider the terms of my celibacy. Just in case he is reading my mind, I decide to distract it with other thoughts.

"So, why is the city being moved?" I ask him. "And where are you taking it?"

"We're moving it out to sea, over an ocean called the Atlantic," he tells me in a rather deadpan voice as he continues to watch me. "Ann ... Empress Anna decided it would be safer to leave the city we're usually stationed above in case the rebellion angels decide to attack us again here in Cirrus. She doesn't want what happened in Virga to happen here."

"Virga," I say, pondering the name. "Isn't that the cloud city Helena blew up? The destruction of which she tried to lay the blame for on your empress?"

Ethan nods. "Yes. When Virga was destroyed, what was left of it landed on the city it was stationed above, rendering it uninhabitable for the foreseeable future. Empress Anna doesn't want something similar to happen to New York City or its people."

"Rather pragmatic of her," I say.

"She likes to prepare for the worst-case scenario when she can," he agrees. "I think any good leader should if they have the resources and the time."

"Speaking of resources, are you the one who's supposed to decide whether or not you guys are going to pay the price I set for my help?"

"I need for you to answer a few questions before I'm willing to give you our counteroffer," he says.

"Counteroffer?" I ask in confusion. "I never said the price was negotiable."

"I think we both know that a person like you always starts out high, asking for the impossible because you know you'll more than likely get exactly what you want in the end."

"What I want are fifty gold bars up front," I say testily. "I don't think I could have been any clearer to Roan on the fee for my help."

"And you should have known that we would never give you that much just on a maybe," he retorts. "We don't even know if your tracking device will work. For all we know, this is some sort of ploy you've set up to steal the gold and scamper off to some distant planet with Evelyn and Enis."

"Are you seriously standing there calling the honor of my mother and uncle into question?" I ask as my voice rises to a fever pitch. "Calling me a thief is one thing. *Possibly* even something I could eventually forgive, but don't ever ... and I mean *ever* ... talk badly about my family to my face. Are we understanding one another, *Commander* Knight?"

I hear a new voice join the conversation with a deep throaty chortle after my outburst.

I look to my right and see a man standing in the far corner of the veranda watching me. He's handsome with long dark hair that hangs down to his chest. The white shirt he's wearing is designed to remain open in the front with a long wide slit in the middle that ends in a point right above where his belly button should be, leaving his rather impressive chest slightly exposed to all who look at him. His tight black slacks hug his hips and legs like a second skin. Although his physique is certainly worth taking note of, it's his blue eyes that capture my attention. The light of the sun filtering through Cirrus' shield makes them sparkle with obvious amusement.

"I don't care what Gideon says," the man tells me, as a lazy grin stretches his lips, "I like you, Jules."

"And you would be ..." I say, leaving my question open to be answered by him.

"Emperor Malcolm Devereaux," he replies, walking up to join the conversation Ethan and I are having.

It's been my experience when dealing with royalty that they think way too much of themselves and their station in life. However, with Emperor Malcolm, I get the distinct impression that the title doesn't hold much meaning for him. He carries himself with a self-confidence not many people reach in life. From the stories my mother has told me about him, I know that he's had to face a large number of trials and tribulations in order to become the man he is today.

"I respect the fact that you just took up for your family," Emperor Malcolm says to me. "It's the same reaction I would have had. But would you allow me to ask you a question before we agree to your terms for this arrangement?"

"I suppose that would be all right," I say hesitantly, unsure if I'm about to be played by someone who has probably made thousands of lucrative deals with people within his lifetime.

I know exactly who Emperor Malcolm Xavier Devereaux is. My mother told me all about Empress Anna's husband. He is a Watcher, an angel who was sent to Earth by God to watch over the development of humanity thousands of years ago. He and his fellow Watchers made the grave error of falling in love and taking human wives, which was in direct defiance of God's orders to them. They were cursed with an uncontrollable bloodlust, and their children were forced to live dual lives: humans by day and bloodthirsty creatures at the rising of the moon each night. There are only a handful of Watchers left on Earth now, and oddly enough, three of them are currently emperors of cloud cities.

"Do you truly believe that you will be able to help us find Helena?" he asks me.

"Yes," I say without hesitation. "I wouldn't be here if I wasn't confident I can finish the job I've started. I don't go into anything half-assed, Emperor Malcolm. I'm either all in or all out, and with this job, I'm all in. I'll find her for you. It's just a matter of time."

He smiles at me, showing perfectly white teeth. "You can call me Malcolm, Jules. I don't care much for the emperor part." Malcolm turns his head to look at Ethan. "I think we can accommodate Jules with her request to receive half of her payment upfront, Ethan. I don't have any doubts now that she'll help us locate Helena."

Ethan doesn't look pleased with Malcolm's decision. "Shouldn't we discuss this with Anna before we just hand over fifty gold bars to this woman?"

"The gold bars are coming from my private reserves, not Cirrus' coffers, and I can damn well do what I want to with them," Malcolm says rather forcefully. "Do you sense Jules is lying to us?"

I look away from Malcom and back at Ethan only to find the surly War Angel staring daggers straight into my soul. At least, that's what it feels like to me.

"No," he finally answers. "I don't sense that she's being deceitful, and she may very well believe she's speaking the truth. But that doesn't mean she'll actually deliver on her promise."

"Listen," I say to Ethan, doing my best to keep my temper under control with him, "I have never failed to find someone once I take on the job to bring them in. I understand that finding Helena is really important to you guys for personal reasons, but this is just a job to me. I have no emotional attachments here, and I can remain impartial and clearheaded. I think if you weren't so personally invested, you would be able to get past the money issue and realize I'm your best bet to find her before she has the baby. Like I told Roan and Gideon earlier, she looks really close to giving birth. I wouldn't be surprised if she has the kid within the next week or even sooner."

"Did she tell you anything about the child?" Malcolm asks me. "Is it healthy? Has she had any problems with the pregnancy?"

I shake my head. "She really didn't say all that much. The closest she came was to tell me that it hasn't been like a regular pregnancy."

"Did she elaborate on that at all?" Ethan asks, looking worried. "What's been unnatural about it?"

I shrug. "I have no idea. From what I was able to gather, it's been painful for her."

"Good," Ethan retorts like a snake shooting out venom. "I hope it has been. She deserves it for what she did."

"Ethan, we've been over this before. Helena didn't mean to kill Cade," Malcolm admonishes him. "You know that as well as anyone."

"If she hadn't blown up Virga, she never would have had the strength to kill Cade. Blowing that cloud city out of the sky and blaming it on Anna *was* intentional! And Cade was the one who ended up paying the price for her actions."

"She's Hell," I say in Helena's defense. "What did you expect her to do? Be someone who sits around and knits doilies all day? It's just her nature to cause turmoil whenever and wherever she can to serve her own needs. That's just who she is."

"What are you? Her best friend?" Ethan practically accuses. "If you have so much empathy for her, maybe you're not the right person to hire to bring her in for us."

"I'm the only person who can do what you and your War Angels have failed to do for months now," I state, lifting my head up a notch in defiance because I'm stating the truth. "And maybe you should learn how to be more empathetic where she's concerned. You're so mad at her for killing your friend that you can't seem to think about her without immediately seeing red. What exactly is your plan to get the baby away from her anyway? Dazzle her with your winning charm?" I scoff.

Ethan's expression turns as dark as a thundercloud. "If she won't listen to reason, I plan to cut her head off and rip the baby out of her womb."

I hear myself gasp before I can even stop it.

"Ethan ..." Malcolm chastises him harshly. "You know that's a last resort move. We promised Anna we would try to convince Helena to give us the baby because it's the best option for everyone concerned."

"Either way," Ethan says, only barely acknowledging what Malcolm just said, "I can't allow her to raise Cade's child. I wasn't able to save him from her, but I can damn well save his baby. I owe him at least that much."

It's then that I realize Ethan and I share something in common: survivor's guilt. His guilt over Cade's death is so great he can't see that it's eating him alive and driving him to make rash decisions where Helena is concerned. I can see it though, and I understand where his anger is coming from.

"I hate to say it, but it might very well come down to you chopping her head off," I tell Ethan. "From what I saw, I don't think she's going to hand over her baby to you just because you ask her to. She'll fight you for him. In fact, I think she's resigned to that fact."

"I hope she does," Ethan states. "I think it would save us both a lot of time. I seriously doubt the two of us will be able to talk out our differences and come to an arrangement we can both live with."

"Did you just refer to the baby as a 'him'?" Malcolm questions me.

"Yes," I reply. "She told me that the baby is a boy."

Both men fall silent as they take in this news.

"Why?" I ask. "Is that important?"

Malcolm slowly shakes his head. "Not in any significant way. It just seems to make the situation feel more urgent knowing the sex of the baby. Now all I can see is a miniature version of Cade running around Hell if Helena is allowed to raise it."

"That isn't going to happen," Ethan states with finality.

He can't seem to envision a scenario where he fails to take Helena's baby away from her. I suppose it might be because he's an angel. I don't think he can fully comprehend the strength of a mother's love for her child.

"Have any of you considered the possibility that she might just stay in Hell until the baby is born?" I ask them. "That's what I would do if I were her."

"As you pointed out," Ethan says, "it's just part of her nature to cause chaos. She can't do that if she isolates herself in Hell. Plus, she worked really hard to become corporeal and have the ability to roam freely through the universe. Pregnant or not, I'm sure she hasn't been sitting around twiddling her thumbs all this time. Whatever planet or planets she's traveled to the last few months have had to suffer through her grief over losing Cade."

"Whatever the case may be," Malcolm says, "we have to do everything within our power to find her, and right now, Jules, you're our best bet. So I suggest we stop talking about what needs to be done and start doing it instead."

"Agreed," Ethan says, looking over at me. "Roan said that you can tell if she's on any planet that we go to. How exactly does this tracker of yours work?"

"The tracer I placed on her emits a signal. I have a handheld device back home that can home in on the signal's unique frequency. I'll be able to give you the direction the signal is coming from and the approximate distance we are away from it. It'll be up to you guys to figure out exactly where on the planet she is."

"That shouldn't be a problem," Ethan tells me. "We've been able to map all of the worlds we've been to so far. If you can give me the direction and distance, that should be enough."

"When do you want to start, and who will be phasing me to these planets?"

"I think we should start searching immediately," Ethan says. "And I'll be taking you to the various worlds."

"You will?" Malcolm questions in surprise. "I thought you were going to ..."

Ethan cuts off the emperor's next words by saying, "If we're going to give her fifty gold bars, I want to make sure we're getting our money's worth."

"If I didn't know any better, I would say you just insulted me," I say.

Ethan looks me straight in the eyes and says, "Well, it wasn't a compliment."

Malcolm clears his throat in the uncomfortable tension that follows.

"Uh, are you sure this is the way you want to handle this, Ethan? Roan said he would be more than willing to escort Jules."

"Having me go with her saves time in the long run. I have the sword," he says, placing his hand on the hilt of the blade sheathed in the black leather sword belt fastened around his hips. "I can confront her and try to bargain for the baby."

"Just remember to talk first," Malcolm reminds him. "For all we know, killing Helena's body might inadvertently kill the baby too. Don't go there to pick a fight with her, Ethan. And remember that this is someone Cade loved. I don't think he would want you to stab first and ask permission later. You may despise Helena, but keep in mind that she's hurting too. We're not the only ones who lost Cade. She lost him and her one chance at finding happiness. Try to keep that in mind when you see her."

"I'll try," Ethan responds, but his sincerity leaves a lot to be desired.

"I'll remind him," I promise Malcolm, earning a grateful smile from Anna's husband.

"I assume the device we need to track her down with is back on Sierra?" Ethan asks me.

"Yes. It's in my apartment. If you can phase us to the street Grace House is on, we can walk to it from there."

Ethan nods curtly, telling me without any words that my instructions are clear.

As Ethan walks up to me and gently grabs hold of the top of my right arm, Malcolm says, "Good luck and Godspeed."

From Malcolm's lips to God's ears, I think to myself just as Ethan phases us to Sierra.

CHAPTER 4

Ethan phases us directly onto the sidewalk in front of Grace House. It's still early in the morning, and the street is virtually empty in front of my mother's nightclub. I know around five in the afternoon that won't be the case. People will begin to line up just for the chance to enter her establishment. Being granted entry into Grace House is a difficult thing to accomplish for those among the general population, but if you can manage an invitation inside by the guards, your social standing can take a giant leap forward in the city of Arcas. As a teenager, I never quite knew if my friends liked me or the fact that I could get them inside the city's most exclusive nightclub. I suppose since none of those people are still my friends, I can assume it was the latter reason.

"My apartment is a couple of blocks up the street by the city park," I tell Ethan as I begin to take off the jacket I was wearing. In the mountains last night, it was chilly, but now that we're in the valley where Arcas was built, the summer humidity is starting to make me sweat. I wrap the thin black jacket around my hips and tie the sleeves together at the front of my waist.

As Ethan and I walk down the sidewalk together, I notice him giving me the occasional sideways glance as if he wants to ask me something but isn't sure if he should or not. I almost stop and ask him what his problem is, but I think better of doing that. Considering our track record with each other so far, we would probably end up fighting over something stupid. I don't feel like fighting or having to defend myself. All I want to do is help him find Helena and earn the rest of the bounty.

I didn't realize the gold bars being offered up as a reward for Helena's capture were part of Emperor Malcolm's personal wealth. I just assumed the gold was a portion of the riches Cirrus had accumulated over the years from the enslavement of their down-worlders.

"How is it that Malcolm is so wealthy?" I ask Ethan. It seems like an innocuous topic that shouldn't cause us to get into an argument.

"He's lived a long time on Earth, and he was sensible enough to save his wealth as gold instead of regular currency. Gold is a universal commodity. There are very few planets that won't exchange it for legal tender."

"That was pretty smart," I say, finding myself respecting Anna's husband even more. "A lot of people would have just squandered wealth like that. Since he's willing to part with it so easily, I assume he probably has a lot more than just a hundred gold bars stashed away."

"You seem awfully curious about how much money he has. Why?" Ethan asks, sounding as if my curiosity means I have some nefarious reason for broaching the subject.

"Geesh, I was just trying to make small talk with you," I say defensively. "Why do you keep taking everything I say the wrong way? I'm not a criminal, you know."

"And yet you basically extorted fifty gold bars from a man who is only trying to save the life of a child."

Ouch. Now I can see why Ethan looks at me like I just crawled out from underneath a rock. He sees me as a coldhearted, money-grubbing mongrel.

"I'm sorry," I say, feeling as if I need to explain my side of this situation. "I wasn't even thinking about it like that. All I'm trying to do is the job I've been hired for. That's all this is to me: a job."

Ethan sighs, and I can see his shoulders begin to relax some from their usual uptightness.

"I realize that," he admits. "It was my idea to put a bounty on Helena's head. I guess I shouldn't feel resentful for you wanting to collect it.

I think I'm just exhausted from looking for her for so long and worried that we won't find her in time to save the baby. From what you witnessed last night, it sounds like she's close to giving birth. I honestly thought we would have found her before now."

"Do you really believe she might kill her own son if she touches him after he's born?"

"I honestly don't know," he says with a weary shake of his head, "but I can't take the chance that she might. I don't think I would be able to look Cade in the eyes again if I let her kill his son. I can't fail him. I *refuse* to fail him a second time."

The fierce determination behind Ethan's words makes me feel guilty for making a profit off this misadventure. But if it wasn't me earning the bounty, it would be someone else who might not be as scrupulous.

"I hope you realize that what happened to Cade wasn't your fault. It wasn't anyone's fault. Not even Helena's, even though you seem fixated on placing the blame squarely on her shoulders."

"I suppose it's easier for me to view her as the enemy in case I need to take the baby away from her by force. If I start to humanize her, I might not be able to do what needs to be done in the end."

"Do you genuinely believe you'll be able to do what you said?" I ask as an imaginary movie of Ethan slicing Helena's head off and ripping open her belly to get the baby out plays inside my head. The gruesome details of such a violent act make me shiver slightly in total revulsion. I just pray that if a showdown between Ethan and Helena does take place, I'm nowhere near when it happens.

"I'll do whatever I have to in order to protect Cade's son," Ethan replies ominously, leaving no doubt in my mind that he will follow through with his plan if Helena leaves him no other option.

"Remind me never to piss you off," I say, meaning my words wholeheartedly.

Oddly enough, this earns me a small smile from the rock-hard War Angel.

"Oh wow," I say in amazement as I openly gawk at him, "you do have teeth! I wasn't too sure since all I've seen you do is scowl at me."

"I don't normally smile a lot," he confesses. "It doesn't exactly promote an aura of authority to others."

"Yes, but a smile can open a lot of doors if you use it at the right moment and on the right people."

"And has your smile opened a lot of doors for you?"

"Bunches," I say with a toothy grin to punctuate my point.

"How did someone like you choose to become a bounty hunter?" he asks, sounding mystified by my chosen profession.

"I used to be a police detective here in Arcas," I tell him. "After my husband died, I left the force and picked up work hunting down some bail jumpers for a buddy of mine who's still a cop. Since then, I've become the go-to bounty hunter for the Arcas police force. They come to me if they need some help because they know I'll always get the job done."

"Do you always work alone?"

"Yes," I reply and leave it at that.

"That seems a bit lonely."

"You're just used to working with your men," I reason. "It's all you know."

"True," he agrees. "We've always worked together."

"So why didn't you bring any of them along with you this time? It seems like it would be easier to compel Helena to do what you want if you present a show of force when you confront her."

"Some of my brothers aren't quite as levelheaded as I am."

I have to laugh at that one. "If you're the calmest one of the bunch, then I say you've made a wise decision to leave the others behind." Before Ethan can make a reply, I announce, "We're here."

I walk up the three steps to the glass door at the front of my apartment complex. I place my hand against the biometric reader on the panel next to the entrance. Once it recognizes me, the locks on the door disengage and it slides open to allow us entry. Ethan follows me to the elevator located directly opposite the door. Once we get in, I push the button for the seventh floor, which is the top floor of my building.

As we're riding up in the elevator, I notice Ethan look over at me again as if he wants to ask me a question.

"Why do you keep looking at me like that?" I ask him point blank. "You're starting to creep me out a little."

"I'm sorry," he says. "I don't mean to."

"You keep looking at me like you want to ask me a question. Spit it out already and get it over with."

"I'll stop looking at you," he promises, turning his head away and staring at the closed elevator doors instead.

"Well, that's not any better," I say in slight exasperation. "Why don't you just ask me your question?"

Ethan doesn't turn his head. He just gives me a sideways glance out of the corners of his eyes.

"I will after I have a better understanding about something," he says cryptically. "Until that time, I would rather not."

I let out an involuntary huff of irritation but decide to let the matter drop for now. Whatever he wants to ask can't be all that important in the grand scheme of things.

I feel relieved when the elevator doors open and we both step out. I turn to my right and begin to walk down the hallway toward my apartment. If my mind wasn't so preoccupied with Ethan's odd behavior, I probably would have noticed the unusual state of my front door before we reached it.

"I assume you don't usually leave your door slightly ajar," Ethan says, resting his hand on the hilt of his sword as a precaution.

"No," I say, looking over at the fingerprint keyless entry and finding the screen smashed in. "Someone broke in."

Cautiously, I open the door only to find the interior of my apartment in shambles.

I vaguely notice Ethan tighten his grip around his sword as he follows me across the threshold. Almost everything in my apartment has been overturned. The cushions from the couch and chairs in the living room have been tossed haphazardly onto the floor. My coffee table is upside down. The table and chairs of the small dinette next to the kitchen area are all on their sides. It's a mess, but strangely, I don't see anything permanently damaged.

"Are any of your belongings missing?" Ethan asks, as he takes in the carnage of what used to be a tidy home.

I quickly scan the area but don't notice anything missing. Items are simply not where they should be.

"Not that I can tell," I reply as I step farther into my apartment. "I don't own a lot of expensive things. There really wasn't anything of much value here except ..."

I make a mad dash into my bedroom where a similar mess was left behind by my intruder. I run over to my closet and have to step over the clothes that were left in a pile in front of it to grab a red shoe box that's thankfully still sitting where I left it on the top shelf. I pull it down into my arms and lift the lid.

"Damn it!" I yell in frustration, throwing the empty box onto the floor with everything else that was once in my closet.

"What's missing?" Ethan asks, but I can tell from his knowing tone that he's already deduced what's been stolen. He just needs me to confirm it.

"The tracking device," I tell him. "The only thing of any value in here."

"Who else knew it was in your apartment?" he asks. "I assume you wouldn't have told a lot of people about it."

I begin to shake my head as I realize exactly who stole it.

"Only Uncle Enis and my mom knew anything about it," I say, just as I sniff something in the air that answers which of the two culprits it was who took the tracker. "My mother has it. I can still smell her perfume."

"Why would Evelyn take it?" Ethan asks. "Do you think she's trying to cheat you out of the bounty?"

I look at Ethan like he's lost his mind.

"Of course I don't think that," I say, appalled by his suggestion. "Are you always this suspicious of people, or just my family?"

"She's a rebellion angel," Ethan states like that should be enough of a reason to not put much faith in my mother's moral character.

"Look, I understand that War Angels were made by God to win the war in Heaven and that you're probably still hardwired to distrust any and all rebellion angels. But you need to realize that my mother and uncle aren't like that anymore. They're not your enemies now."

"Then your mother has an odd way of showing it. She just stole the one thing we need in order to find Helena," he points out.

"She didn't do it to prevent you from finding her." I sigh. "She did it to prevent me from getting hurt. I know my mother. Keeping me safe is all she cares about."

"Then how do you suggest we get the tracker back? For all we know, she might have already destroyed it to make sure you can't use it."

"No, I don't think she would have destroyed it," I say, knowing exactly what my mother is doing with it. "Can you phase us inside Grace House?"

Ethan nods and walks over to take hold of my arm again. He phases us directly onto the dancefloor.

I can't prevent myself from saying, "Now I know you angels can only phase to places that you've been to before. Does this mean you've come to the nightclub and danced here? Because I would have paid good money to witness that happen."

Ethan lets out a half laugh. "No. I have most certainly not danced here. I had Xander bring me here once, so that I could phase to this planet if I ever needed to."

"Ah Xander," I say, making my way across the dancefloor to the kitchen area. "From what I hear and from what I've seen personally, he has a serious drinking problem."

"He's trying to work through it," Ethan says in a voice that doesn't sound too confident his fellow angel is going about his rehabilitation in the correct way.

"You realize that if he truly wants to kick the habit, he'll actually have to stop drinking alcohol one day."

"I'm fully aware of that fact, but until he decides to do that for himself, there isn't much I can do to force him to change. I thought you of all people would have more sympathy for his predicament."

"Me?" I ask as I stop in front of the swinging door to the kitchen to look back at Ethan. "Why would you think I'm addicted to alcohol?"

"I was told you get drunk on a regular basis," he answers, looking confused. "Was I misinformed?"

"Oh, no, I drink a lot, but I'm not addicted. To be honest, I hate the taste of alcohol. I just like the way it makes me forget things for a while."

"Aren't there various drugs you could use instead that would produce the same effect?"

"Sure, but I might become addicted to those. The way I see it, if I use something I hate, there's no way I'll become hooked on it."

"That's very odd logic," Ethan replies, looking confused.

I shrug. "It's worked for me so far. I don't see any reason to go changing my strategy now."

I push the door to the kitchen open and step inside with Ethan following close behind me.

We find my uncle sitting at the counter I ate my breakfast at just a little while ago. He's watching a cartoon on the tablet in his hand and laughing at something on the screen. When he sees us walk in, he greets me with his usual affable smile.

"Don't smile at me like that," I say sternly. "Where's Mom? And don't tell me she's at some meeting with an alcohol supplier, because I was just at my apartment."

Uncle Enis' smile slips from his face. "Oh, figured that small lie out already, have you?"

"What is she thinking?" I ask, unable to hide my frustration.

"She's thinking that she's saving your life, Jules," he answers. "You don't know what Helena is capable of doing to you. She could end your life on a whim just for looking at her funny. What do you think she's going to do when she learns you're helping her enemies hunt her down? I can tell you one thing: it won't be pretty."

"I won't let Helena touch her," Ethan tells Uncle Enis.

The conviction with which he said his words takes me by surprise. He didn't say it like a random promise. It sounded more like a solemn oath.

Uncle Enis begins to shake his head. "You can't make a promise like that, Ethan. Do you know how powerful Helena is right now? Do you even know what she's done?"

"What she's done?" Ethan asks, sounding confused. "Do you mean since killing Cade?"

"She has become a destroyer of worlds," he tells Ethan. For the first time in my life, I see fear in my uncle's eyes. "I don't know what killing Cade did to her exactly, but I do know that she's gone nuclear on at least one planet that I know of, more than likely more. I can't be sure. All I know is what I heard secondhand."

"Heard from who exactly?" Ethan asks.

"A fellow rebellion angel who used to live on the planet she destroyed. He said he felt her presence the moment she arrived on his world. In fact, it was the very same day she killed Cade. David told me that he had never felt darkness like that before, and that's saying a lot considering the fact we used to work for Lucifer. He said that it was so strong he was able to pinpoint her exact location on his planet. When he phased to where she was, he found her floating over a dune in the desert within a sphere of what he thought was pure energy at first. As he continued to watch her sob inside it, he slowly realized it was a ball formed from her own tears. Over a short period of time, the power emanating from Helena's grief became so strong it started to produce shockwaves that made it impossible for him to keep standing. Eventually, the shockwaves grew in intensity and frequency until there was a final flash of bright white light. Apparently, it was the release all of the energy Helena had produced within the ball. David wasn't able to phase away quickly enough and lost the body he was inhabiting at the time, but it wasn't strong enough to kill him in angelic form. He wasn't sure how long he had been knocked unconscious, but when he came to, there wasn't a living thing—human, plant, or animal—left on the world. All he could find was scorched earth. Everything else had been turned to ash."

"Why didn't you tell Roan this story after you heard it?" Ethan asks, sounding suspicious of the tale since it's only being retold now when we're so close to finding Helena.

"We never thought she would slip up and do something stupid—like going back to the cabin—that would let you find her."

"You should have at least told me," I say. "You and Mom have never kept secrets from me before. Why not tell me this? You knew I was looking for her."

"We wanted to, but we weren't sure you were in the right state of mind to know how easily Helena can kill."

"What exactly do you mean by that?" Ethan asks, looking between Uncle Enis and me curiously.

Neither of us make a reply. Uncle Enis simply looks at me since it's my secret to tell, but for some reason I don't want Ethan to know about my death wish. I'm not even sure I really want to die. If I did, I could have ended my life a dozen different ways by now, but I chose to drink my problems into oblivion.

"Nothing," I reply, keeping my gaze fixed on Uncle Enis. I fear if I look into Ethan's eyes, I might say more than he needs to know, and right now, he doesn't need to know anything about my personal demons. "Where's Mom, Uncle Enis? We need the tracking device to help us look for Helena."

"I think I know where she is," Ethan says, eyeing something over to his right where the large industrial-size refrigerator stands.

I know she isn't hiding in it, so I ask, "Can you see her phase trail?"

"I see *a* phase trail." Ethan looks back at my uncle. "I assume it belongs to Evelyn?"

Uncle Enis just nods his head reluctantly. "You'll go through it anyway. There's no reason for me to lie about it."

I hate seeing my uncle look so crestfallen. All he and my mother were trying to do was protect me. I can't fault them for caring so much about my safety. I walk over to my uncle and wrap my arms around his shoulders.

"I'll be careful," I whisper to him. "I promise."

He wraps his arms around my waist and holds me tight.

"You better, Jules. Otherwise your mother will never let me hear the end of it."

I laugh and lean back to give him a peck on the cheek.

"I'll be home for supper," I tell him.

"I'll be waiting."

I walk over to Ethan, who takes hold of my arm again before he follows my mother's phase trail to a whole new world.

CHAPTER 5

There have been very few times in my life when I've been rendered utterly speechless. When we phase onto the planet where my mother traveled to, I end up having one of those rare moments.

We're standing on a beach with black sand, and a vast magenta-tinted ocean stretches out into the horizon before us. The sun for this planet is setting, causing a spectacle of tangerine orange hues to meld with the raspberry red tones in the sky. The colors themselves are gorgeous, but it's the sight of two large planets floating next to the one we're on that causes me to lose my breath. One is alive with vibrant blues and greens, reminding me of pictures I've seen of Earth taken from space. The other one is lavender and white with a silver belt of rings encircling its equator. I turn around to view some of the vegetation on this planet and see tall gangly tan trees with large fluffy green leaves. For some strange reason, they remind me of a feather duster. Red, orange, and mint green bushes fill out the floor of the jungle.

When I look along the sandy beach, I spot my mother sitting on a black rock jetty holding my tracking device loosely in her right hand. As she stares out across the ocean toward the setting sun, a heady breeze blows over the water and lifts her long blonde hair away from her face. With her still being dressed in her white suit and the wind blowing around her, she is the picture-perfect representation of an angel.

"Can you give me a few minutes alone with my mom?" I ask Ethan. "I would like to talk to her in private."

"That's fine," Ethan says readily, surprising me with his willingness to delay our search for Helena in order to give me a personal moment with my mother.

"Thank you," I reply, sincerely grateful that he isn't pushing matters to satisfy his own agenda.

As I walk along the beach, I keep my gaze fixed on my mother. I witness her hand tighten around the handle of the tracking device, ensuring a firmer grip. It's a sure sign that she knows I'm here without even having to confirm it by looking over at me. She continues to stare out toward the sunset, even as I climb up the rocks and take a seat beside her.

"I didn't realize you had this stupid thing fitted with a biometric sensor," she says, flexing her wrist slightly to indicate the tracker.

"I couldn't very well have someone waltz in and take credit for all my hard work," I tell her in a joking manner. "It seems like you can't trust people to keep their hands off your personal property these days."

My mother smiles wanly and tilts her head down slightly as she takes my jab at her invasion of my privacy good-naturedly.

"Here," she says, handing me the small black handheld device. "I thought about throwing it into the ocean, but I knew you would just jump in there and fish it out. Sorry about breaking the fingerprint lock for your apartment. I thought it might buy me some time by making you believe a regular burglar broke into your home. I should have known you wouldn't be fooled by something so simple."

I accept the tracker from her and simply hold it in my hands, giving her the opportunity to say her piece. I know she'll want to caution me to be careful as we search for Helena. She'll tell me the job is too dangerous and that I should just let the War Angels handle things from here on out, but she also knows that I'm not someone who leaves a job half finished. I need to see this through. I need to know how the story ends.

"Just be careful, Jules," she says in a resigned voice, averting her gaze from the spectacle of this planet's sunset to look into my eyes. "Helena was unstable before; now she's completely unhinged. She isn't in complete control of her emotions, and that's dangerous for anyone who gets around her. Promise me that you'll let the War Angels handle her. Don't try to be a hero, because it might just cost you your life."

"I'm always careful," I remind her. "You know that."

"Yes, but you've never had to deal with someone as powerful as Helena either."

"Uncle Enis told me and Ethan what she did to that planet your friend used to live on. I wish you had told me that story before."

"Would it have stopped you from searching for her?" she asks doubtfully.

I shake my head. "No. I guess it wouldn't have, but it tells me how much Helena still loves Cade. That information might be useful when the time comes to ask her to give up the baby. She might do it if she believes it will protect his child."

"You can't reason with a creature like her, Jules. She isn't rational like most normal people. The fact that she was able to find a way to love someone other than herself is still something I can't quite fathom. Hell wasn't meant to become a living, sentient being. It was only supposed to be a repository of power for Lucifer to use as he saw fit. Sure, she was able to decimate that planet with just the power of her grief, but what will she be able to do if she consciously focuses all of her energy on purpose? She has the potential to obliterate entire solar systems."

"You really believe she's that powerful?"

"I think she has the potential to be, yes. Right now, she's too distraught and hormonal to concentrate on such an endeavor, but after the birth, I fear she may doom us all. The more worlds she destroys, the more powerful she will become. I think that was proven after she killed all of those people in Virga, and that was just one cloud city. She's probably thought about the destruction she can cause now, but her grief has been keeping her at bay. Once the baby is born, there won't be anything to stop her from gaining more power for herself."

"To what end?"

"To end the universe and all life in it. That was Lucifer's goal in the beginning. I'm sure that remains Helena's goal now."

"But won't destroying the universe destroy her too?"

"Do you honestly think she cares about that anymore? She might even welcome obliteration."

"But what about her child? She can't wipe out the universe without ending his life too."

"I think her love for the baby may be our only hope. Either that or the final nail in all of our coffins."

Well, that seemed like an odd thing for my mother to say.

"What makes you think his birth might end up dooming us?" I ask her.

"If the War Angels take the child away from her by force, why should she care what happens to him? They'll never let her see him again. That's not something she will be able to handle emotionally. I think it would simply drive her deeper into madness and cause her to act out violently."

"Ethan's pretty determined to take the baby away from her," I say, looking back over to where he stands watching us from afar. The distance is too great for him to hear what we're saying, but even if he could, I'm not sure he would change his mind about taking Cade's son away from Helena. Odds are he and the others have discussed the possible outcomes of forcing Helena to give up her child. They obviously believe what they're doing is still the best course of action.

"I don't really care about them or anyone else in the universe, Jules," my mother says, reaching out one of her hands for me to take. "All I care about is you."

As I twine the fingers of my hand with hers, I say, "You know I'll be careful, and after hearing what you think might happen, I'll see what I can do to help the situation. I'm not sure any of them will listen to me, but I'll at least give them my thoughts on the matter."

"Just try to stay away from Helena if at all possible, Jules. Stay safe, if not for yourself, then for me."

I see my mother look at my hair and my clothes with a critical eye, like all mothers do to their daughters.

"You might want to rethink the grunge look you have going on though," she advises me. "No one is going to take you seriously looking like someone who just spent the night on the street."

Self-consciously, I use both of my hands to tuck the sides of my long hair behind my ears.

"I might be able to talk Ethan into taking me back home to shower and change clothes," I say.

"I'm sure he would appreciate that," my mother replies with a little scrunch of her nose as if to say I stink to high heaven.

I know I'm not lemony fresh, but come on, I can't possibly smell that bad.

"Okay, Mom. I get the hint," I say.

It seems like it doesn't matter how old I get, a part of me will always want to please my mother.

There's one more thing I need to do before I leave this world. I hold the tracking device up to look at the blank screen. Involuntarily, I hesitate before turning it on and allowing it to scan the iris of my eye to activate. What are the odds of finding Helena on the first planet I search? I'm thinking they're slim to none, but you never know. Stranger things have happened in the universe.

I take a deep breath in a vain attempt to ease my tenseness and help steady my nerves. I squeeze the handle on the tracking device to switch it on while holding the screen up to my right eye so the scanner can unlock my security measures. Once I'm in, I watch as three little red dots light up sequentially on the screen, letting me know the device is scanning the planet for the tracer's unique signal. If Helena is here, they'll all blink green at the same time before giving me the direction and exact distance of my target. I find myself holding my breath, awaiting the results of the search.

When the words "no signal" pop up on the screen, I feel my body instantly relax. After the talk I just had with my mother, I don't feel like I'm ready to come face to face with Helena just yet.

"She's not here," I tell my mother, unable to hide the relief I feel.

"A small blessing, I suppose. Just remember what I've told you and be careful," she begs me. "I love you, Jules. You're my heart. I can't live without you."

"I love you too, Mom," I say, leaning in and giving her a hug around the shoulders. "I promise to be careful when we run into Helena."

"I guess that's all that I can ask from you," my mom replies, sounding resigned to the fact that she won't be able to change my mind.

I step off the rocks to walk back over to Ethan.

As soon as he sees me heading toward him, he begins to walk too in order to shorten the distance more quickly.

"Hey! I'm not getting a signal for Helena here," I say once I'm within shouting distance of him. "Before we go to another planet, would you mind making a small detour and taking me back to my apartment for a little while?"

"Can I ask why?"

I stop just a couple of feet away from Ethan, because now I'm paranoid my body odor might offend his sense of smell.

"My mother suggested that I go tidy up before I travel around the universe with you," I say. "I haven't showered in a couple of days, and apparently it's showing ... and smelling."

Ethan grins, looking rather amused by my frankness but refrains from outright laughing at my predicament.

"I think we can spare a few minutes for personal hygiene purposes," he replies diplomatically.

He closes the distance between us and takes hold of one of my arms, phasing us directly to the living room of my apartment.

"I would tell you to make yourself at home, but I think the best I can offer right now is find yourself somewhere clean to sit while you wait."

"Actually," he says hesitantly, "I would like to return to Cirrus before we leave. Will you be all right here by yourself since the lock on your door is broken?"

"Oh yeah, I'll be fine," I assure him with an unworried wave of my hand. "The people in this building are nice. They won't just barge in on me. Go do what you need to do. I should be ready in about thirty minutes. Is that enough time for you?"

"Plenty. I'll be back before then," he promises.

Ethan phases, and I head directly to my bedroom. I quickly shed my clothes and walk into the connecting bathroom. While I wait for the water in the shower to warm up, I look at my reflection in the mirror above the vanity and physically cringe at what I see. My hair is as limp as a noodle, and my normally clear blue eyes are bloodshot red. With all that going for me and my normally pale skin, I remind myself of a zombie. I bare my teeth in the mirror like a fiend on the prowl and quickly discover I need to brush my teeth too. I'm pretty sure I have a piece of ham from breakfast stuck in between my top front teeth.

"Snap out of it, Jules," I berate my reflection. "You can do better than this."

After properly chastising myself for my unkempt appearance, I step into the warmth of a welcoming shower and begin the disinfection process of my hair and skin.

It takes me about twenty minutes to shower, put some makeup on to conjure the illusion that I'm a real girl, and find a clean pair of jeans and a gray three-quarter sleeve shirt in the pile my mother left on the floor when she demolished my closet. I really don't have time to do anything about the mess my apartment is in though. Right now, I have to help a handsome War Angel go steal Hell's baby away from her.

Who in the world thought that this would be how my day turned out? Oh well, at least I'm officially filthy rich. There's an orphanage downtown that will definitely reap a financial reward from all my hard work.

I grab my cell phone and call Uncle Enis to ask him to come over sometime during the day and replace the fingerprint scanner my mother broke earlier. I would rather leave my apartment locked up while I'm gallivanting across the universe with my angelic escort. He promises to take care of it for me within the next hour and lock it up once he's finished. After that, I walk back into the living room and discover miracles really can happen in modern times.

As if by magic, all of my possessions have been put back in their original place. In fact, the room looks cleaner now than when I left it yesterday.

Ethan is just setting down a framed photograph of me and Timothy on the glass end table by the couch when I enter. It's a picture of the two of us when we were in kindergarten together. When he hears me enter the room, Ethan turns around and looks me up and down.

"You look refreshed," he says, obviously pleased to know that I can in fact groom myself properly.

"And not like the walking dead?" I joke, knowing his response was meant to be complimentary without sounding rude about the state of my appearance earlier.

I let my gaze slowly travel around the living room and can't help but smile at how nice it looks.

"Thank you for doing all of this," I say, truly impressed by his act of kindness. I'm sort of at a loss for words on how to tell Ethan how happy he's made me. Then my inner devil whispers in my ear that all may not be what it seems. "Do you mind me asking if you had an ulterior motive for being so nice? Is there something that you want from me?"

"I didn't clean to soften you up, if that's what you're implying," Ethan is quick to say, looking somewhat miffed that I questioned his motives for being nice. "But there is a request I'm supposed to relay to you from Empress Anna."

"Does this have to do with my money?" I ask, crossing my arms in front of me, waiting for his response. "Because if she's reneging on the deal ..."

"She has no intentions of backing out of the agreement you made with Malcolm," Ethan tells me, sounding slightly annoyed that my thoughts were immediately negative ones. "You'll get your money. All she wants is for you to come to the palace and meet with her so she can give it to you in person."

"Oh," I say, feeling stupid for accusing the empress of something that probably never even crossed her mind. Add in the fact that I just proved to Ethan that I *am* the money-grubbing mongrel he believes me to be and you have the makings of an awkward situation. "I'm sorry. I shouldn't have jumped to conclusions like that. I'm just not used to people doing nice things for me without wanting me to reciprocate the favor. I apologize."

"That's all right," Ethan says hesitantly, but I can tell he's not sure what to think of me now, and for some reason, I care about the way he sees me.

"I plan to give most of the money away," I blurt out. The sentence sounded a lot better in my head. Spoken out loud, it makes me sound like I'm trying to justify my earlier outburst. I think a better explanation is required to smooth out this situation. "There's an orphanage not far from here that I plan to donate most of my earnings to. It's the one I probably would have ended up in if Mom and Uncle Enis hadn't taken on the responsibility of raising me."

"Did it ever feel awkward to be raised by angels?" Ethan asks sincerely.

I shake my head. "No. They've just always been my guardians. I've never known anything else."

"It's nice that you want to give your money to the orphanage," he says with an understanding grin, "but it really wasn't necessary for you to tell me."

I sigh. "I know. As soon as I said it, I realized how lame it sounded, but I didn't want you to think that I was doing all of this just for myself. I do plan to keep some of the money but not a lot. As you can see," I say, taking a cursory glance around my apartment, "I don't need that much to get by."

"I don't either," he tells me. "Sometimes I wish I lived in the downworld on Earth instead of Cirrus. Things just seem so much simpler there. Whenever I get the chance to take some time for myself, I like to go to the surface and camp out underneath the stars. I'm always amazed by how many different worlds my father made. I have access to all of the inhabitable planets through the Nexus, but I still haven't been able to visit them all."

"Speaking of planets," I say, "which ones will we be going to first?"

"I have a few in mind." Ethan looks me up and down. "Some of them are rather cold though. I would advise bringing along a jacket."

"Okay, I'll go grab one," I say, heading to my bedroom again. While I'm in there, I retrieve not only my black jacket from off the floor but also the tracking device from my bed before heading back into the living room. When I return, I ask, "When exactly does Empress Anna want to meet with me?"

"She said anytime tomorrow would be fine. Her schedule will be free."

"Should I take something there when I go see her?" I ask.

"Like a gift of some kind?" Ethan inquires uncertainly.

"Yeah. Isn't that what you're supposed to do with royalty? Bring them a tribute when you visit them?"

"Considering the fact that she'll be giving you fifty gold bars, I believe anything you give her in return would automatically seem a bit trivial in comparison."

"Ah, you make a good point there," I admit as I put on my jacket. "So what's the name of the first planet we're going to?"

"It's called Laed-i. All of the planets I want to visit today have humanoid populations who are either involved in a world war or on the brink of one."

"And why exactly would we want to go to planets like that first?" I ask. The idea of walking into a potential battle zone doesn't sound too smart to me.

"Helena naturally craves turmoil and chaos. What better planets to visit than ones that already have that going for them?"

"True enough," I agree. "Let's go."

Ethan walks up to me and places his hand on my left shoulder.

"Stay close to me after we phase in," he requests.

When I look up and see the worry he has for me in his eyes, I feel something stir between us that wasn't there before now.

"I won't leave your side," I promise him in a whisper. "The closer I am to you, the less likely I am to get blown up."

Ethan chuckles, and I earn a smile for my little joke. "Great minds think alike, I guess."

This time I laugh and tighten my grip on the tracking device in my hand.

"I'm ready when you are, fearless leader," I tell him.

"Here we go ..."

CHAPTER 6

The first stop on our search for Helena's whereabouts ends up being a total bust.

"She isn't here," I regret to inform Ethan after I see the "no signal" message appear on the screen.

"I'm not too surprised by that," Ethan replies, as he surveys the forested area he phased us to on Laed-i. "We suspect she's still in Hell."

I lower the tracking device to my side and ask him, "What makes you think she's still there?"

"We've been unable to phase into the Nexus. It's a problem we've encountered before and previously assumed it was because Helena was there blocking our ability to phase into her domain. I think she's been there since she left you last night after your encounter with her at the cabin."

"So why are we doing this today if you're so sure she's not on any of the worlds you're planning to take me to?" I have to ask. "It seems like a colossal waste of time to search for her if you already know where she is."

"She has to come out of hiding eventually," Ethan points out. "Besides, I need to check on a few of my men who are stationed on some of the worlds we'll be visiting today."

"You placed War Angels on other planets?" I ask, finding this curious. "What for?"

"I have a few scattered on various worlds to keep an eye on things for me. It may not look like it," Ethan says, sweeping his gaze around the green forest we're standing in, "but this planet is slowly being torn to pieces by its ruler."

"How can a single man tear a whole world apart?"

"By killing anyone who gets in his way and doing away with any opposition before they can become a threat to his rule. The people of this world are too scared to stand up to their king, so he continues to pillage this planet of its natural resources and to sell them to neighboring planets for a hefty profit."

"Seems a little shortsighted of him," I say. "Which of your men do you have stationed here?"

"Both Xander and Zane are here keeping an eye on the planet's destruction. I believe you already know them."

I nod. "Yeah. They come to Grace House on a regular basis. How come Xander has such a drinking problem anyway? Seems strange for an angel to be an alcoholic."

Ethan looks at me as if he's confused by my remark. "He drinks to forget. Isn't that the reason you gave me for why you drink?"

"What in the world would he need to forget? He hasn't been on Earth long enough to rack up a lengthy list of regrets."

"Yes, but he was involved in the war in Heaven, just like the rest of us. There are things that we each did during that time that's hard to forget. Xander was forced to kill his best friend back then because he betrayed us by siding with Lucifer. Xander kept what he did a secret from the rest of us for a very long time, and by keeping that secret, it damaged his soul in a lot of ways. He's having difficulty forgiving himself for what he did, but I have faith that he'll pull himself together sooner rather than later."

"Why does he come to Grace House to get drunk? Don't they have alcohol on Earth?"

"He doesn't want Anna to know that he's still drinking. He's ashamed that he hasn't been able to break his addiction to it, and he would rather not worry her with his personal problem. The last time he got drunk in Cirrus, Anna had to shame him into leaving the establishment he was in and go home. Xander doesn't want her to feel the need to do that again."

"He must have a lot of respect for her."

"We all do," Ethan states without hesitation. "She's an exceptional woman, mother, and leader. I still have a hard time believing she's Lucifer's daughter, considering how well she turned out."

"My mother told me that Anna used to be a Guardian of the Guf. Aren't those the angels in charge of molding souls?"

"Yes. She was the second soul ever created in Heaven. In fact, Lucifer made her from the light found within his own soul. So she was basically his daughter in Heaven too."

"She was called Seraphina while she was a Guardian, right?"

"Yes. And Seraphina was the Guardian who created the first human soul in the Guf."

"Which pissed Lucifer off and started the war," I conclude.

"Lucifer simply didn't like the fact that God wanted him to serve humanity. His ego wouldn't allow him to even consider bowing down to creatures he considered beneath him."

"My mother told me that after Lucifer and the other rebellion angels were cast out of Heaven, Seraphina asked the Guardians of the Guf to transform her angelic soul into a human one."

"Yes, she did. She knew that the only way to save Lucifer was to become human and show him how wonderful a species they are. Her love for him changed everything. It just took a very long time for all the pieces to fall into place and for Seraphina's original plan to finally work."

"Did you ever resent being made a War Angel?" I ask.

"Resent it?" Ethan questions, as if the thought has never even crossed his mind. "Why would I resent being what I am?"

"If you hadn't been made into a War Angel, you wouldn't have had to fight in the war. The energy your soul was made out of could have been molded into a Guardian or even a human."

"I like myself just the way I am," he replies with a troubled frown. "Do you think less of me for being a War Angel?"

"No!" I'm quick to say. "But haven't you ever wondered what it might have been like if you hadn't been specifically created to be a warrior?"

"It's honestly never crossed my mind until this moment. I wouldn't want to be anyone else besides myself, but from your question, I take it that you believe being a War Angel is a bad thing."

"That isn't what I said," I tell him.

"But you implied it with your question."

"It's just that you don't strike me as someone who would take pleasure in killing others. Am I wrong about that?"

Ethan hesitates before answering my question. "No. You're not wrong, but you have to understand that we were made to prevent Lucifer and the rebellion angels from tearing Heaven apart. Of course I didn't enjoy killing other angels, especially since killing an angel in Heaven is a true death for them."

"True death?" I ask, having never heard this part of the story before. "What do you mean by that?"

"The angels who died during the war in Heaven were lost forever. Their souls were basically sucked back into the vortex of energy that makes up the Well of Souls."

"I didn't know that," I say, extremely thankful now that my mom and Uncle Enis were fortunate enough to survive the war.

"It's a time most of us would rather forget," Ethan tells me, returning his gaze to the forest around us as he seems to search for something. I also get the feeling he would rather drop the subject of our conversation.

"What are you looking for?" I ask.

"Xander and Zane were supposed to meet us here and give me a report. It's not like them to be late."

"Do you think something is wrong?"

"That's the only conclusion I can make."

"Do they have a home here?"

"Zane does." Ethan looks back at me. "He married a woman on this planet a few months ago."

"He's married?" I ask in total shock, wondering if I misheard Ethan's statement.

Ethan nods. "He's the first of us to marry and the second of us to have a child on the way. I believe his wife is two months along in her pregnancy."

"I had no idea," I say, "but I don't talk to Xander and Zane that much when I see them at Grace House either. We normally just give a passing hello to be nice."

"Do you have any children?" Ethan asks.

"No," I reply with a small shake of my head, leaving it at that. It's a topic of conversation I would rather not delve into right now with Ethan. "Do you know where Zane and his wife live? Have you been to their house?"

"Yes."

From the questioning way Ethan is looking at me, I can tell he senses my brusque change of subject was meant to deflect the conversation away from me and my past. Whatever. As long as he doesn't push things, we'll be just fine.

"Then maybe we should go there to see if they're having a problem," I suggest. I thought he would have gotten the hint with my mention of their house, but apparently not.

"I suppose we should," he says, but he doesn't make a move right away to touch me so he can phase us both there.

He may not be saying anything, but his silence is speaking for him. He wants to ask me more questions, but he senses now isn't the time.

Finally, he reaches out and places his hand on my shoulder to phase us to Zane's house.

As soon as we arrive, I instantly feel a strange sense of being home. The house Zane and his wife live in is built on top of a rocky mountain. The landscaping in front of it is filled with a lush green lawn and flowers ranging from red to purple and every color in between. Green trees with leaves that look like lace fans stand tall on each side of the house. The front porch is made out of polished wood boards and is about four feet wide. The home itself is mostly constructed out of white stone, and the front is totally exposed to the outside world, since it's predominantly comprised of large panes of glass held into place by steel beams.

Ethan raps his knuckles against the darkly stained double wooden doors we're standing in front of, and we wait in mutual silence for someone to answer it.

A harried looking Zane yanks the door open. He's wearing a white linen sleeveless shirt and matching long pants. His usually slicked back short blond hair looks natural and free flowing today, unlike the times I've seen him in Grace House. I assume this must be his casual look while he's at home with his wife. When he sees Ethan and me, his expression changes to one of remorse.

"I'm so sorry, Ethan," he says, opening the door wider. "I completely forgot about our meeting today. Verati has been sick all morning. I just sent Xander back to Earth to track down Desmond so he can bring him here to examine her."

"Do you think anything is seriously wrong?" Ethan asks with concern.

Zane shakes his head, and I audibly hear Ethan sigh in relief.

"I think it's just regular morning sickness, but you know Desmond. He wants us to keep him up to date on everything about her pregnancy."

Zane looks over at me and smiles. "Hey, Jules, are you starting to regret you got caught up in the search for Helena yet?"

"Not yet," I say, smiling back at him. "But the day's still young."

Zane laughs and takes a couple of steps back to allow us entry into his residence.

As soon as I step over the threshold, I smell the sweet aroma of lavender. All around the room are vases of a purple flower with large petals and a bright green center. It may not look anything like the plant I'm used to, but it certainly smells the same.

Zane's home is spotlessly clean and decorated in such a way that I feel comfortable in my surroundings. Most of the furniture in the living room to my right is white with touches of purple and peach thrown in for an accent color in the pillows and other odds and ends, such as candles and picture frames. To our left is a dining room, which has a white-washed dining table and matching chairs. Straight out from the front entry is a cable-suspended staircase, which leads up to the second floor.

"Zane!" I hear a woman call out from the back of the house. "Is that Desmond?"

"No!" he shouts back. "It's Ethan and Julia Grace!"

"Come on," Zane tells us with a wave of his hand, indicating that we should follow him. "Verati is out on the back porch. She said she needed some fresh air to calm her stomach."

We follow Zane to the rear of his house, and I instantly see why his wife prefers to sit on the patio. Stretched out before them is a blue-green ocean in the distance. We're too far away to hear the crash of the waves against the shoreline, but that doesn't detract from the beauty of the scenery surrounding us. Verati is lying out on a lounge chair on the large wooden back porch with her eyes closed, basking in the sun's rays as she allows her skin to soak up its warmth.

My first impression of Zane's wife is that she looks far too petite to be having a baby. I know Ethan said she was only two months pregnant, but for some reason, I still expected to see her with a baby bump. Her slim frame will certainly fill out in another month or two as the child begins to grow exponentially inside her womb.

With her tanned skin and short black pixie style hair, Verati is the picture of tranquility in her relaxed pose. She's dressed similarly to Zane, except her sleeveless white linen outfit is a summer dress. When she hears us step onto the porch, she immediately opens her eyes and turns her head to look our way. A welcoming smile lights up her face and her brown eyes. She swings her legs onto the wooden planks of the porch to stand up and greet us.

"Ethan!" she says excitedly before walking over to him and giving him a hug around the waist. "It's so good to see you again. I was disappointed when you couldn't make it to dinner the other night."

"I'm sorry, Verati," Ethan apologizes, returning her hug. "Something came up that I had to attend to."

Verati steps back from Ethan, which places her right beside her husband.

"I'll let it slide this time," she says as if she's making a grand gesture of forgiveness on her part, "but I will expect you to come over the next time you're invited to dine with us. My friend was extremely disappointed that she didn't get to meet you."

Ethan suddenly looks uncomfortable with the turn of the conversation.

"Verati, I would like to introduce you to Julia Grace," Ethan says to her, quickly changing the subject and expertly steering the chat in another direction.

Verati smiles at me and extends her hand, which I automatically shake. "My husband has mentioned you to me before. It's a pleasure to finally meet you."

"It's nice to meet you too, and congratulations on the pregnancy," I say.

"Zane says you're feeling sick to your stomach," Ethan says.

"It's just the baby," she replies, protectively placing her hands over her belly. "But it has Zane worried, so he asked Xander to bring Desmond over here."

"And who is Desmond?" I ask to no one in particular, since it's obvious they can all answer the question.

"He's one of the last remaining Watchers," Verati tells me. "Have you met any of the other ones yet?"

"I've only met Malcolm so far," I admit.

"Oh yes, Malcolm," Verati says with a sly grin. "I swear, every time I see that man, I think he gets more handsome."

"If I didn't know you were madly in love with me," Zane says, bringing his wife into his arms, "I might get jealous with you talking about another man like that."

Verati places her arms over Zane's shoulders and gently begins to play with the hair at the nape of his neck.

"My heart only belongs to one man, and I'm looking straight at him," she declares.

I feel sure that if Ethan and I weren't standing right in front of them that Zane would have kissed his wife for her sweet words.

Quite suddenly, but not unexpectedly, Verati's smile slips from her face and she places her hands over her mouth before running back into the house.

"Sorry," Zane tells us hurriedly before chasing after his wife, "we'll be back as soon as we can."

"Poor thing," I say sympathetically. "Morning sickness can be the worst. You feel like your body's betraying you and there's nothing you can do about it."

Ethan doesn't say anything, but I can feel his eyes on me. When I look into his face, I can tell he's debating on whether or not to ask me a question. Before he can make a decision, I decide to ask him one instead.

"How long has Verati been trying to fix you up with one of her friends?" I ask.

"Ah ..." Ethan turns his gaze away from mine and looks out toward the distant ocean. "Caught onto that, did you?"

"It was blatantly obvious," I say. "I assume you knew that was the reason she invited you for dinner, but what I want to know is if you purposely found an excuse not to come here that night so you didn't have to spend the evening getting to know her friend."

"Something did come up that night," Ethan says as he looks back at me. In a lower voice he says, "But it wasn't something that couldn't have waited until the next morning. I just didn't feel like being introduced to one of her friends again and having to turn down her advances. Situations like that can become extremely awkward."

I have to laugh a small bit about that. "How many friends of hers has she tried to set you up with?"

"Five so far," he answers with a heavy sigh.

"And none of them met your requirements for a potential mate?"

"No. They did not."

Ethan's response was so quick, I have to ask, "And what exactly *are* you looking for in a future life partner?"

"I only have one set criterion," he tells me, staring into my eyes as if I should know what he's referring to.

Unfortunately, I have no clue. So I have to ask, "And no one has met this mystery criterion of yours yet?"

Ethan takes a deep breath and says, "Actually ..."

"Ethan!"

We both turn to look inside the house. I see Xander walking alongside a man I can only presume to be Desmond. The Watcher is handsome in a rugged sort of way with shoulder-length curly brown hair. He smiles at me with an ease not many people can manage when first meeting a stranger.

"Glad to see you, Desmond," Ethan greets him, holding his hand out to the other man. "Verati is in the bathroom with Zane. They should be back out shortly though."

Desmond looks at me and smiles. "And you must be the much talked about Julia Grace."

"Yes," I say, confused. "Who exactly has been talking about me?"

"Malcolm told us you would be traveling with Ethan to track down Helena's whereabouts," he replies. "I hope you can find her. We haven't had much luck in that area since she went off the grid. I was also informed that she told you she hasn't sought any medical assistance with the pregnancy. Is that correct?"

I nod. "That's what she told me. I don't think she was lying. She had no reason to."

"I doubt she was either, lass," Desmond agrees. "Knowing Helena, she believes she can handle having the baby on her own, but I would much prefer to be there for the delivery. Please tell her that, if you see her again, and let her know that all I'm concerned about is the child's welfare. Nothing else."

"I understand," I say, letting him know I can read between the lines. Desmond may want Cade's child to be raised by anyone other than Helena, but he won't actively try to take her son away from her, unlike the War Angels standing around us. "I'll let her know if I get the chance."

Desmond nods. "Good."

I look over at Xander. "I honestly can't say that I've ever seen you sober."

Desmond lets out a chortle at my remark, but Xander simply raises a dubious eyebrow in my direction.

"I could say the same about you, Jules," he replies smoothly with a satisfied grin.

"Touché," I reply. "I guess we're both full of surprises today."

"Xander," Ethan says, "maybe you can give me a report on the state of this world while Zane is attending to his wife. Jules and I have other planets we need to visit today. I would like to get going as soon as possible."

"King Manas has increased his demand for iron ore," Xander tells us. "It's only a matter of years before he's harvested all he can from this planet's crust. I've tried to talk him into slowing down, but he refuses."

Ethan sighs deeply. "Do what you can, Xander. We can only advise him on what's best for his world. The rest is up to him."

"This is Zane's home now," Xander stresses. "Why can't we do more? It wouldn't take much to force Manas off the throne."

"We can't do that," Ethan says in such a way that Xander should know better than to try to argue.

"Yes, we can," Xander replies, attempting to change his leader's mind on the subject, even though we can all see it's an act of futility. "Just a few War Angels could take this whole planet away from him."

"You know as well as I do that the people of this world are scared of change. They've been conditioned by the Manas family for generations to be followers and not to think for themselves. We need to find them a strong leader to replace Manas before we completely revolutionize their world."

"What if we started laying the groundwork for a regime change? We could help those who want to rebel against Manas' reign. Or is that against the rules too?"

"We were not sent here to become the caretakers of the universe or its law enforcers, Xander. Our father sent us here to help Anna solve her Helena problem and facilitate the evolution of humanity."

"But we can do so much more, Ethan. Why won't you let us?" Xander questions desperately.

"Because it's not what our father asked us to do!" Ethan thunders. "Now drop the subject. I won't argue this point with you again."

Xander scowls at Ethan, but he keeps his mouth shut.

All righty then. I guess even angels have tempers and get mad with one another. Not that it's any surprise to me. I've seen my mom and Uncle Enis argue a lot over the years, but it was usually about something petty, like what color to paint the living room or something similarly trivial. They never debated whether or not to change the fate of an entire planet.

To be honest, I'm on Xander's side of the argument. I mean, if they know this King Manas is about to destroy the planet's ability to sustain its inhabitants, why not stop him in his tracks and change things for the better? Although I can also see Ethan's point too. If Anna's War Angel contingent starts policing the entire universe, they'll be so spread out that they won't be able to help Anna if she needs it. But Ethan has drawn his line in the sand, and Xander doesn't look like he's about to cross it. I'm not sure if that's because Xander knows Ethan would whip his ass in a fight, or if he simply respects his commander enough to follow all of his orders. My gut instinct tells me that it's a mixture of those two reasons.

The tension between the two War Angels isn't broken until Zane and Verati walk back onto the porch. The conversation quickly turns to the subject of her pregnancy. I feel like an intruder listening to them talk about such a private matter and decide to walk over to the railing on the porch to gaze out at the beautiful scenery. I'm soon joined by Ethan, who must feel as out of place as I do.

"We can leave as soon as they get through talking," he tells me, not wanting to be rude to his friends by interrupting their conversation just to say good-bye.

As I continue to observe the beauty of this world, I have to ask Ethan something.

"Why won't you let Xander save this planet? It sounds like he could, and you can't argue that it's not a world worth saving. I mean, just look at it, Ethan. It's paradise."

"There are thousands, if not millions, of worlds just like this one whose people need help. We can't save them all," Ethan reasons.

"Yes, but you could save some of them," I argue. "You told me that you like to go to the down-world on Earth and look up at the stars to see all of the worlds God has made. Don't you think He would want you to save as many of them as you and your men can while you're here? Surely He didn't just send you down to help Anna and bed as many women as possible to spread your seed throughout the universe. Why not do more?"

Ethan remains quiet, and I can tell he's thinking over what I just said before answering.

"Like I told Xander," he begins, "our primary reason for being sent here is to help Anna. Until we've completed that mission, I don't see how we can add on any more responsibilities to the duties we already have. If that changes, perhaps we can do more to help, but until things get resolved, Anna needs us. I won't abandon her. Not now. Not ever."

Ethan's loyalty to his empress is commendable, but I can't help but believe it's a bit shortsighted. I decide not to push the issue any further though. It's obvious he's made up his mind on the subject, and I know I don't have enough influence over him to change his way of thinking.

"Ethan ..." I hear Verati say in a singsong voice. It's one that tells me she's about to ask him to do something for her. "I was wondering if you are free for dinner tonight. I'm sure if I call my friend she would be more than willing to join us this evening."

"I'm sorry, Verati," Ethan says, sounding believable, "but I already have plans for this evening."

"Oh, surely you can rearrange things and join us," she insists.

"I really can't," he says apologetically. "Certain arrangements have already been set into motion. I can't back out of them now."

"And what is so important that you can't come back here to have dinner with your friends?" she asks, clearly suspicious that Ethan is simply making up an excuse not to come.

"Jules and I are having dinner together this evening," he lies smoothly.

I thought angels weren't supposed to lie. I know my mom told me that the War Angels can tell the truth from a lie, but I don't see either Xander or Zane calling Ethan out for telling a fib. Did he ask me to dinner earlier and I just didn't realize it? I don't remember being asked out on a date, and I haven't been drunk since last night. I don't say anything because I'm not completely sure what's going on.

Verati looks at me with newfound interest ... and dare I say it ... hope?

"Well then, I sincerely wish the two of you a marvelous time together this evening," she says with what looks like a conspiratorial wink at me.

What exactly is that supposed to mean? Does she think I am going to get lucky tonight? Fat chance of that happening. I'm not even sure Ethan plans for us to go on this convenient date he seemed to pull out of thin air on the spot.

"I'm sure we'll have an interesting time," Ethan tells her before he starts making the rounds to the others and saying his good-byes to everyone.

While Ethan is talking to the other men, Verati sidles up to me and says in a whisper, "You will have to tell me what happens on this date of yours. I've been trying to fix Ethan up with some of my friends for the past few months, but he doesn't seem interested in any of them. I suppose he's waiting until he finds his soul mate."

"Soul mate?" I ask, never having heard the term used before now. "What is that?"

Verati looks at me in complete surprise. "No one has told you about soul mates yet?"

I shake my head. "No. Why? Should they have?"

"Well, I would advise you to ask Ethan to tell you about them tonight. It's an interesting story if you have time to listen to it."

Ethan walks back over to us and asks me, "Are you ready to go to the next planet?"

"Sure," I reply, taking a step forward so he can place his hand on my shoulder.

"You two have fun tonight!" Verati says enthusiastically.

I look up at Ethan's face just before he phases us and swear I see him blush.

CHAPTER 7

When we phase to the next planet on Ethan's agenda, I find myself standing on top of a lush green hill in an isolated part of this world. Before I even activate my tracking device, I look up at Ethan.

"So what was that all about?" I ask him curtly. "I really don't like being used as an excuse to get you out of a blind date."

"I wasn't using you as an excuse," Ethan tells me, looking a bit taken aback by the ferocity of my reaction to what he just did. "Verati simply took me by surprise. I was planning to ask if you wanted to have dinner with me this evening after we're through today."

I cross my arms in front of me. "And you just assumed that I would say yes to your invitation? What if I already have plans for my evening?"

"I would never presume to know your answer to any question or expect you to change your own plans," he states on the edge of being terse himself. "I simply hoped that you would accept my invitation. If we're going to be working together, I think it's a good idea if we get to know one another better. Don't you?"

I feel a bit let down by his answer for some reason. I suppose it's because he makes the evening sound more like a business meeting than an actual date. I'm not sure why that bothers me, but it does.

"I told Uncle Enis that I would be home for supper," I tell him, not quite sure I want to use it as an excuse to get out of spending time alone with Ethan in a casual setting. I quickly decide that I don't. "But I guess I can let him know my plans have changed. He'll probably be happy that he doesn't have to cook for me tonight."

"Does he always cook for you?"

"He does if he doesn't want me to have a meal from a fast food restaurant or reheated in my microwave."

"I take it that you don't like to cook, then."

"It's not so much that I don't like it or can't do it myself. It's more like I don't have the patience to cook a decent meal. If it takes more than five minutes to prepare, forget it. I've got better things to do with my time."

"I do like to cook. See, we're getting to know things about each other already."

Ethan grins at me, and for some odd reason, I just can't come up with a reason to refuse his offer to dine with him.

"So, are you cooking for me?" I ask, definitely intrigued by the notion. "If you are, I can't refuse your invitation."

"Then, yes," he says as his grin grows wider, "I will be cooking for you this evening. Do you have any preferences?"

"Seafood!" I automatically respond, or was it a shout? Probably a shout because this dinner just got *way* more exciting for me. "I heard Earth has more ocean covering the planet than land. Sierra is the complete opposite, and it's against the law to fish in our oceans. I would *love* to try some seafood."

"Seafood it is then," Ethan readily agrees. "Anything in particular for dessert?"

"Nah, surprise me. I like surprises. Well, of the good variety anyway."

"Duly noted."

"So ..." I say as I look around the world we're standing on. "How come you keep phasing us to isolated parts of these planets we're visiting? Are you afraid someone might see us?"

"These are the safest places on each planet to phase to," he answers. "They're also the predesignated spots my men have been instructed to meet me at."

"Who are we meeting on this planet?"

"Their names are Atticus and Marcus," he replies.

"Do you always send your men out in pairs?"

"Usually, yes, but not always. On the more volatile planets, it's safer to have two stationed. If one of them runs into trouble, the other one can either help or come get me. You never did tell me why you don't work with a partner in your bounty hunter business."

"Having to look after someone else would be too much trouble for me. They would just get in my way."

"Considering you hunt down criminals on a regular basis, it sounds like you should have someone who can watch your back," Ethan says, sounding concerned about my physical safety.

I shrug his worry off. "It's worked for me so far. I don't see any reason to bring someone new into my life if I don't have to."

"Well, what about Enis? He would certainly be able to help you."

"More like hover over me like a mother hen. *No* thank you."

Ethan still looks less than pleased about my insistence to work alone, but to be honest, it's really none of his business what I do. After this job is over, we'll both go back to how things were before and probably never see each other again. The thought of that eventuality makes me pause before bringing the tracking device up and turning it on.

"Is there something wrong with it?" Ethan asks. "It's not broken, is it?"

"No," I answer, as I squeeze the button on the handle to turn it on. "It's fine."

As I watch the little red dots flash on the screen, I find myself strangely hoping to see a "no signal" message appear. If Helena isn't here, then I don't have to worry about my adventure with Ethan ending too soon, which isn't like me at all. Normally, I can't wait to finish a job. I glance up to look at Ethan's face and notice him watching the screen too with a worried frown crinkling his forehead. When the message on the screen reads "no signal," I notice that his wrinkles vanish as he appears to be as relieved as I am that she's not here. I find his reaction curious, but not in a bad way.

"Sorry," I tell him, trying to emote that emotion. "She isn't here either."

"I'm sure we'll find her eventually," he says. "I have a feeling that she'll at least resurface when it's time for the baby to be born, if not sooner."

"Why would she do that?" I have to ask. "The safest place for her to give birth would be Hell. She can keep everyone out of there if she wants to."

"True," Ethan agrees, "but I don't believe she'll want Cade's son to be born there. She knows how much he hated her domain. It was one of the reasons they were on your planet. Apparently she wanted him to stay in Hell while she blew Virga up so he wouldn't know what she had done, but he talked her into letting him stay in your cabin instead of Hell."

"It seems like he had a lot of influence over her."

"He did. More than anyone else she's ever had in her life so far."

Two men phase in front of us on the hill. I can only assume one is Atticus and one is Marcus.

Ethan holds out his hand to the War Angel to the left of us who has curly short brown hair and intense blue eyes. It's not so much the color of his eyes that make them stand out. It's the strength behind them that causes you to notice them first. He wears a serious scowl on his face, and I have to wonder if it's a permanent facial expression since the creases of his skin conform to it so naturally.

"Atticus," Ethan addresses the man, "it's good to see you. We miss you back on Earth."

Atticus shakes Ethan's hand and replies. "I would definitely rather be there than on this planet. I swear the leaders here act like squabbling children fighting over a piece of candy."

Ethan holds his hand out to the other man who looks somewhat similar to Atticus, but rather than a scowl, his expression is more relaxed and self-confident. The two angels could pass for brothers, if you didn't know any better: Atticus as the older brooding sibling who wears the weight of the world on his shoulders for all to see, and Marcus as the young rogue always looking for a good time no matter where he's at.

"So have the two of you been able to smooth things over between President Lauder and Prime Minister Arden?" Ethan asks.

"Yes," Atticus answers, "but the peace between them is tenuous at best. Neither of them seems to want to budge or share this land." Atticus briefly looks around the area we're standing in. "It seems to be an all or nothing situation for them, and they're both willing to do whatever it takes to claim it. I'm afraid it's just a matter of time before an all-out war breaks out here."

"I see," Ethan says, sounding disappointed. "Well, do the best you can. That's all I can ask from either of you."

Both Atticus and Marcus look at me with undisguised curiosity.

"So you're the one who planted a tracer on Helena?" Atticus asks gruffly. "How did you manage that?"

"By allowing her to believe I wasn't a threat," I answer. "I was drunk at the time, so I suspect she didn't view me as a worthy adversary."

"Remind me never to underestimate you then," Marcus tells me with a flirtatious twinkle in his light brown eyes. From the self-confident way he holds himself, I can tell Marcus isn't used to being rebuffed by the fairer sex. He is good-looking and perhaps even charming to other women, but I need more than that to draw my interest.

"I doubt I'll need to remind you of anything, unless you're becoming prematurely senile. Odds are we'll never have reason to see each other again after I help Ethan capture Helena," I tell him. When I see his well-practiced, lady-killing smile falter, I can't help but feel as though I've taught him a small lesson in humility.

Oddly enough, I hear Atticus chuckle and see him slap Marcus on the back.

"Well, I'll be damned, Marcus," he says to his friend. "I think we actually found a woman who is immune to your charms."

"More like apathetic," I clarify, "but we can go with immune if that makes you feel any better."

Atticus begins to laugh harder, obviously enjoying Marcus' sudden discomfort.

"I don't say this to many people," Atticus tells me, "but I like you, Julia Grace."

"Call me Jules," I tell him. "All my friends do."

"I'm glad I could help the two of you bond so quickly," Marcus says, obviously not taking my gentle jab at his ego to heart. I'm glad to see that he has a sense of humor and doesn't take himself too seriously. That at least gives him some friend potential.

"Have you had any luck tracking down Helena?" Atticus asks me. I can already tell from the expression on his face that he isn't expecting me to have news concerning her whereabouts and that his question was more out of politeness than anything else.

"Not yet," I answer. "But we'll find her. Don't worry about that."

Atticus nods but doesn't look as if he has much faith in me finding Helena anytime soon. I don't take any offense. They've been searching for her for months. Why would I be able to find her on my first day?

"I don't suppose either of you have eaten Ethan's cooking?" I ask in an attempt to lighten the mood. "He's making me dinner tonight, and I want to know what to expect."

"Ethan's cooking for you?" Atticus asks as if I've said the strangest thing he's heard in a long time. "He's never cooked for anyone, as far as I know."

"I know how to cook," Ethan assures me. "Malcolm's been teaching me so I would be prepared."

"Prepared for what?" I have to ask. "Do you plan to wow your enemies with your culinary skills instead of fighting them?"

Ethan grins. "Not exactly, but close."

I look at Atticus and Marcus. "Since neither of you have tasted Ethan's cooking, why don't you join us this evening?"

"They have work to do here," Ethan is quick to say before either man can give an answer of their own.

"I thought this was going to be a business meal," I reply, testing him to see what he says next. From the way he's acting, our meal might actually be a date and not just a "let's get acquainted" dinner like he implied. Either way, I want to know what the deal is. "Shouldn't I get to know as many of your men as I can?"

"If I wanted them there, I would have asked them myself," Ethan tells me. "Unless you have a problem dining with me alone."

"I didn't say that," I reply.

"Ethan's right," Atticus pipes up before things can get more intense between me and Ethan, "we have work to do here. If we can prevent this war, we need to try. I would hate to leave this planet wondering if I could have done more to help."

"I suppose we'll have to take a rain check," Marcus says to me with a wink. "But thanks for asking."

"We should probably get going," Ethan says to me.

I hold my hand out to Atticus. "It was nice meeting you. I hope this isn't the last time we get to see each other."

Atticus shakes my hand and says, "I'm sure it won't be. In fact, I'll make sure it isn't."

I turn to Marcus and say, "And it was interesting meeting you."

Marcus smiles and shakes my hand. "Have fun tonight, but not too much fun."

I am about to ask him what he means by that but don't get a chance to. Ethan places his hand on my shoulder and phases us to yet another strange new world.

Only this time, we don't phase onto a peaceful part of the planet. We phase directly into the middle of a battlefield.

I probably do one of the dumbest things I've ever done in my life. I duck and run to take cover. Why is this a colossal mistake on my part? What I should have done was grab ahold of Ethan and relied on him to phase us away. *That* would have been the smart thing to do. Yet I let my natural instincts take control of my body and run behind a large boulder on the rocky terrain we phased onto. Ethan has no other choice but to follow me.

"I thought you said all the places we were going to were safe!" I yell at Ethan. I'm not yelling because I'm mad. I'm yelling because the noise of the battle raging around us is so loud I can barely hear myself over the bedlam.

"They're supposed to be!" he shouts back, cautiously looking over the top of the boulder we're hiding behind to survey the fighting that's happening all around us. I notice him go stock-still as if something unexpected catches his eyes. "Silas?"

"Is that the War Angel we were supposed to meet here?" I ask him.

Ethan crouches back down next to me shaking his head. "No. He's one of Helena's men. Check the tracker and tell me if she's here."

The urgency in Ethan's voice spurs me into action. I hold the tracker out so we can both see the screen. I find myself holding my breath as we wait to find out if Helena is on this planet.

The red dots only have a chance to blink once in sequence before they all turn green. Only a second later, we're given a direction and a distance to our target.

"She's north of us and ..." I blink to make sure my eyes aren't playing tricks on me before I check the distance again. "She's only one hundred feet away from us, Ethan," I say, looking over at him. "That means she's directly behind us."

"Hide the tracker in your jacket pocket so she doesn't see it," he advises me.

I notice Ethan place his right hand on the hilt of the sword hanging against his hip. He grips it tightly as if preparing to draw it out.

"Stay here," he tells me just as he's about to stand up.

I quickly grab his left arm and say, "You promised Malcolm you would try to talk to Helena first. How are you going to do that with a firefight happening directly between us and her?"

"I'll give her an ultimatum," he says hurriedly. "If she doesn't agree to give me the baby when it's born, then I'll take him from her now."

"You can't do that," I argue, gripping his arm even more firmly. "It's not right, Ethan."

"And letting her keep him is the right thing to do?" he questions incredulously. "That's not a solution either, Jules. She can't be allowed to raise Cade's child and turn him into a monster."

"If she loves him, she won't let that happen," I say. "At least talk to her and see what her plans are for the child."

"Even her best intentions can't be trusted. Look at what happened to Cade. She planned for them to make a fresh start on a new planet, yet she killed him because she loved him too much. I can't let her do that to the baby too."

"But she's his mother, Ethan! Every child deserves to know that he's loved by at least one of his parents."

"I couldn't agree with you more" we both hear Helena say.

We look directly in front of us and spot Helena standing only about ten feet away from where we're crouched. Gunfire still rings through the air all around us, ricocheting off of the rocky terrain. Helena stands proudly before us with her shoulders pulled back and her long blonde hair flowing in the breeze of battle like it's her natural element. The black chiffon dress she's wearing billows out around her as if it is made of smoke. I take a brief moment to appreciate her gown with its diamond and pearl encrusted cap sleeves and matching empire waist. The dress is pleated in the front, allowing her swollen belly plenty of space to grow.

Ethan stands to his full height from his position behind our rock to face Helena.

"And what exactly will your kind of love do to the child, Helena?" Ethan questions her. "Will it kill him as easily as it did Cade?"

"What happens to *my* child is none of your concern," Helena replies angrily. "You and your merry band of War Angels seem to think you know what's best for my son when the exact opposite is true! Do you honestly believe that a child born from me will be someone you can control? He'll be more powerful than you can imagine, Ethan. What will you do to Cade's baby if it turns out to be more of a monster than you believe me to be? Do you imagine you'll have the strength to kill him in order to protect the ones you love?"

Ethan doesn't answer right away, and I can tell that he's carefully thinking about his response before he gives it.

"The boy may be half you, but he's also half his father. Cade was the best of us all. He had the purest heart, and I have to believe part of his gentle nature was passed on to his son, despite who his mother is."

Helena doesn't say anything right away. She simply stands there defiantly, staring Ethan down. I'm not even sure she realizes I'm present, which is probably a good thing. Of the three of us, I'm the most vulnerable to Helena's powers. I clearly remember my mother's warning to keep my distance from the embodiment of Hell if at all possible. I've always listened to my mom's advice, and I don't intend to stop now.

"Then listen to me carefully, Ethan Knight," Helena begins. "If you think for one moment that I will ..."

And then she vanishes.

"Did she just phase?" I call out to Ethan. I assume that's what she did, but why would she do it mid-sentence? It sounded to me like she was about to tell Ethan he was crazy if he thought she would give him her baby freely. But why phase just before she said it?

Ethan stares at what I presume is Helena's phase trail. After a few seconds, he turns back around and bends down on one knee in front of me to speak.

"She's gone back to Hell," he tells me, sounding just as confused as I am about her abrupt departure.

"Why did she leave so quickly?" I ask. "If I didn't know any better, I would say something phased her away against her will."

Ethan stares at me, and I see a look of dawning enter his eyes.

"That might be exactly what happened," he says.

"What do you mean?"

A bullet from the battle that's still raging around us strikes the top of the rock we're behind.

"First things first," Ethan says, grabbing one of my arms and phasing me back to the safety of my apartment.

The sudden quiet of my home compared to where we just phased from gives me a brief moment of panic that I've gone deaf.

Ethan and I both stand up.

"You didn't get hurt while we were there, did you?" he asks, quickly looking me over to check for any obvious injuries.

"No," I tell him, secretly pleased by his worry for me. "I'm not hurt."

Ethan continues to look at me as if he wants to say something but doesn't really want to. Finally, he tells me, "I need to go back to Cirrus to discuss something with Anna and Malcolm. I think it's safe to say that Helena won't be venturing out of Hell again today, so I think we should resume the search tomorrow, if that's all right with you."

"Sure," I say with a small shrug.

"Good." Ethan gives a small nod of his head. I can tell his mind is racing with thoughts, but he doesn't seem to want to share any of them with me, at least not yet.

"Are we still having dinner together this evening?" I ask, finding myself hoping that what just happened hasn't altered those plans. For the first time in a while, I'm looking forward to an evening not spent alone with a bottle in my hands and memories haunting me until I pass out drunk.

Ethan smiles, and I take that as a good sign. "Yes. I'll be back in about four hours to pick you up."

"Are we eating inside or outside?"

"Outside."

"And will it be cold or hot?"

"Warm with a breeze," Ethan replies, continuing to grin at me.

"Formal or casual?" I have to ask, because how else will I know how to dress myself?

"Casual."

Ethan stands there looking at me expectantly for a moment before asking, "Is there anything else you need to know?"

I shake my head. "Nah, I think I've got it."

"Okay, I'll be back to pick you up exactly four hours from now. I look forward to seeing you then."

Ethan phases, and I find myself alone in my apartment. For some reason, the space feels emptier with his departure. I walk over to the picture frame window facing the city just to feel some sort of connection to the outside world. Usually this is one of the few places where I can find some peace, but now it just seems too quiet, too desolate.

My loneliness swiftly comes to an end when I hear Helena ask, "Why do you choose to live in such squalor?"

CHAPTER 8

I spin around and come face to face with Helena. I won't lie to myself and say that she doesn't scare me. She does. And with good reason. I have Hell standing smack dab in the middle of my living room looking slightly pissed off about something. I consider my options for calling for help, but none of them seem likely to work. I left my cell phone in my bedroom earlier and walking past Helena to go get it would certainly tip her off to my intentions. The best thing I can do in this situation is not let her think she scares me, because I believe a show of fear would simply encourage her wrath. I decide to treat her like anyone else who just showed up to my apartment unannounced.

The first and most obvious question I have to ask is, "How did you get in here?"

Helena snorts derisively. "Ethan was stupid enough to phase directly here from the battlefield. I thought I might be able to finish my conversation with him by following, but I see that he's already left." Helena looks to her right and squints slightly, presumably looking through Ethan's phase trail. "Scurried back home to Cirrus and my sister, Anna, I see."

"If you wanted to finish your conversation with him, why did you leave earlier?" I ask.

"Frankly, that's none of your business," she replies brusquely. She looks me up and down like I'm a specimen on a petri dish "I'm glad to see that you've finally bathed. The smell of alcohol and uncleanliness on you last night was not very becoming."

"My mother already pointed that out to me," I say with a roll of my eyes. All I need is another unwanted lecture. "I didn't realize I was offending so many people with my personal hygiene habits."

"Humans tend to be overly polite about such things and allow their friends to run around unkempt. I suggest you find better friends who are more truthful with you."

I don't make a reply, because I expect Helena to phase away since Ethan isn't here.

But she doesn't. She simply stands where she is examining my apartment with a look of total disdain on her face.

"Is there something else I can help you with?" I ask her.

"I thought Evelyn was quite wealthy in this world," she says, returning her gaze to me but keeping her upper lip curled in open disgust. "Why is it that you live like a beggar?"

I look around my apartment and see nothing wrong with it. Sure, it's a little sparse on décor, but it's clean and functional.

"What exactly does my mother having money have to do with the way I live?" I ask her.

"Is Evelyn so greedy that she won't share her wealth with her own daughter?" Helena asks snidely. "Not very progressive of her, if that's the case."

"My mother would give me everything she owns, if I asked her to," I say defensively. "But I don't need her money. I can take care of myself."

Helena raises a dubious eyebrow in my direction. "From where I'm standing, your ability to provide a decent living to survive on is questionable."

"Don't you have souls in Hell to torture or something?" I ask her. "Surely you have something better to do than goad me into an argument."

"Why do I need to go there when I can stay here and accomplish the same thing?"

The smile that appears on Helena's face tells me that she just made a little joke at my expense and that she finds herself immensely amusing.

I decide to transition the subject away from torture before Helena gets any ideas about switching tactics and turning to a more physical expression of her sadistic side.

"Do you really believe what you told Ethan back on that planet? Do you think your child will turn out to be a monster that no one can control but you?" I ask.

Helena doesn't respond right away, and I can see her wavering between giving me an answer to my question and remaining mute on the subject. Finally, she makes a decision.

"It's possible," she tells me in a reserved voice that gives nothing away about her true feelings concerning her son's powers.

"Anything is *possible*," I point out, taking her response as the non-answer that it was meant to be. "You must have an educated guess on the abilities he'll be born with or you wouldn't have said anything to Ethan."

I witness a flash of worry cross Helena's face as she self-consciously places her hands on her belly in a protective manner.

"I don't know what powers he'll have. All I know is that he's different," she tells me, "and not knowing how he's different worries me somewhat."

For the first time, I feel a strange sort of connection with Helena. I understand what it feels like to worry over your unborn child when so many things can go wrong, even circumstances that are completely out of your control. I may not be able to assuage her concerns over what powers her son will have after he is born, but I can at least try to ease her worry over his birth.

"I have a message for you," I tell her. "Do you know Desmond? He's one of the Watchers from Earth."

Helena nods. "Yes. I know who you are referring to. What about him?"

"Apparently, he's a doctor. He asked me to tell you that all he wants to do is help in the delivery of your son when the time comes. He won't be there to take him away from you. All he's interested in is the welfare of the child."

"And did you believe him when he said that to you?" she asks warily.

"I did. I truly believe he's only concerned about the baby being born healthy. He may wish for you to give it up, but he won't force the issue. He only wants to help."

Helena nods, letting me know she heard my words. I expect her to go on a tirade about how she can't trust any of the angels on Earth, but she doesn't.

"If you see him again," she says instead, "tell him I'll consider his offer."

"I strongly urge you to not have the baby on your own. There are a number of complications that can occur during a delivery, and with your baby, who knows what might happen? Even you don't know if this will be a normal birth. I really don't think it would be a wise decision to try and deliver him on your own."

"Are you scared I might die during childbirth?" she asks disbelievingly. "If you are, you shouldn't waste your worry on me. I can't die ... not really."

"To be honest, it isn't your life that I'm worried about. Do you have any idea if your baby can die? I can assure you that if he ends up dying during his own birth, you'll never be able to forgive yourself. You'll always wonder if he might have lived if you had only swallowed some of your stupid pride and asked for help. Desmond is offering his services to you without any strings attached. I suggest you take him up on his offer when the time comes."

"But if I seek his help, what's to prevent Ethan and his men from following us and killing this body I'm in after my son is born?"

"Not much," I concede, "but at least your son will be alive and well cared for by people who love him. No parent can ask for more than that if they're unable to look after their child themselves."

Helena narrows her eyes on me. "You speak as if you have experience with that sort of dilemma." She looks around the living room and notes, "Yet I see no pictures of loved ones on the walls, only the one of you and that boy as a child on your table. I thought perhaps you might have a baby of your own to have so much insight into the connection between a child and parent. I heard everything you told Ethan. And I wholeheartedly agree that my son should know that at least one of his parents loves him unconditionally. I understand how it feels to be raised without that type of love and support, and I refuse to allow my son to experience what I did."

Helena's confession moves me, and to be honest, I'm not sure why she's opening up to me the way she is. Perhaps she's simply lonely and needs someone to talk to who isn't judging every little thing she says in a derogatory way. Or perhaps she intends to kill me so I can never tell anyone what she just told me. I have no way of knowing what her true intentions are, but I prefer to believe she just needs someone to talk to right now.

I feel a need to cross the threshold where my own inner demons are hidden away, and I can't believe I'm about to do it with Helena. But if my previous experiences can convince her to seek help during the delivery, it will be well worth it.

"I had a child once," I tell her as my heart begins to ache with loss and regret. "But I never got the chance to see him smile or even take his first breath."

Helena frowns.

"Why not?" she asks in a quiet voice. "What went wrong?"

"We—my husband and I—were in our mountain cabin when my water broke," I tell her. "We'd spent months learning everything we could about home births and thought we could handle things on our own. As soon as the contractions started, I began to panic because I knew something was wrong. Once we realized that we were in over our heads, we decided not to take any chances and got into our car to head to the hospital. It wasn't that far away, just at the base of the mountain. So we didn't even think to bother my mom or Uncle Enis to help us out and phase us there instead. Timothy and I were always very independent and rarely ever asked them for help. Anyway, on the way down the mountain, it began to rain so hard we could hardly see five feet in front of us. I told Timothy to take us back to the cabin so I could call my mom, but he kept telling me he could get me to the hospital faster if we just kept going. The storm never let up, and Timothy lost control of the car when it hydroplaned. We ended up sliding off the road and into a shallow ravine. He and I were lucky enough to survive the crash, but our son wasn't."

I have to stop and collect myself as the terror and utter helplessness I felt when we drove off the cliff flashes through my mind.

"Some people say that mothers have a sixth sense about their children," I continue, "that they can tell when they're in trouble. I guess I developed mine even before my son was born. It wasn't until the next morning that we were rescued, but by that time, my son was already dead. The doctors called it umbilical cord prolapse. It caused my son to be deprived of oxygen for too long, and he ended up dying inside me," I say in a hollow voice as I recall that moment in the hospital when we were told how our baby died. "If I had only stayed in the city, we could have gotten the help we needed and saved my son's life. I don't want to see you make the same mistake I did. I don't wish that kind of grief on anyone. So I beg you to take Desmond's offer seriously. No matter what you might want, you need to put the welfare of your son first before anything else."

I suddenly feel as if I'm standing emotionally naked in front of Helena. I've bared one of my deepest regrets to her but kept my darkest secret out of her grasp. She's the embodiment of Hell, and I know I can't trust her. I meant what I said to her last night back at the cabin. I'm not sure if my soul is destined to travel to her domain after I die, or not, for the things I've done and the person I wronged. If I can't forgive myself for what I did, how can I ever expect God to forgive me?

Helena continues to stare at me with a completely blank expression on her face. Most people would immediately say how sorry they are for my loss and how terrible it is that I had to experience such pain. But I didn't tell her my story to gain her sympathy. My only motivation was to give her an example of how the birth of her own son could go terribly wrong in a very short amount of time. Some people don't see the pitfalls to a situation until it's too late. By that time, they're buried so deeply in their mistake that no one can help pull them out of it.

I suppose I should have been prepared for what she says next, but I'm not.

"How exactly did your husband die?" she asks with a small tilt of her head. "Obviously, he survived the crash from what you just told me, but I remember Evelyn saying that he's dead now. How did it happen?"

I brace myself emotionally, because I know she isn't going to like my answer, and I'm not sure how she's going to react to it.

"That's really none of your business," I state. "I only told you the story about my son because I don't want you to be as stupid as I was. You have a chance to ensure that your child doesn't suffer the same fate as mine. I suggest you take it and count your blessings that Desmond only wants to help you. I don't think you can say that about a lot of people in your life."

"No, I can't," she agrees as she continues to study me. "Although I can't help but wonder if there is something else that you want from me. For instance, why were you with Ethan earlier? I don't believe he makes it a habit of dragging girls along with him wherever he goes, even though I know for a fact that he hasn't led a celibate life since he's been on Earth. You don't exactly strike me as the type of woman who would sleep with someone you just met, so your presence seems oddly timed. What possible reason would he have to allow you to tag along on his search for me?"

I swallow and pray to God that some sort of miracle happens within the next few seconds that gets me out of this conversation.

"Jules!" I hear Uncle Enis call out as he knocks on my front door. "Are you in there? I tried to call but didn't get an answer!"

I automatically break my eye contact with Helena and look toward the door like anyone would do in the same situation. By the time I turn my head back around to look at her again, she's gone.

Cautiously, I look up toward the heavens, wondering if God is actually watching everything that happens here. Just in case, I say a quiet but grateful "thank you."

I take in a deep breath to ease the tension I feel after my unexpected encounter with Helena.

When I open the door and look at Uncle Enis, I must be wearing an expression on my face that tells him something is very wrong.

"What happened?" he immediately asks. "Why do you look like you just saw a ghost, Jules?"

I begin to slowly shake my head. "Unfortunately, she isn't a ghost. She's all too real."

My uncle has always been rather astute when it comes to figuring things out on his own with little information given.

"Helena was here?" he asks worriedly. "Inside your apartment?"

I nod my head.

Before I can protest, Uncle Enis grabs ahold of my arm and phases me to my mom's apartment.

"Evelyn!" he calls out, which automatically causes my mother to phase to our position in the living room.

"What's wrong?" she asks, looking between the two of us for an answer.

"Helena was in Jules' apartment," he tells her, sounding incensed by the notion. "She can't live there anymore. We'll need to move her."

"Wait a minute ..." I begin to protest before my mother interrupts me.

"She has free reign to enter your home now, Jules," my mother says like it should be obvious that I need to pack all my belongings and switch apartments immediately.

All I can do is let out a hollow laugh. "Do you honestly believe that if Hell wants to have a chat with me that she can't just knock down the door to wherever I live? Come on, you two. I know you're smarter than this. That apartment is my home. I refuse to leave it."

Neither of them says anything. They just look at me disapprovingly, making me feel like I'm a teenager again who stayed out a little too late with my friends.

"Why was she even there?" my mother asks. "How did she discover where you live?"

Now that part of the story is something I don't want to tell them, because I know exactly what their reactions will be.

"Ethan and I were on a planet where Helena was. She phased away unexpectedly, and he phased me back to my apartment, because there was a battle going on where we were. He was just trying to get me somewhere safe before I got shot by a stray bullet. It wasn't his fault."

"Ethan should have known better!" my mother erupts. "It was careless of him to not consider the possibility that she would return and follow his phase trail. Where is he now? I need to have a talk with him."

"No," I say absolutely. "You are not hunting him down just to yell at him about this. Do you honestly believe that will do anything but cause tension to form between the four of us? He'll feel bad enough after he learns what happened, Mom. Don't make matters worse by playing the overbearing mother hen and chastising him because you think he put your little chick's life in danger. I'm not a child. I fully understood the dangers of taking on this job. So if you want to blame someone for what happened, blame me."

My mother's face remains scrunched up in anger, but it slowly dissipates as she lets her rage go.

"Fine," she says reluctantly, looking anything but all right about the situation. "But you better tell him what happened, Jules. He needs to know what he did so he doesn't make another mistake where your safety is concerned. I won't allow you to place your life in danger over this. You may consider this an overreaction on my part, but it isn't. She's dangerous. More dangerous than anyone you've ever met in your life. I know she looks beautiful and vulnerable, especially since she's pregnant, but she isn't. If anything, she's more lethal than ever."

"I understand your concern," I tell her. "And maybe it's naïve of me, but I get the feeling she just wants someone she can talk to right now. I think she feels isolated, and if she's as dangerous as you think, that isn't a good thing. You always taught me to help those who need it. Why shouldn't that rule apply to Helena?"

"Because she's a homicidal maniac!" Uncle Enis shouts in frustration. "You just don't know her like we do, Jules. She's nuts!"

"You're always telling me that people can change for the better," I tell him. "At least that's what you said about you and Mom. Are you telling me that's not true? I know you both did things in the past that you're not particularly proud of. Why are you placing a restriction on Helena? Is she the only person in the universe who is immune to change? Even Mom said she shouldn't have been able to find a way to love someone, but we all know how much she loved Cade. Isn't that proof that she can be better than what she was originally designed to be by Lucifer?"

"You listen too closely to the things we say to you," my mother grumbles.

"I listen to good advice," I reply with a small smile, because I can see that my words are finally sinking in. "And you've always given me that. Just because I'm putting it into practice isn't any reason for you to get upset. You both need to trust me. You didn't raise a fool, and I've learned from the mistakes I've made in the past. I can handle this. Let me deal with Helena in my own way."

"I hate it that you're all grown up," Uncle Enis grouses. "I can't just send you to your room anymore. Plus, you're starting to make more sense than we are now."

I have to laugh. "I was taught by the best. What else can I say?"

Uncle Enis brings me into his arms and hugs me like he never intends to let me go.

"Just be careful," he whispers to me. "That's all I ask."

"You know I will," I promise him.

"When do you plan to see Ethan again?" my mother inquires. "He should know about his stupidity as soon as possible."

"Actually ..." I say, quickly trying to decide if I should tell them about my upcoming dinner with Ethan or not. I decide full disclosure is called for in this instance. "We're having dinner together this evening."

"Like a date?" Uncle Enis asks, sounding surprised that Ethan asked me out.

"It's more of a 'let's get acquainted' type of meal," I reply, not wanting to place the "date" label on a simple dinner.

"Where is he taking you?" my mother asks, clearly curious about the details.

"He didn't really say," I admit. "All I know is that it will be warm and breezy there and that he will be cooking some seafood for me from Earth."

"He's cooking for you?" Uncle Enis questions as if the fact is totally unexpected.

"Somebody has to cook the food," I say with a small shrug, finding this a reasonable explanation. "You know I don't even cook for myself, much less someone else."

"Yes, I'm fully aware of that fact," he replies. "Still, it seems a bit intimate for him to be cooking for you. Sounds like a date to me."

"Whatever it is," my mom says, "I'm just happy to see you willing to try something new. It's been so long since you went out with someone besides me or Enis."

"Yeah, I know."

No one says it, but we're all thinking about the fact that this will be the first time I've gone out with a man since Timothy's death.

Finally, my mother breaks the tension by asking, "What do you plan to wear?"

Excellent question.

"I have no idea," I admit. "I probably don't have a dress that fits anymore. I'm pretty sure I've lost weight in the past five years."

My mom's face lights up with excitement. "Then let's go shopping! How much time do we have?"

"He said he would be back in four hours to pick me up. I guess that was about twenty minutes ago."

"Then we can make a day of it," my mother says, looking happier than she has in quite a while. "We should find you a new dress, get your hair done," she looks at the hair on my head as if something dangerous might crawl out of it, "and a manicure certainly wouldn't hurt."

"It's not a *date*, Mom," I try to stress. "We're just having a meal together."

My mother simply waves her hand in the air at me to brush off my claim.

"Call it whatever you want. I call it an excuse to go shopping and be pampered. Let me go get my purse and we can go."

As my mother walks toward the back of her apartment, presumably to her bedroom to get the mentioned purse, Uncle Enis looks at me with a certain amount of pity.

"You know she's going to try to doll you up for this date," he tells me, as if I should just go ahead and resign myself to my doomed fate.

I sigh. "Yes. I know. But it's not a date."

Uncle Enis pats me on the back. "Go ahead and let yourself think that way if it makes you feel less nervous, but eventually, you'll realize Ethan asked you out on a date."

I shake my head. "It's not a date."

"Okay," he says again with another reassuring pat on the back, but he's doing nothing to hide the fact that he believes I'm simply deluding myself.

I feel my heart start to pound a little harder inside my chest as the realization begins to sink in.

I'm going on a date with Ethan Knight, commander of the War Angels and undoubtedly one of the most handsome men I've ever met.

What in the world have I gotten myself into?

CHAPTER 9

My mother decides that since it's so close to my birthday the occasion provides her with an excuse to go overboard on our shopping spree. She takes me to the most expensive clothing store in Arcas and buys me not one outfit, but three, and shoes to match. I silently wonder if she believes my dinner with Ethan will lead to more dates in the not so distant future. Honestly, I'm not sure what I think about the possibility of that happening and decide not to dwell on a maybe.

I have to admit that shopping with my mom has its perks. It's nice to go out with someone who can phase all your packages home within a split second, saving you the hassle of lugging a bunch of bags everywhere you go. Plus, my mother has impeccable taste. She knows what will look good on me even before I try things on. I trust her implicitly and simply allow her to choose my outfits for me. I'm not much of a fashionista anyway. I could care less what I wear most of the time, as long as it covers the important parts of my body and is comfortable.

Since I didn't argue with her about spending so much money on my new clothes, she seems to take that as permission to spoil me for the rest of the day. After we get through having facials, manicures, pedicures, and our hair styled, I only have about thirty minutes left to get ready before Ethan is expected to arrive. By the time my mother is through primping me, I feel as though I've been primed to enter a beauty pageant instead of going out on a simple dinner date.

"I didn't realize I had so much wrong with me that I needed a full makeover," I tell her, half joking, half not, while I put on one of the dresses we bought earlier in the day.

"Jules, you're a natural beauty," my mom tells me from her seat on the side of her bed. "The only thing we did today was get rid of the grime beneath your fingernails and excise the split ends from that gorgeous head of blonde hair you have. You didn't need a makeover, just a sprucing up. And ..."

My mother's long pause prompts me to turn around to face her as I'm zipping up the back of my dress. She looks uncertain on whether or not to say what else is on her mind, which is odd for her. It's a rare occasion when she doesn't say what she believes you should know.

"And what?" I gently prod her, seeing that she needs some encouragement to finish her statement.

"And," she begins hesitantly, "I'm glad to see you take an interest in yourself again. It's not just the fact that you let me primp you today and buy you pretty clothes either. I was happy to see you enjoy the time we spent together. You acted like your old self while we were out. I know you've never cared much about shopping for clothes or going to the salon to be pampered, but today was one of the first days in a long time when I felt like you were having as much fun as I was. You made me feel like you wanted to be with me instead of just going through the motions because you thought it would make me happy."

"I love spending time with you, Mom," I tell her, walking the few feet to her. "I'm sorry if I've been making you feel like I don't lately. It's just ..." This time it's my turn to make a long pause.

"I know," she says understandingly with a smile to match. "Things have been hard for you the past few years. I'm just relieved to see you open up to people again, even if one of those people is Helena."

During our extravagant day of shopping, I told my mom about the conversation I had with Helena in my apartment. She didn't say it in so many words, but I knew she thought I was nuts for telling her about the death of my son, which was the start of a downward spiral that led to Timothy's death. Even knowing how much my mother disapproves of me sharing such a private tragedy with Helena, I still have no regrets that I did it. Strangely enough, telling her about my own loss helped me feel less alone in my grief. I'm not exactly sure why. Perhaps forcing myself to say the words out loud was therapeutic in a way that I couldn't have foreseen. Whatever the reason, I'm glad I did it, and I hope it made Helena reconsider trying to handle the birth of her son all alone.

"Anyway," I say, shaking off the morbid turn our conversation was taking, "how do I look?"

I make a complete turn in front of my mom so she can view the dress from all angles. When I look at her again, she's wearing a proud smile on her face.

"You look stunning," she tells me. "You may in fact render Ethan speechless when he sees you."

I walk over to the full-length mirror in my mother's room and examine my reflection.

I have to admit that the dress I'm wearing isn't something I would have normally picked out for myself. Yet my mother's flair for fashion allowed her to know the halter lace sheath dress would look perfect on me. The cocktail dress is the color of champagne and has a cutaway leaf design with an open back and sheer illusion hem, which accentuates the details in the lace while revealing a little bit more of my legs. We decided to keep my hair simple and straight with just a few layers to frame my face and accentuate my high cheekbones. My makeup is barely there, because my mom knows how much I hate having to fuss with lipstick and powder.

"I do clean up nicely," I have to admit, which earns me a hearty laugh from my mom.

I turn back around to face her and ask, "How much time do I have left?"

My mom looks at the clock on the mantel of the fireplace and says, "Just a few minutes."

She stands up and pulls out a pair of strappy high heels from their box that we bought to match the dress. I walk over and take them from her, quickly sliding them on my feet. Once that's done, she touches me on the arm and phases me back to the living room in my apartment. When we get there, I receive another surprise.

"Why are you here, Uncle Enis?" I ask him.

He stands from his seat on my couch and uses the remote in his hand to turn down the volume of the television program he was watching.

"I just thought I would see you off," he tells me, but even I can see through his obvious ruse.

"You do realize I'm not sixteen, right?" I ask. "Ethan doesn't need 'the talk.' I'm sure he'll be a perfect gentleman with me this evening."

Uncle Enis clears his throat. "It wasn't really him I wanted to talk to before you left. It was you."

"Me?" I ask in total confusion. "I can assure you that I won't be making any overt sexual overtures to Ethan tonight."

"I wasn't talking about sex, Jules," Uncle Enis says, looking uncomfortable about the turn of the conversation. "I wanted to encourage you to let yourself have a good time with him this evening. Don't overthink things like you sometimes do. Just go with the flow and let yourself have some fun."

"I'll try to," I say, feeling a little uncertain as to why he felt the need to tell me what he did. "But I'm not planning to make a lifelong commitment to the man on our first date."

"Aha!" Uncle Enis says triumphantly, punctuating his words by spearing the air with an index finger. "You finally admitted it's a date!"

"Date. Casual dinner. Whatever. It all amounts to the same thing," I reply, trying to play off the fact that I did in fact finally call my evening with Ethan a date.

"Excuse me," I hear Ethan say unexpectedly.

I turn slightly to find him standing to my right between me and the front door of my apartment. He's dressed in a soft blue linen shirt with the sleeves rolled up to his elbows, a pair of white linen pants, and white sandals. He looks between the three of us with a degree of uncertainty.

"Have I arrived at a bad time?" he asks me. "Should I have used the door and knocked first?"

"Knocking isn't necessary when I'm expecting you," I tell him. "My mom and uncle were just leaving."

I'm not sure I could have given them a bigger hint than that but, apparently, my uncle needs a sign to help him find the door.

"So, what do you have planned to do tonight, Ethan?" Uncle Enis asks in a manner that appears laidback but definitely isn't. He has that too "casual" pose going on that screams he's trying to be nonchalant about the whole situation.

"I'm making dinner for Jules this evening," Ethan replies, stating a fact that my uncle already knows.

"And after you eat," Uncle Enis presses a little harder, "do you have anything special planned?"

Ethan only pauses for a moment as he considers the question.

"Well, afterwards I thought I would use my considerable talent of seducing women into my bed on Jules and ravish her until morning," Ethan says with a completely straight face. "Is that plan all right with you, or do I need to ask for your permission first?"

"And on that note," I say, looping one of my arms around one of Ethan's while my uncle is still wearing a stunned expression on his face, "I think we'll be leaving."

I expect Ethan to phase us to wherever he plans to take me straight away, but instead he looks over at my mother first and tells her, "I'll have Jules home before midnight, Evelyn. I promise."

My mother smiles at Ethan and inclines her head in his direction. "Thank you for letting me know."

Ethan then phases us to the location of our dinner date.

I soon find myself standing inside a large white painted gazebo on a world I've already visited once that day. It's the same planet that we followed my mother to after she stole my tracking device from my apartment.

I let go of Ethan's arm and walk the two steps it takes for me to stand at the edge of the entrance to the gazebo. It's already nighttime on this world. When I look up into the sky, I can still see the two other planets I spied earlier hovering close by. My eyes are instantly drawn to the illumination of the magenta ocean.

"Do you know why the water glows like that?" I ask Ethan, unable to take my eyes off of the natural wonder.

"I've been told that the water is filled with little organisms similar to plankton on Earth. They're bioluminescent creatures, which is why you can see them so clearly at night."

"I've never seen anything so beautiful," I say not only meaning just the water, but the entire corner of this world. I turn around to face Ethan and catch him looking at me instead of our surroundings. "Is the rest of this planet as beautiful as this?"

"I can show you more of it after we eat, if you would like that," he offers.

"I would love it!" I reply enthusiastically. "What else is there to see?"

Ethan grins. "I don't want to ruin the surprises this world has to share by telling you ahead of time what to expect. I would much rather show you and let you discover them for yourself."

"Then I look forward to finishing our meal," I say, looking around the interior of the gazebo for the food. All I see is a small round table covered by a white tablecloth with two place settings and an arrangement of red and white flowers set in the middle.

"Um ... where is the food hiding?" I have to ask.

"I was running a bit late," Ethan begins to explain. "I had to ask for some help to get everything here, but my assistants should be arriving any minute now with the rest of what we'll need."

I consider the gazebo and the white floating glowing orbs, which provide a soft, but clear, light for us to see by.

"I don't remember this structure being here earlier," I note. "You didn't build it in the four hours since you left me, did you?"

Ethan shakes his head and smiles like I said something funny. "No. I didn't build it. I borrowed it from Malcolm and Anna and phased it here for us to use."

"It was nice of them to let you use it," I say as I consider whether or not I should ask my next question. I decide there's no reason not to. "What have you been doing since you left me in my apartment?"

"I went fishing."

I stand there for a moment, wondering if I heard him correctly.

"Did you say you went fishing?" I have to ask, just to clarify.

Ethan nods. "Yes. You said you wanted seafood, so I went out and got some."

"From the sea?" As soon as I ask the question, I realize how stupid it sounds. Of course he fished in the sea. Where else would you get seafood? Duh.

"Yes," he answers, looking amused by my question and not doubting my intelligence for asking such an idiotic one. "I was able to talk a shrimper into taking me out to catch some shrimp and fish. Afterwards, I located a man who traps lobsters near Maine for a pair of those."

I could almost squeal with glee at the prospect of eating shellfish because such a delicacy is forbidden on my planet, but I refrain from acting so childish in front of Ethan. He probably eats like this every day. Or does he?

"Why did you have to catch the shrimp yourself?" I have to ask. "Don't you have stores in Cirrus where you can buy groceries like that?"

"I could have asked the staff in the palace for them, but such things are considered a luxury for the aristocracy. I decided to go to the down-world and pay for them myself. The shrimper I went to see was on his way out, so I volunteered to go help him. I like to work, and I love the sea. It was actually a lot of fun for me, but it put me a little behind my schedule. That's why I had to ask some friends to help me out a little bit."

As if his friends heard him mention their participation in our dinner, I see Malcolm and Roan phase in with items to help with our evening and a pint-sized companion who seems to be holding the most important part of the meal: dessert.

Malcolm phased in with the little man carrying our dessert and what looks like a rather large stainless steel outdoor grill with an attached stove and small sink. Roan phased in with a small white clothed table, which has two small closed ceramic containers sitting on top of it and a rather large white plastic box.

"Ready for your big date, Jules?" Malcolm asks with a large grin on his face like I'm missing some sort of inside joke between the men.

"It's just dinner," both Ethan and I say at the same exact time.

I look at him, and he looks at me. Then we both begin to laugh a little. I can only assume Malcolm, and possibly even Roan since he's smiling too, have been giving Ethan as hard a time as my mom and uncle did me about our evening together.

"You sure look pretty, Ms. Jules," the little gentleman standing beside Malcom tells me.

I walk over to him and say, "Thank you for the compliment ..."

"This is my son, Lucas," Malcolm tells me, placing a hand on his son's shoulder.

"Well, thank you for the compliment, Lucas. I appreciate it."

I don't ask why Malcolm has a son who appears to be around the age of seven or eight. As far as I know, Anna and her husband have only been married a little over a year. Around the time all this business with Helena started, Anna gave birth to fraternal twins (a boy named Liam and a girl named Liana). My mother didn't tell me they had more children, but considering Lucas' dark skin, I have to assume that either his mother is someone from Malcolm's past or Lucas is adopted. Whatever the case may be, he's absolutely adorable. I resist the urge to pinch his cheeks because I'm sure that would just embarrass him.

"I have to agree with Lucas," Malcolm says. "You do look nice, Jules. I barely recognized you."

From the twinkle of amusement in Malcolm's eyes, I know he's joking, but to be honest, he's not that far from the truth.

"Dad," Lucas says to his father with a disapproving shake of his head as he looks up at Malcolm, "you're not supposed to say things like that to a lady. You would never say anything like that to Mommy. It would make her feel bad."

Malcolm smiles down at his son with pride. "You are right, as usual. I shouldn't pick on Jules. I'm sure she wanted to look as nice as she could for her date with Ethan."

"It's ..." I begin, but decide to not protest that I'm not on a date with Ethan. We all know that's exactly what this is and denying the fact is just ridiculous at this point. "It's always nice to have an excuse to dress up."

"It is a very nice dress, Jules," Roan says with an appreciative look. "I can't say I've ever seen you in one before now."

"I don't wear them often," I reply, suddenly feeling self-conscious about the way I look.

Ethan must notice, because the next words out of his mouth are: "Thank you all for helping me out with things. Let Anna know when you get back that I appreciate her making the dessert. It looks delicious."

I look down at the fruit tart Lucas is holding and ask, "Are you saying the empress made that for us? With her own hands?"

"She received a cookbook from a special person to us both as a wedding gift, and she's been cooking one new recipe a day from it for the past month. A fruit tart was today's recipe, so she offered it to Ethan for your meal."

"Please tell her thank you for me," I say. "That was very nice of her."

Malcolm smiles. "I believe you'll be seeing her tomorrow. You can tell her whether or not you liked it. I'm sure she'll want to know."

"I will," I promise. "Anything that looks that beautiful has to taste good."

Lucas holds the tart out for me to take.

"I hope you have fun tonight," he says. "My mom said this is the first real date Ethan has ever been on, so don't get mad if he messes something up. He's trying really hard, and that's what counts."

I hear Ethan clear his throat as if what Lucas just told me has embarrassed him a bit.

"Your mother sounds like a very wise woman," I tell Lucas, secretly pleased by what he just revealed about Ethan. "Please let her know that I look forward to meeting her tomorrow."

"I will," Lucas promises. "See you later, Ms. Jules! Have fun!"

The three of them phase, presumably back to Cirrus, while I stand there holding the tart in my hands. I turn around to face my date.

"That boy may end up ruling his own cloud city one day," I declare.

"What makes you think he's not already calling the shots in Cirrus?" Ethan questions me with a smile.

"I wouldn't doubt it if he was," I reply truthfully.

Ethan walks up to me and takes the tart from my hands.

"I hope you're hungry," he says as he walks over to the small table Roan phased in and sets the tart down on it. "I prepared a couple of side dishes for us, but I thought the shrimp and lobster would taste better if I grilled them here."

"To be honest, I'm starving," I admit. "Sometimes I think my mom forgets that I'm human and need to eat on a regular basis. Either that or she was just having too much fun today shopping with me."

I notice Ethan's eyes look me up and down in a slow manner. It's the first time he's allowed himself to consider me in my new outfit. The intensity of his gaze makes me wonder if he has x-ray vision because I suddenly feel like I'm standing in front of him in the buff.

"If that's one of your purchases from today, I have to say it was money well spent," he tells me.

Ethan doesn't smile as he says these words, which makes the moment feel more intimate. He does, however, allow his eyes to sweep me from head to toe once again as he awaits my response.

"Thank you," I tell him in a soft voice because there's no need for me to say it any louder. The air between us has suddenly become filled with an electrical charge that seems to cause every look and word said to carry more meaning. I can honestly say I've never felt such a strong attraction to a man, not even Timothy.

"Well," Ethan says with a small grin to break the sudden, but not unpleasant, tension between us, "I suppose I should start cooking before you waste away. I brought plenty of food, so don't feel shy about eating as much as you want. That's what it's here for."

"If there is one thing you should know about me," I declare, "it's that I'm not shy when it comes to food. In fact, would you be terribly upset if I had a slice of Anna's fruit tart for an appetizer?"

Ethan chuckles. "Please, be my guest. I'm sure she'll love to hear whether you like it or not."

"I have a feeling I'm going to love it," I say as I walk over to the dining table and pick up the small dessert plate sitting on top of the dinner one.

As I'm cutting a slice of the tart and Ethan walks over to the grill to prepare to cook, I see a man phase into the gazebo. He's handsome in a very classic sort of way with brown hair and dressed in a well-tailored black suit with a white undershirt. I've never seen the man before and can only assume he's either a War Angel or one of the Watchers from Earth. Whoever he is, he looks haggard and anxious, causing me to immediately wonder what horrible tragedy has befallen him.

Ethan looks over at the man who is standing at the entrance of the gazebo.

"Jered, what's wrong?" Ethan says to him in surprise. "What are you doing here?"

"I need you to help me," Jered says desperately, his voice quavering slightly. "I need you to help me find my son."

CHAPTER 10

I have no idea what's going on, so I decide to stand still and listen.

"Malcolm just told me you saw him on Cephas," Jered says anxiously. "Where exactly did you see him? What was he doing? How can I find him there?"

Ethan turns away from the grill and walks over to Jered.

"I tried to find you earlier to tell you myself that I saw Silas, but Malcolm said you were busy doing something in the down-world. I figured that by the time I found you and took you to Cephas, he would most likely already be gone."

"But what if he's still there?" Jered asks desperately. "You don't know that he isn't. Where exactly did you see him?"

"I went to meet Alex there to get his report but found a firefight happening in our usual meeting spot instead. I saw Silas shooting on one side of the fight; I'm not sure which one. I didn't have time to figure it out before we had to deal with Helena."

It's only after the mention of a "we" that Jered seems to finally notice my existence.

"I'm so sorry," he says as he straightens his shoulders and tries to wipe away the worry from his facial features. It almost works, but I can still see his troubled state of mind in the pools of his eyes. "Please excuse my intrusion, Ms. Grace."

"No apology necessary," I tell Jered, slightly surprised that he knows my name. I can only assume Malcolm told Jered who Ethan was with this evening.

Jered nods his head in my direction, silently letting me know that he appreciates my acceptance of his apology.

"Ethan, do you have a moment to spare to phase me to Cephas so I can look for Silas myself?"

"It's been hours since I saw him there, Jered. I'm sure he's gone by now."

"Nevertheless, I would like to be able to phase to the planet on my own whenever I want. If he went there once, that might mean that he'll go there again. I won't be able to rest until I know for sure that he isn't on that world anymore."

"I think it would be better if I took you to where Alex is staying on the planet," Ethan tells him. "He can escort you around and show you the most likely places that Silas might be. That's better than phasing you to a world you've never been to before and having to walk everywhere you want to go."

"Then I would appreciate you taking me to Alex," Jered replies, sounding as grateful as he looks.

Ethan turns to me and says, "Will you be all right on your own for a few minutes? This shouldn't take me very long."

"Sure, I'll be fine."

"I'll be back as soon as I can," he promises before resting his hand on his friend's shoulder and phasing away.

By the time Ethan returns, I've already eaten my first slice of the fruit tart and am working on my second serving.

"I'm sorry about that," he apologizes. "Jered has been looking for his son for months. This is the first time any of us have seen him for quite a while. Although I guess I shouldn't have been surprised that Silas was on Cephas with Helena."

"Why is that?" I have to ask. "Does he work for her?"

"Sort of," Ethan begins, sounding hesitant to categorize Silas' connection to Helena in such a way. "Jered is a Watcher. I assume your mother probably told you about their curse and the curse their children had to suffer through."

"Yes," I say. "She told me that their children would transform into creatures at night called werewolves."

"Jered wasn't always the man he is today. A long time ago, he sided with Lucifer and used his son to help him accomplish various misguided deeds that ended up killing a lot of people. Anyway, Jered's son died and has been in Hell for over a thousand years. At least he was up until a few months ago. We assumed he was helping Helena in some way after she left Earth, but this is the first time any of us has actually seen him with our own eyes."

"So, is Jered going to try to talk his son out of helping her?"

"That's part of his plan," Ethan says with a heavy sigh. "As you can imagine, Jered feels an enormous amount of guilt for being the reason his son was sent to Hell in the first place. Now, he wants to find a way to break Silas free from Helena's hold over him so he can redeem himself."

"What if Silas isn't interested in asking for God's forgiveness?"

"That isn't a possibility as far as Jered is concerned."

"And what is your opinion on the subject?"

Ethan shrugs. "It doesn't really matter what I think. As long as Jered believes his son can be saved, I have to help him in any way I can."

"What if the only way to help Jered is to make him come to terms with the fact that his son will never change?"

"Then I'll help him with that loss when the time comes. Right now, Jered has hope that he can reason with Silas. I'm not about to take that dream away from him."

I decide to drop the issue because it's really none of my business. I'm sure Jered knows his son. If he thinks Silas can be saved, there has to be a possibility of it happening. If Silas was my child, I would never give up on him either, and I can only assume that Jered feels the same way.

"I see you've already eaten a quarter of the tart," Ethan notes before returning to his position by the grill. "If you will have a little more patience with me, I'll have the rest of our meal cooked in just a few minutes."

"No rush," I tell him from my seat at the table. "I just started eating this slice, and I'm trying to eat it more slowly than I did the first piece so I can savor all the flavors."

"By the time you're through, I should have everything almost cooked," Ethan promises.

From my position at the table, I quietly watch Ethan as he begins to prepare our meal. Apparently the large plastic box on the table contains the fresh seafood he intends to cook. I see him pull out a bag of shrimp and a bag with two lobster tails. He also pulls out two silver-looking pouches and places them directly on the grill without opening them. After he lights a fire underneath the grill, he begins to skewer the shrimp and place them over the low-burning flames.

Every motion Ethan makes is sure with purpose and graceful fluidity. I can't say I've ever seen anyone move like he does. It takes me a moment to figure out what it is about the way he shifts his body that intrigues me. After a few minutes of studying him, I realize what it is. He moves like a man who knows exactly what he's doing and exactly how he intends to accomplish each of his actions. Most people hesitate for at least a few seconds while they work at something, but not Ethan. There is no doubt in his actions, and for some reason, I find it fascinating to watch him move.

He must feel me watching him, because while he's basting the shrimp and lobster tails with melted butter, he turns around to meet my gaze.

"How was the tart?" he asks me. "I assume it was good since you ate two slices of it."

"It was one of the most delicious things I've ever eaten," I declare truthfully. "Anna is a great cook."

Ethan smiles at my remark like I've said something that amused him.

"Did I say something funny?" I ask, unsure how my statement could be considered humorous.

"Anna comes from a long line of really bad cooks," Ethan answers. "She's the only one of the descendants who was able to break the curse and learn how to do it."

"Ah, well, she definitely knows how. That's for sure. I just wish I had the patience to do it."

"I'm sure you're good at other things," he says, hinting for me to divulge a plethora of my secret talents to him.

"I always hit my target when I shoot my gun," I tell him. It may not be something a normal girl would say, but if whatever this is between me and Ethan has a chance of progressing to something more than just a dinner date, he needs to know I'm not like a lot of other women he's met on other worlds. "And I always bring in a bounty once I've accepted the job."

Ethan grins. "I take it you're not the type of woman who sits at home knitting scarves and baking cookies then."

"Sometimes I wish I were," I half laugh. "Life would be a lot simpler."

"Why did you leave the police force to become a bounty hunter?"

I stare at Ethan for a moment, considering whether or not I should answer his question. I don't feel ready to, so I break our eye contact and look down at my nearly empty plate. While I consider my next words, I use my fork to roll a solitary red raspberry around in the left-over crumbs.

"I, uh," I begin so it doesn't seem like I'm ignoring his question while I try to figure out how I'm going to answer it. "I quit after my husband died. I hated the way people would look at me like they pitied me. So I decided to start working alone. I'm basically doing the same job I did on the force. I hunt down criminals and get paid for it. The only difference is that I don't have a badge or a nine-to-five job to go to every day. I like being my own boss and setting my own schedule. It makes life easier not to have to answer to someone else."

"I can understand that," he says, turning back around to face the grill to flip over the shrimp and lobster tails.

I suddenly feel an overwhelming urge to be closer to Ethan, so I stand from the table and walk over to him. As soon as I approach the grill, the delectable scent of the shrimp and lobster assail my nostrils, filling them with their sweet aroma.

"That seriously smells delicious," I tell him, unable to prevent myself from inhaling deeply. I look over at the two foil-wrapped items he first put on the grill. "What's in those?"

"Sea trout," he answers. "We caught a few while we were shrimping.

I have some white wine, melted butter, lemon juice, parsley, and pepper in there with the fish. I thought you might like to try it."

"It all smells wonderful," I tell him as I walk over to the small table Roan brought earlier to look at the two small closed containers sitting on top of it. "Can I ask what you cooked for side dishes?"

"I made some lemon rosemary roasted potatoes and sautéed asparagus spears with mushrooms. I hope those are all right. I wasn't sure what you would prefer."

"Everything you brought sounds yummy to me," I say, turning sideways slightly to meet his gaze again.

"Good," he replies with a pleased nod of his head. "My culinary skills are limited, but I try to expand them by learning new recipes when I have the time. Lately, we've been so busy trying to find Helena that I haven't had much of an opportunity to cook."

With the mention of Helena, I realize I haven't told Ethan about my encounter with her in my apartment after he left me earlier. I almost don't want to, because I know as soon as I do, he'll feel guilty for leading her directly to where I live. But if I don't tell him now, I'll feel like I'm keeping a secret from him, and that's not any better of a solution for me.

"I have to tell you something," I begin, drawing his attention away from the grill and back to me. "Helena came to my apartment not long after you left it today."

Ethan's body goes completely still. I don't even think he blinks as he considers my words.

Finally, he seems to snap out of his shock and asks, "Has she ever been there before? Perhaps during the time she and Cade spent on Sierra?"

I shake my head and wish I didn't have to say my next words. "They never visited my apartment. She followed your phase trail there from Cephas."

Ethan grips the wooden handle of the brush he was using to baste the shrimp and lobster with so tightly that it snaps into two pieces.

"That," he says in a deep voice, "was stupid of me."

I assume he's talking about leading Helena to my apartment and not the fact that he just broke his basting brush.

"She didn't hurt me or even try to," I'm quick to tell him. "In fact, I was able to use the opportunity to talk to her about asking for Desmond's help when it's time for her son to be born."

"But I led her straight to you, Jules," he says agitatedly as he throws the now ruined brush into the sink beside the grill. "It was thoughtless of me, and I'm never careless, especially when it comes to people I care about."

"Seriously, don't beat yourself up about it," I tell him in an attempt to take away the sting he obviously feels for making a mistake. "I think it might have worked out in our favor, actually. She opened up to me a little bit, and that might help us later on, particularly if you want to convince her to hand over her son to you. I know you're used to fighting for what you want and what you believe to be right, but I don't believe this will be a situation you'll be able to win with a sword. You're going to have to reason with Helena and prove to her that giving up her son is the best thing she can do for him."

"You can't reason with a creature like her," Ethan says without a note of doubt in his voice. "She's pure evil."

"Do you truly believe that?" I have to ask. "From what I've been told, Cade loved her very much. Do you think he was the type of person who could love someone who has zero redeemable qualities?"

My question seems to bring Ethan up short. His lips press together tightly like he's doing his best not to start a verbal fight with me about Helena's virtues ... or lack thereof. I remember him telling me earlier that if he starts to humanize Helena, he might not be able to do what he feels like he has to in order to save Cade's child from her. I can't imagine Ethan cutting Helena open and ripping her baby right out of her womb, but it's obvious he can, and I'm not sure how I feel about that side of him.

"I'm sorry I absentmindedly gave her access to your apartment," Ethan says in a low voice. Apparently he's decided not to answer my question about Helena's possible good traits. Cade must have seen something worth loving in Helena before his untimely demise or she wouldn't be pregnant with his child right now. "I'll try to be more cautious in the future. I suppose I was so concerned about your safety,

I didn't consider all of the repercussions of taking you directly home from the battlefield."

"Why were they fighting there anyway?" I ask. "I thought you said the places where you meet your men are out of the way on each planet."

"They were when we originally picked them. Apparently two of the warring clans on Cephas found a mineral deposit in that location within the last week and decided to have a fight to see who would earn the right to claim it as their own."

"And your friend—Alex, was it?—where was he in all of that mess? I assume he knew what time to meet us there."

"He phased in a few minutes earlier and discovered the fighting. He was helping tend to the wounded when you and I arrived. That's why we didn't see him."

"I take it from what you said to Jered that you don't believe Silas is on that planet anymore. Why do you think his son was participating in the fight?"

"To encourage a larger fight to break out, most likely. Helena uses people to promote chaos in the universe. I'm sure starting a war on Cephas simply progresses whatever agenda she has at the moment."

"Do you think she's on a crusade of some sort?"

Ethan begins to shake his head. "I don't know if she has a particular plan in mind or if she simply wants to cause as much destruction as she can. There's no telling what's going on in that twisted sense of logic of hers."

Ethan glances down at the grill before walking over to the table to retrieve our dinner plates. I take this as meaning that the meal is finally cooked and we can eat! I'm so excited I begin to smile like an idiot.

"I can't believe I'm about to eat shrimp," I tell him in awe of the meal he's prepared.

"I'm surprised your mother or Enis never went to Earth to get some for you if you wanted to try it so desperately," he says while placing two of the shrimp skewers on my plate.

"You might as well add an extra one," I tell him, already knowing two won't be enough for me.

Ethan smiles and obliges my request for a third skewer.

"I'm sure they would have, but while Lucifer was full-on evil, they were ordered by him to stay on Sierra and to not return to Earth unless they were told to come. I guess they just got used to not being on Earth and lost their desire to go back there. They both seem to want to return now, though, since Anna is being threatened by the other rebellion angels, or at least the ones who decided to remain on Hale's side. I still can't believe some of them didn't accept God's forgiveness when He offered it to them."

"Rebellion angels have always been stupid and stubborn," Ethan says with complete disdain for his fellow angels. "I've never understood them, but then again, I suppose I wasn't built to comprehend that level of idiocy."

"Hey now," I warn good-naturedly, "watch how you talk about rebellion angels around me. My mom and uncle used to be on the wrong side of the argument you know."

"Yes, but they've recovered and realize which side of the fight they should actually be on."

I can't really argue against that point.

After Ethan loads my plate with shrimp, a lobster tail, and the sea trout, I know I don't have room for a sampling of his side dishes. I guess I should have known he would have already thought about that. After I sit down at the table, he brings over the two covered dishes and sets them down. When he removes their covers, I see that they contain two smaller plates filled with each side dish, stacked one over the other to prevent them from touching. Ethan sets a plate of the potatoes and a plate of the asparagus and mushroom dish on either side of my dinner plate.

"I hope you like everything," he says, taking the remaining side dish plates and placing them beside his own table setting.

Once he takes his seat, I see no reason not to dig into the meal with gusto.

As soon as the first succulently sweet shrimp enters my mouth, I feel like I must have died and stepped straight through the pearly white gates.

"Oh dear Lord in Heaven, this tastes so good!" I practically squeal, which earns me a smile of pride from Ethan.

"I'm glad you like it, and I feel privileged to be the first person to introduce you to seafood."

"Honestly, I don't think I've ever tasted anything po pood ..."

Po pood? What the ...

I immediately lift my hands to my lips and notice they feel hot and swollen.

"Jules?" Ethan says in alarm as he stares at me like I've grown a second head out of my shoulders.

At the moment, that feels like exactly what's happened.

"Meh pung's mowen!" I say in alarm, but even I wouldn't have been able to decipher my gibberish as meaning "my tongue's swollen."

Apparently Ethan doesn't need me to tell him what's wrong. From the expression of horror on his face, I can tell he knows I'm in trouble.

His next movements are so quick all I see is a blur of motion. Before I know it, I'm safely cradled in Ethan's arms, and he phases us to what looks like the interior of a well-kept, but unassuming, kitchen in the lower part of an old house.

"Desmond!" Ethan shouts, unintentionally causing my ears to ring and my head to hurt with the volume of his booming voice.

Ethan takes another lungful of air in to shout out Desmond's name again, but luckily for my ears and head, Desmond phases into the kitchen beside us.

"What's wrong, Ethan?" he immediately asks, looking between Ethan and my face.

Desmond's eyes show his shock, and I wonder if my head has ballooned to the size of a watermelon.

"What happened?" Desmond quickly asks Ethan.

"She ate some shrimp," he replies in a rush to get the words out. "I think she's having an allergic reaction to it."

"A quite severe one if you ask me," Desmond says. "Jules, are you having any trouble breathing?"

I feel sure the sound of my newly acquired wheeze is answer enough for Desmond.

He wastes no time and phases away but returns within just a few seconds holding a small black metallic tube of some sort.

"Sit her down," Desmond orders Ethan.

Ethan sets me in one of the wooden kitchen chairs at the table. He makes to move away, but I grab ahold of one of his hands, needing the reassurance of his touch in that moment. Without questioning me, he squeezes my hand, letting me know that he's not going anywhere.

Desmond bends down on a knee in front of me and places one end of the black tube he's holding against a patch of the skin on my thigh that's peeking through the illusion hem of my skirt.

"This is going to sting a little bit," he warns me, "but you should feel better almost instantly."

When Desmond presses down on the other end of the tube, I feel a slight bit of pressure and a stinging sensation as what I presume to be medicine enters into my bloodstream. Almost instantly, I feel the constriction of my throat lessen and find it much easier to breathe.

"Are you feeling better?" Desmond asks me, showing me his winning grin and soothing bedside manner.

I nod my head. I know if I try to talk, I'll just end up embarrassing myself because my tongue is still swollen.

"Good," Desmond says before standing back up. "Luckily, Ethan brought you to me instead of the doctors on your world. They don't have access to the drug I just gave you, which should clear everything up and have you feeling better by morning. If you had had this reaction on your world, they probably would have kept you in a hospital for a few days hooked up to an IV bag and administered a good dose of antihistamines. The only side effects you should feel from what I just gave you is dizziness and perhaps some nausea. It's also going to make you feel drowsy, so I suggest you go home and get some rest. Tomorrow you'll feel a lot better. I promise."

My heart sinks at the thought of his orders. I've totally screwed up my first date with Ethan, and he'll probably just chalk it up to a catastrophe averted with me. The odds of him asking me out again are slim to none, and just the thought of that possibility makes me sadder than I thought it would. I can't even make myself look up at Ethan I feel so embarrassed by the whole situation. All I want to do is go home, get out of my fancy dress, and crawl underneath the covers of my bed to hide from the world for a little while.

"Thanks for your help," Ethan says to Desmond, shaking his friend's hand.

"Anytime, brother," he replies. "I'm just glad you got her here before things got any worse. I can't say I've ever seen a food allergy that severe before."

"It's all my fault," Ethan says, sounding like a man guilty of a heinous crime. "I never should have fed her shellfish. I didn't even consider the possibility that she might be allergic to it."

"Bon't," I tell him, squeezing the hand he still holds and hoping he understands that I really mean "*don't*." He shouldn't feel an ounce of guilt for something that was my idea. I was the one who begged him to make seafood. He didn't force it down my throat. At least I was able to taste the succulent meat once in my life, because now I know I never will again.

"She's right," Desmond tells Ethan. "None of this was your fault or hers for that matter. It was just an accident. Now, why don't you take her home so she can get some rest? That's the best remedy for her right now. Her body has literally gone through a shock, and it needs some time to recover from it."

Ethan nods and leans down to pick me up into his arms again. I would protest, but, well, for one, I can't even speak well enough for him to understand what I would say, and secondly, I like having him hold me. It makes me feel safe, and that's a sensation I haven't felt in quite some time. It may not be the "woman of modern times" thing to admit, but being held by someone who seems to care about your well-being is comforting. It makes Ethan even more attractive to me to know that he seems to feel protective of me.

"I'll make sure she gets plenty of rest. I won't leave her side tonight," Ethan promises Desmond.

"Good. Just let me know if anything unexpected happens. I don't foresee any complications arising, but you never know. I'll be here if you need me."

"Thank you," Ethan says before phasing me back home.

Thankfully, my mom and Uncle Enis aren't in my apartment anymore. I really don't have the energy to deal with their worry.

Without asking permission, Ethan carries me into my dark bedroom and lays me down on the bed with my head resting on a pillow. He reaches over toward my nightstand and turns on the lamp there, giving the area surrounding us a soft glow. He then turns back toward me and slips off my shoes, setting them down on the floor next to the bed.

When he looks me in the eyes again, he asks, "Where can I find some pajamas for you to change into?"

I point directly behind him to a chest of drawers.

"Second drawer," I'm able to say intelligibly. It wasn't exactly the clearest speech since my tongue is still slightly swollen, but it was at least understandable.

Ethan walks over and opens the drawer, pulling out the top T-shirt and matching shorts he finds there. I don't actually own a pair of fancy pajamas. I prefer shirts and shorts. For one thing, you never know what might happen in the middle of the night. What if there was a fire and I had to run out of the building? I would rather be in regular clothes than silky pink pajamas and fluffy house shoes.

I see Ethan take notice of what's printed on the front of the black T-shirt he's holding.

"Twisted Fate," he reads, looking at the words and the guitar embroidered with white thread. "Is that a music group here?"

"Yes," I say sitting up on the bed and swinging my legs over the side. "They're my favorite rock band."

Ethan hands me the clothing.

"Do you need any help changing clothes?" he asks in such a way that I know he only wants to be helpful. He isn't trying to use the situation to his advantage in any other respect.

"I think I can manage," I tell him. "But thank you for the offer."

"All right then, I guess I'll go sit out in the living room and check up on you from time to time. If you need me, just call out my name. I'll hear you."

Ethan walks out of the room and closes the door behind him. I do almost call out his name but not because I feel sick. I begin to have the same strange sensation of loneliness that I felt earlier in the day when he brought me home from the battlefield. There's an emptiness to the room now that he's left it that I don't like.

I quickly change clothes and go to the bathroom to brush my teeth and put my hair up into a ponytail. Once I'm done, I walk into the living room and find Ethan reading a book that I don't remember ever owning. Obviously, he phased home and retrieved it to pass the time with.

"What are you reading?" I ask as I walk over and sit down beside him on the couch, curling my legs up and pulling the throw blanket I had draped over the back of it to cover me.

"It's a book about the last Great War on Earth," he tells me.

"Are you a history buff?"

"About Earth's history, yes," he admits, closing the book so he can give me his undivided attention. "Are you feeling all right? Is something wrong?"

I shrug my shoulders and look away from him for a moment before working up my courage to look back at him. The concern I see in his eyes for my welfare compels me to be more truthful than I normally would be in this situation. Or perhaps it's simply because I feel strangely comfortable enough to tell him the real reason I came out here.

"Every time you leave me," I say, feeling a little nervous and excited by his response to my words, "I start to feel lonely. It's almost like you're not supposed to leave me. Does that make any sense?"

Ethan grins understandingly, and I have to wonder if he feels the same way too.

"Yes," he tells me. "It makes perfect sense."

He stretches out his left arm as if silently beckoning me to lean up against him to rest my head. I don't need a verbal invitation. A physical one works just fine.

As I snuggle up next to his warmth, he reopens his book and asks, "Would you like me to read to you?"

"Well, if anything is a surefire bet to put me to sleep, it's definitely a history book," I confess.

I hear and feel Ethan chuckle at my words, but I think he appreciates my honesty. As he begins to read, I find the cadence of his voice comforting and the material in the book about as dry as I thought it would be. Within a few minutes, my eyes begin to droop of their own accord. Just before I fall asleep, I feel Ethan kiss the top of my head, which is resting comfortably against his shoulder.

"Sweet dreams," he murmurs.

I smile. It isn't exactly the type of kiss I was hoping we would end our first date with, but I'll take it.

CHAPTER 11

When I wake up the next morning, I find myself lying on my side in bed safely tucked underneath the covers. I only need one guess as to who carried me to bed and made sure I stayed warm throughout the night. My heart aches with a slight emptiness I don't fully understand. I lift a hand to cover my chest, trying to figure out if I'm still feeling the aftereffects of my food allergy or if something else is wrong. I quickly come to the conclusion that it's something else. Luckily, I know just how to fix my dilemma.

I toss my covers aside and get out of bed. I'm relieved to find that Desmond was right about my quick recovery. I don't even feel drowsy anymore, for which I'm grateful. Today is the day I'm finally supposed to meet the Empress of Cirrus and receive the down payment for my tracking services. I've heard so much said about Empress Anna Devereaux that I feel a little nervous about meeting her. Not only does she control the most powerful cloud city on Earth, but she is also Ethan's commander. My mom told me that Ethan only takes orders from God and Anna, in that order. Anyone who is strong enough to control a regiment of War Angels has to be someone formidable. I just pray I can hold my own while I'm with her.

I decide to take a quick shower and spruce myself up for the day ahead. Normally, I wouldn't put on much makeup, but considering the company I'll be keeping today, I put on just a touch more than I normally would so I don't look completely washed out. For some reason, I'm a bit paler than usual this morning. I can only assume it's a side effect from the fiasco that was my first date with Ethan the night before.

My hair still looks good though, so I just run a brush through it to straighten it back out. I keep my clothing simple with a plain white button up, black jeans, and matching boots. I'm almost positive Ethan will want to travel among the stars after my meeting with Anna and search for Helena's whereabouts for a while. However, I have a feeling it will be a waste of time. I doubt she lets anyone find her unless she wants to be found. But if I'm out tracking Helena down, that means I'm spending time with Ethan, which is just fine by me.

The ache in my chest when I first woke up completely disappears when I walk into my living room and hear the laughter of my mother. I look over at the small dinette I have to the left of the kitchen area and see her sitting there with Uncle Enis and Ethan. All of them are smiling and laughing while they eat what looks and smells like breakfast.

Ethan is the first one to see me enter the room, since his vantage point from the table offers him a view of my bedroom door. It makes me wonder if he did that on purpose so he could watch for my emergence this morning.

After spying my reentry into the world, he stands from his chair and walks over to me while asking, "How are you feeling? Did you sleep well?"

"I feel great, actually," I tell him, not having to lie.

I truly feel quite wonderful now that I'm in the same room with him. However, that tidbit of information I don't reveal to Ethan. I've only known the man for one day, yet I feel like the rest of the days of my life will always need him in them. I have no idea what's wrong with me. I'm usually not one of those women who feels incomplete without a man in her life, but I can't seem to shake the feeling that Ethan isn't just a man or an angel; he's something else to me that I can't quite put a label on yet. All I know is that the ache in my chest has been replaced with joy and contentment, and the reason for that is Ethan.

"Did your face really blow up like a puffer fish, Jules?" Uncle Enis asks from his seat at the table, unable to control his chuckling at my expense. "I would have given good money to see that happen."

I witness my mother playfully slap Uncle Enis on the arm, but I can tell she's just barely able to stifle her own laughter.

"Now, Enis," she tells him, "an allergic reaction like that could have been fatal if Ethan hadn't reacted as quickly as he did."

"Oh, I know," Uncle Enis says to her, "but we never would have let her go on that date if we didn't trust him to take care of her."

"You two do realize that I'm a grown woman who can take care of herself," I say as Ethan and I make our way back to the table to join them.

When we reach my chair, Ethan holds it out for me to sit in. No one has done that for me since Timothy, and the thought of him causes me to feel a pang of guilt for finding a reason to enjoy my life again. He's dead because of what I did to him. Maybe I don't deserve to feel happy or content when he's nothing more than ash in the wind.

"Jules," I hear my mother say, drawing me out of my morbid reverie. From the inflection of her voice, it sounds like this isn't the first time she's called my name in the last few seconds to get my attention.

"I'm sorry," I tell her as I notice Ethan retake his seat beside me, "my mind drifted off. Did you ask me something?"

"I was wondering what time you're supposed to meet Anna today," she says. The look of worry on my mother's face is a sure indication that she recognizes something is wrong with me, but I know she won't ask me about it until we're alone.

For years now, my mom has tried to convince me that I'm not responsible for Timothy's death. A part of me wants to trust her words, but there is also a part of me that can't let go of my guilt. If it wasn't for me, I know Timothy would still be alive today. If I shrug the responsibility of his death from my shoulders, it will be like I am spitting in his face. He may be dead, but the memories of our last year together still haunt me. Those are the moments I try to forget by drowning them out with bottles of alcohol. I just wish I could wash them away completely with the liquid poison.

"I assume I'll be meeting with Anna this morning," I say, looking over at Ethan for confirmation.

"I told her I would bring you to her quarters right after you ate breakfast," he tells me. "That is, if you feel up to eating."

I look at the food on their plates and see pancakes, eggs, bacon, and fruit.

"I think my stomach can handle some pancakes, fruit, and three slices of bacon," I say.

"Coming right up then." Ethan stands from his chair and heads into the kitchen, presumably to make me a plate of food.

While Ethan is otherwise occupied, my mother leans in slightly across the table and asks, "What's wrong, Jules? I know that look on your face and you're overthinking something."

Sometimes, I wish my mother didn't know me so damn well.

"Timothy," I reply because I don't need to say anything more than that for her to understand what's troubling my mind.

"I wish you had never met that boy," Uncle Enis says with more venom than I thought possible from him.

"*Enis*," my mother hisses in a low voice, chastising him for his remark.

"Well, it's true, Evelyn," Uncle Enis replies, not showing an ounce of remorse for his remark. "It was his half-witted idea to have Jules give birth naturally up in that cabin. He didn't even want us around when the baby was born. If you ask me ..."

"No one's asking you," I interrupt harshly. "Can we please just drop the subject? I don't want to get into the same old argument we've been having for the past five years while Ethan is around."

My uncle doesn't look pleased with my request, but he sits back in his chair and remains mute, even though I can clearly see his unending anger toward Timothy simmering just below the surface.

When Ethan returns with my plate of food, he looks between the three of us as he sets my breakfast down in front of me and retakes his seat.

"Did I miss something?" he asks, not being shy about letting us know he realizes things are not the way he left them just a few minutes ago.

"Nothing important," I tell him, picking up my fork from the plate and cutting into the stack of fluffy pancakes. Their buttery deliciousness makes me giggle as soon as they touch my tongue. "Oh my goodness, did you make these?"

Ethan grins. "I did. I take it from the smile on your face that you like them."

"They're awesome," I say, stuffing my mouth with more because I realize how hungry I am. It shouldn't come as any big surprise though. All I ate last night was a shrimp that almost killed me. "I'm sorry I didn't get to try any of the fish or side dishes you made last night. I hate knowing all that food and effort went to waste because of me."

"It was just food," Ethan assures me. "All of that can be replaced. You can't."

"Amen to that," Uncle Enis wholeheartedly agrees.

"So tell me, how are Anna and the babies doing?" my mother asks Ethan. "I haven't seen her in quite a while."

"Oh, that reminds me," Ethan says. "Anna asked me to invite you all to Cirrus for a party being thrown in the twins' honor."

"When is it?" my mom asks, her interest in such an event obviously piqued.

"Tomorrow night," Ethan tells her. "It will be a formal event held in the ballroom. Anna and Malcolm decided it was time to stop shielding the children quite so much. Although after everything that happened before and after their birth, I can't say I blame them for wanting to keep the twins away from people."

Ethan looks over at me. "I was hoping we could go together, if you're interested in attending it."

I swallow the pancake in my mouth as I consider his invitation, but who am I fooling? There's only one answer to give.

"I would love to go with you," I tell him.

I spy a smile grace my mother's face. I'm not sure if it's because I've agreed to go on a second date with Ethan or if it's because we'll need to go shopping for formal wear. More than likely, both of those reasons are causing her to feel happy.

I eat the remainder of my meal in record time because I want to go to Cirrus as soon as possible and finally meet Empress Anna. I've seen a picture of her, but something so two-dimensional can't truly give you a clear image of someone's soul. Having already met her husband and Lucas, I can't imagine her being anything but strong spirited, just like them.

"Are we going to see if we can track Helena down after my meeting with the empress?" I ask Ethan.

He nods. "That was my plan, if you don't have something else to do today."

"Considering how much money your empress is about to give me," I say, standing from my chair, "I'm pretty much at your beck and call until the situation with Helena is resolved. Give me a minute to go get my jacket and the tracking device."

I walk into my bedroom and make a quick detour to the bathroom to brush my teeth. I definitely don't want to meet the empress with bad breath. First impressions are always important, at least that's what my mother taught me.

After I'm through in the bathroom, I grab my black jacket and the tracking device, which I tuck safely into one of the jacket's pockets. When I walk back out into the living room, I notice that Uncle Enis and my mom are already gone.

"They left without saying good-bye?" I say out loud, finding it curious that they would do such a thing. Normally, I have to practically push them out the door to make them leave after a visit.

"I asked them if I could have a private moment with you before we go to Cirrus," Ethan tells me, looking slightly uncomfortable, as if what he has to say isn't easy for him to put into words.

I walk up to him and ask, "Is something wrong? You look fidgety. Did Uncle Enis say something to you? That man does not know when, or maybe it's just how, to mind his own business."

Ethan grins and shakes his head slightly. "No. It's nothing either of them said or did. I just wanted to apologize about last night again. It should have occurred to me that you might not be able to eat the food. It was the first time you had ever had it, and I should have been better prepared for anything to happen. It all took me by surprise when it shouldn't have."

"Listen," I say, taking a step forward, "last night was nobody's fault, least of all yours, and I'm fine now. Don't keep beating yourself up about it. Seriously, let's just not mention it again because it depresses me too much to think about."

"Depresses you?" Ethan asks in confusion. "Why does it depress you?"

I sigh exaggeratedly. "It's depressing to know what shrimp tastes like and that I will never be able to eat it again. I might get more depressed if I keep thinking about it because I didn't even get to taste the lobster! Do you think I would have the same reaction to it? Maybe we should try ..."

"No!" Ethan says rather adamantly. "Don't even think about trying to eat lobster. I can assure you the same thing would happen, and my heart just can't go through that again. I just found you. I'm not about to lose you to a shellfish fetish."

I have to smile at his use of the word fetish. Usually that's a word used in a sexual context, but I suppose it can be used correctly in this instance as well. Yet that isn't the only thing that he said that caught my attention.

"How long have you been looking for me?" I ask, sounding as confused by his statement as I am.

Ethan seems somewhat caught off guard by my question. I'm not even sure he realized what he said before I pointed it out to him. I can see an inner turmoil play behind his eyes on whether or not he should answer my question. He finally decides, but he doesn't look certain about whether or not he's making the right decision.

"Practically since time began," he replies.

If it wasn't for the earnest expression on his face, I would have thought he was being humorous, but I don't believe he is. His words seem heartfelt, and the strength of his sincerity causes the darkest corner of my soul to welcome the light his words are offering it.

I don't know how to respond. I mean, when a man says something like that to you, it has to mean he at least likes you. I almost feel like a school girl who has been given the verbal equivalent of a small note by a boy she's interested in where I'm supposed to either check the box that says "*I like you too*" or the one that says "*Get away from me now*."

"We should probably go," Ethan says rather abruptly, not allowing me a chance to respond to what he said, which seems to be the point of our hasty departure. "Anna's expecting us."

He holds out his right hand for me to take, and without giving it much thought, I place my hand into his. Ethan phases us, and I mentally try to prepare myself in that split second for my first meeting with the Empress of Cirrus.

We phase into what looks like a fancy living room. Although I suppose the rich probably call it a sitting room to make it sound grander.

When I see Empress Anna for the very first time, I instantly believe she's a goddess from another time and place. No one can radiate such natural beauty and still be human. Then I remember that Anna is only partially human. She is a descendant of the Archangel Michael on her mother's side, and of course her father is Lucifer, the first and most powerful Archangel ever created.

We find her sitting on an area rug in the room, which is situated between an opulent white marble fireplace mantel and a white couch. She's wearing a lavender dress made of material that shines in the light of day, adding to the illusion that she's not from this world. Lucas is sitting beside her as they both play with two babies who are sitting up in front of them. As if the scene didn't look surreal enough, I see a hellhound lying down beside Lucas with its thick white coat ablaze with yellow-orange flames, which I know are just for show, and a medium-sized orange and white coated dog sitting next to the empress.

Empress Anna notices our presence first and bestows upon me a smile that has probably melted the hearts of many a man and woman in Cirrus. I can think of one man in particular that it has more than likely charmed quite a bit over the last year and a half of marriage.

"Anna," Ethan says, as she stands to her feet to greet us, "I would like to introduce you to Julia Grace."

Anna walks over to us and immediately holds out her hand for me to shake.

"I'm so glad you came," she tells me, instantly making me feel welcomed and wanted in her home. "I told Ethan that I had to meet the woman who bested Helena without her knowing it."

"I'm not sure if I bested her, Empress Anna. I think I just got lucky is all," I humbly protest, even though I do appreciate the praise.

"Oh, don't be so modest," she tells me. "And please, just call me Anna. The only people who use my title are acquaintances, and I would much rather count you as a friend once we get to know each other a little better. Malcolm told me that you prefer to be called Jules. Is it all right if I address you as such?"

I nod. "Of course you can."

"Wonderful," she says, continuing to smile at me. "I also heard you had a bit of a hiccup on your date with Ethan last night. Are you feeling well? You look a little pale."

I knew it. I knew I looked pallid this morning, and now that I'm standing next to Anna, I feel like the poor relative who's come to visit her rich, beautiful, and charming cousin for a handout.

"I'm much better now. Thank you for asking though."

"Mommy," Lucas calls from his spot on the floor, "I think Liam needs his diaper changed. He's smelling awfully ripe."

"I'll do it, Anna," Ethan volunteers, taking me by surprise with his offer to do something so domestic.

When I think of War Angels, the changing of a baby's dirty diaper doesn't readily come to mind.

"Thank you, Ethan," Anna says. "I would appreciate that a great deal. It'll give me a chance to speak with Jules in private."

"Uh oh," Lucas says as he stands up from the floor and picks one of the babies up. "That means I need to leave too I guess. Come on, Ethan. We can go to the nursery so Mommy and Ms. Jules can talk."

"I won't be gone long," Ethan tells me. "I've become pretty good at changing a diaper over the last few months."

I hear Anna giggle. "Yes, he has," she declares with a certain amount of pride in his newly acquired skill. "All of the War Angels in my personal guard are quite proficient at it now."

"Only because you insisted that we should be," Ethan grumbles, even though I can tell by the small twitch of an almost smile at the corners of his mouth that he doesn't mind helping Anna out at all with her babies.

"Come on, Ethan!" Lucas encourages him as he makes his way

down a hallway to the left of the room with the hellhound following close behind him. "Let's get Liam clean before he starts crying. We don't have the magic rattle anymore to stop it."

"I'll be right back," Ethan promises before following Lucas to who knows where. That's where people generally keep supplies for their young ones.

"Come sit with me on the sofa while they're busy," Anna encourages me as she walks back over to the little girl still sitting on the rug and picks her up in her arms. "They'll probably be longer than they think. Liam may need a bath in addition to a diaper change from what I just smelled."

As we sit on the sofa together, Anna places the little girl on her lap, facing me. Anna's daughter is as beautiful as her mother, but she doesn't share the same hair color as either of her parents. When I first saw her playing with her dark haired brother, I thought her hair was blonde. Now that I can see it more clearly, it appears to be white. Her eye color doesn't match either of her parents' eyes. Malcolm does have blue eyes, but their daughter's eyes practically glow with an otherworldly blue. I watch as she places the thumb of one of her hands in her mouth as she observes me. The glint of something shiny catches my eyes, and I notice the silver bracelet she's wearing. Anna gently pulls on her daughter's hand to make her stop sucking her thumb.

"She has to be the cutest baby I've ever seen in my life," I declare truthfully.

Anna smiles with a mother's pride. "I have to admit, I think Liana is too. Although I would never say that in front of my other children."

"It's almost like she has a little extra something inside her that I can't quite put my finger on," I say, studying Liana carefully and trying to figure out what it is that's different about her besides her hair color and eyes.

I notice the smile on Anna's face slip away and a look of worry replace her happiness.

"I'm sorry. Did I say something wrong?" I ask, feeling as though I must have stumbled across a problem with the baby that perhaps Anna didn't want to be reminded about.

Anna shakes her head. "It's nothing. I try not to dwell on things that I can't possibly change. Besides, I would love to hear how you and Ethan are getting along. I heard the two of you got off to a rocky start, but that seems to have disappeared rather quickly."

"Ah, I guess you heard about our first meeting from Malcolm," I reply, feeling embarrassed about the way Ethan and I argued in front of Anna's husband yesterday. "We're doing a lot better now that we've gotten to know one another. Sometimes when you think too much like someone else, your personalities clash. But I don't want you to worry that it will interfere with the job you're paying me to do. We shouldn't have any problems locating Helena if she's on a planet that we visit. We've already found her once. I'm sure we'll find her again."

"Can you show me how you're tracking her?" she asks, full of eager curiosity.

I pull out the small tracking device from my jacket pocket and hold it up to show Anna.

"How does it work?" she asks.

I find it a little hard to believe that Anna would care about such a thing, but I decide to go through the motions of showing her how the device functions. This could just be her way of forming a connection with me through a shared interest, and if it is, I'm grateful. I don't have many friends. Scratch that. I have zero friends besides my mom and Uncle Enis. The ones I did have before Timothy's death ended up abandoning me because they couldn't handle my dark side. Good riddance to them. True friends stay with you during the happy and the sad times. They're not supposed to turn their backs on you the moment your life starts to careen off a cliff. None of my so-called friends decided to stick around and help lift me up to the light to remind me that I was still alive.

"It will only work for me," I tell her, holding the screen up to my face and pressing the button on the side to turn the machine on so it can scan my retina. Once it's functional, I face the screen toward her so she can see it. "The red dots show that the device is attempting to track down the signal on Helena's tracer."

Anna's brow furrows as she looks at the screen. "And what does it mean if the dots turn green?"

"How did you know they can turn green?"

Anna shifts her gaze away from the tracker's screen and looks directly at me.

"Because they just did."

I quickly face the screen toward me. When I do, the green dots vanish and the direction and distance of our target appears on the screen.

"Holy ..." I stop myself from cursing because I remember a baby is present. "She's here!"

"Shh," Anna says, craning her head to the side to look down the hallway Ethan and Lucas just walked down. "Don't say it so loud."

"Why not?" I ask, leaning forward to get up so I can go find Ethan and tell him Helena is on Earth.

With a lot more strength than I thought someone as petite and genteel looking as Anna would possess, she yanks me back down onto the sofa.

"Don't tell Ethan," she orders in a whisper. "If he goes to her, they'll just argue, and that's not what I want right now. I need to go speak with her myself and try to reason with her."

"Anna," the medium-sized orange and white dog says in an admonishing tone. "You shouldn't go alone. There's no telling what she might do to you. I simply won't allow it."

"You can talk!" I say to Anna's dog. At least I thought it was a dog, but as far as I know, dogs can't talk.

"Yes, I am a sentient robot who can talk and reason quite well, unlike some people in this room," she says looking toward Anna accusingly.

"I'm sorry, Vala," Anna replies, standing up and placing Liana on the floor in front of her robotic friend. "I have to go to her. This might be my only chance to convince her to give the baby up peacefully." Anna looks at me and asks, "Where is she?"

I hesitate because I'm not sure what to do in this situation. I seem to be damned if I give Anna the information she wants and damned if I don't. I can just imagine how mad Ethan will be with me if I don't tell him Anna is about to go talk to Helena, and I know Anna will get upset if I allow her window of opportunity to speak with Helena alone close. Luckily, the decision about whether or not to tell her is taken out of my hands as Malcolm walks in through the double doors of the room that lead in from the hallway of the palace.

He looks at Anna when he walks in and immediately asks, "What's wrong?"

"Helena is here on Earth," Anna whispers to him. "And I want to go speak with her before Ethan finds out. You know I need to, Malcolm. I might be the only one she'll listen to."

Malcolm closes the door behind him, not looking the least bit pleased about what Anna is proposing to do.

"I know you feel as though you owe it to Cade to try and reason with her," Malcolm says, "but I also don't believe she's in any state of mind to act rationally right now, Anna. It's too dangerous."

"Please, Malcolm," Anna practically begs. "You know I'll go with or without your blessing, but I would rather go with it, and right now I need your help. I need you to keep Ethan busy while I speak with her."

"I'm not about to let you talk to her by yourself!" he thunders.

"Stop yelling!" Anna says forcefully, but in a whisper. "Fine. I won't go alone. I'll take Jules with me for backup."

I'm not sure what superpowers Anna has been led to believe that I have, but fighting the embodiment of Hell isn't one of them.

"Malcolm would probably be a better candidate to help keep you safe," I tell Anna, finding this a reasonable excuse to stay put.

"Helena won't talk to me if Malcolm is there," Anna states. "I don't think she'll care if you're with me."

"Why? Because I'm a puny human she can squash like a bug if she wants to?"

"Precisely," Anna confirms, not sounding the least bit apologetic about wanting to use me in such a way. "But I won't let her touch you, Jules. You have my word on that. Neither of us," she says, looking over at Malcolm, "will get hurt."

Malcolm sighs in resignation. "I know I won't be able to talk you out of it, so go. But if you're not back here in ten minutes, I'm coming after you. Where is she exactly?"

I stand up and show Malcolm the screen of the tracker. He looks at the direction and distance in relation to where we're standing.

"We know this spot," he says in a surprised voice, which is exactly how I feel hearing his words. I thought he would need to look at a map to figure out where she is, but then again, he *has* been on Earth a very long time. He probably knows every nook and cranny on this planet. "It's the cemetery where we placed Cade's memorial. The one he liked to go to sometimes to think."

"I'm surprised Helena even knows about that place," Anna says.

"Maybe Cade took her there at some point or she found out about the memorial," Malcolm suggests. "But if you insist on going without Ethan finding out, I suggest you go out onto the balcony to phase. He's sure to see your trail if you do it in here. Where is he anyway?"

"In the nursery changing Liam's diaper," Anna answers, grabbing me by the right arm and practically dragging me toward the balcony connected to the room. "We'll be back as soon as possible. Just keep Ethan occupied and take care of Liana while we're gone."

Once we're out on the veranda, Anna tells me, "You should put that tracker back in your pocket. We don't want her to know that you were able to pinpoint her location with it."

I do as she says but have to ask, "How are you going to explain that we knew exactly where she is?"

"Hopefully, she won't ask," Anna says. "But if she does, I'll come up with something plausible. Do you mind doing this with me? If you're too scared to go, I'll understand."

"I'm not scared of Helena," I tell her, earning myself an incredulous look from Anna. I don't really have time to explain it, so I just say, "It's a long story."

"One I would like to hear soon," Anna replies, sounding intrigued. "But right now, we need to go to her. Are you ready?"

I nod. "Yes. Let's go. I would much rather talk to her about giving the baby up voluntarily than watch Ethan rip it out of her."

"Me too." Anna nods, seeing that I understand the reason behind her desperation to speak with Helena alone.

Anna phases us, and I soon find myself staring straight into Helena's eyes.

CHAPTER 12

(Helena's Point of View)

The specter of sorrow surrounds me like a clingy, unwanted visitor whose stay is endless and whose gift is everlasting pain. The life-size alabaster statue Anna and her family erected to memorialize Cade's passing almost looks real. He stands tall with his shoulders straight and proud as his gaze is directed toward some unknown object in the distance. He's shirtless but wearing his War Angel feather cloak, pants, and boots.

I reach up and touch the replica of his lips, allowing the tips of my fingers to glide across the smooth, cold stone. I close my eyes and picture Cade's face smiling at me. I can almost feel the warmth of his skin beneath my fingers as I caress the side of the statue's face, but I know what I'm feeling is just an illusion that I desperately want to believe is real.

I open my eyes and force myself to face the fact that Cade is dead. His soul is safely tucked away behind Heaven's veil, and no matter how powerful I become, I will never be able to reach him.

I let my hand fall back to my side, knowing wishes don't come true for creatures like me. They never have and they never will.

Unexpectedly, I see Anna phase in with Evelyn Grace's daughter, Jules. They stand only a few feet behind Cade's statue staring at me but not looking the least bit surprised to find me in this cemetery.

"Hello, sister," I say to Anna, finding the timing of her visit curious. It can't be by coincidence. "What happens to bring you here?"

Anna lets go of Jules' arm and walks closer to me.

"I wanted to talk to you," she tells me, her face full of pity that I neither want nor need. I see her eyes drop down to my stomach as if needing to prove to herself that I am indeed with child.

"Really?" I ask, feigning ignorance. "About what exactly?"

Anna looks at me knowingly. "You know full well what I want to talk to you about, Helena."

"Then say what you have to say, if it will make you feel better. I would hate for your conscience to be rife with guilt because you don't believe you did enough for Cade's baby. Or are you here to rip my little bundle of joy out of my womb yourself instead of sending your henchmen to do the dirty work for you?"

"That was never my plan, Helena. I have no desire to see you hurt, but I also don't believe you're the best person to raise Cade's son."

"That's rich of you, Anna," I scoff. "Aren't you my polar opposite in this universe? At least I thought you were supposed to be the good one in the family. It doesn't seem very sisterly of you to suggest that I should hand my baby over to you because you deem it the right thing to do."

"And do you believe you're capable of taking care of him on your own?" she questions me, sounding doubtful that I have one motherly bone in my body. "You haven't even been to see a doctor to make sure he's all right. Desmond would be more than happy to do an examination at any place and time of your choosing. All he wants to do is make sure the baby is healthy. If you won't even do that one simple thing for your child, why should I believe you'll raise him right?"

"He's *my* child, Anna!" I scream, sick and tired of her holier-than-thou attitude toward me. "He is the only thing I have left of Cade, and I will not give him up without a fight! Trust me, sister, you don't want to push me on this. If it's a war of mutual destruction that you want, I am more than willing to do it because I have very little to live for these days. My son and the promise I made to Cade not to harm the ones he loves are the only reasons I haven't destroyed this planet that you cherish so much. But heed my words and take them to heart, I will destroy you and your family if you push my patience too far."

"Helena," my sister says in a placating voice meant to temper my wrath, "what kind of life can you offer him? Do you want him to become as bitter and hateful as you are? Do you really believe Cade would want that sort of life for his only child?"

"You're such an insufferable hypocrite, sister," I say through gritted teeth. "Can you honestly stand there and tell me that you would just hand over one of your own children to me if I asked you to?"

"That isn't the same thing," she protests weakly, but I can see her begin to realize precisely what she's asking me to do.

"It's the exact same thing, and you know it! Remember when I took Liana away from you for a short time? Do you remember how that made you feel? Now multiply that heartbreak a million times over and you'll have a small taste of what it is you are asking me to do. I've lost Cade for an eternity. I will not lose my son!"

From the look of defeat on Anna's face, I can tell she knows trying to convince me to give my baby to her will never work.

"Then at least let me help you with the pregnancy," she begs. "Let Desmond look at the baby, just to make sure he's healthy."

"He's fine!" I reply adamantly. "There's nothing wrong with him."

"Excuse me," Jules says, "but the other night you told me that your pregnancy has been anything but natural. Now, I could be wrong, but that sort of makes it sound like something hasn't been quite right the last few months."

"It's nothing," I say, attempting to wave away my own worries while convincing them that everything is as it should be.

"Please, Helena," Anna begs. "If something feels wrong, go to Desmond. I know for a fact that he's at his home in Stratus right now. I swear I won't follow you there or tell anyone else that you've gone. All I want you to do is make sure the baby is healthy."

"You expect me to believe that you won't tell Malcolm or Ethan that I've gone to him?" I ask her scornfully. "What type of simpleton do you take me for, Anna?"

"If there is one thing I have never questioned you about, it's your intelligence," she assures me. "And if there is one thing you should never question about me, it's my promises. I swear to you on the lives of my children that I will not tell anyone that you've gone there."

I look over at Jules. "And what's to stop her from telling Ethan where I am? Do you think I haven't noticed that sword he carries on his hip? I know exactly what he intends to do with it if I don't give him my son. I know everything, Anna. Why do you think I let those War Angels of yours use the Nexus so freely? They didn't know it, but I was there reading their minds and seeing all their plans."

The flash of surprise in Anna's eyes doesn't shock me. I know that the angels assumed I wasn't in Hell while they used the Nexus to search for me. That's the reason why I sometimes closed entry into my domain off from them. They began to assume I was only there when they couldn't phase into my realm. For being angels of war, they certainly don't think very strategically. Of course I would learn everything I could about their plans for me. I'm not an idiot, and it made it far simpler to keep them preoccupied during their search if I happened to stir up trouble on some of the planets that they keep a watch over.

"I won't tell Ethan," Jules says to me like a promise. "I told you last night that I'm only concerned about the baby's welfare, and if my story wasn't enough to convince you of that fact, I really don't see how else I can prove to you that all I care about is the child. Don't be stubborn when it comes to your baby's life, Helena, or you may live to regret more than just killing Cade."

"Why is it that you feel as if you can talk to me like you're my equal?" I ask her, having found my encounters with Jules almost disturbing.

"I'm nowhere near your equal as far as power goes," she tells me. "I doubt anyone in the universe is, except for maybe Anna. The only thing we have in common is the fact that we both feel responsible for a loved one's death. We share a common guilt, and I know how debilitating that kind of pain can be, but don't make your son pay for your sins. He's an innocent in all of this, and he deserves a chance to live a happy life. A child is a gift that you shouldn't take for granted. Take it from someone who has lost the ability to have another child of her own: don't squander the blessing that you've been given."

"You can't have children?" Anna asks Jules in shock.

Slowly, Jules shakes her head. "No. The accident that caused me to lose my son also forced the doctors to perform a hysterectomy."

Anna looks confused by this information for some reason, but she tells Jules, "I'm so sorry you had to go through something like that."

Jules bobs her shoulders up and down as if she's shrugging Anna's condolences off. The natural action causes me to have a smidge of respect for her.

"Things occur in life that you don't count on. That one just happened to be my life-altering event." Jules looks over at me and says, "Go to Desmond if for nothing else than to ease your own mind that your son is well. Odds are, he's perfectly fine. But if you keep worrying that something is wrong, the stress you cause yourself may end up affecting him too."

I know she's right, but I'm not about to admit it to her.

"Well, I think I've been lectured enough for one day," I tell them both. "Oh, before I go, you never told me how you knew I was here, Anna. How exactly did you know?"

"We have people watching the places we thought you might visit here on Earth," Anna tells me. "This was one of them."

I'm not quite sure I believe her, but I don't see how else she could have known I was in the cemetery.

"I saw the memorial you built for Cade in one of Roan's memories," I tell her. "I thought I would come see it for myself." I pause for a moment, unsure if I want to ask Anna my next question, but curiosity gets the better of me. "Have you seen him? Have you gone to Heaven to speak with Cade?"

Anna shakes her head. "God told me He doesn't want to talk to anyone yet. He's grieving the loss of you just as much as you are him, Helena."

I swallow back the threat of tears because I have to know one more thing.

"Does he know I'm having his child?" I ask my sister. "Does he even know I'm pregnant?"

"I honestly can't answer that because I don't know," she tells me, looking sorry for not having an answer for me. "We haven't seen God in months either, so I haven't been able to ask Him. I wish I could tell you. I truly do."

"It's just as well," I say, acting as if the news doesn't bother me in the slightest when it actually troubles me a great deal. "Even if he knew, it would more than likely only make him sadder."

"I don't think it would," Anna says with a small smile. "I think he would be happy to know he has a son on the way."

"A son you and your War Angel contingent seem determined to take away from me," I say snidely.

Anna sighs. "If you could assure me that you would raise him in a way Cade would approve of, I wouldn't have a problem with you keeping your son. But, to be honest with you, Helena, I don't think you're in any state of mind to take care of a baby. And ..." she pauses as if concerned about voicing her next words, "have you thought about after the baby is born? Have you even considered the possibility that you might unintentionally kill him with your love like you did Cade?"

"You impress me, Anna," I say, feeling a chill run down my spine at the implication of her words, "even I didn't think you could be cruel enough to suggest such a thing happening."

"I'm only trying to make sure you don't make the same mistake twice and live to regret another loss. I know firsthand the strength of a mother's love for her child. All I ask is that you consider the possibility that your love could kill him too. Just think about it, Helena. Promise me you'll consider all of the ramifications of keeping him with you."

"While I would love to stay and chitchat with the two of you more," I say, knowing I need to go before I show Anna just how much I already care for my baby, "but I have business I need to attend to elsewhere." I look over at Jules. "And you might want to suggest to Ethan that he should check up on Xander on Laed-i. If my sources are correct, he's having a bit of a problem over there right now."

And with those words of advice, I leave them in the cemetery to return to my own domain so I can contemplate what was said. At least I think it was me who phased my body to Hell. It's been hard to tell these days. I would have asked Anna about the twins phasing her places she didn't want to go to near the end of her own pregnancy, but I didn't feel like prolonging our unexpected family get-together.

Ethan probably already suspects that I'm not in complete control of my powers since he saw me phase while I was in mid-sentence on Cephas. I know from the memories of some of the War Angels that it was actually the Guardians of the Guf whose souls are attached to the seals who kept phasing Anna to different places. I have no doubt now that the soul of my son is actually a seal too and that it is more than likely the guardian of his seal who takes control of my powers every once in a while. I can't say I like that very much, but there's really nothing I can do to stop it from happening. Until my son is born and the awoken guardian is expunged from my body, I won't be able to regain absolute control over my actions.

As I sit down on the wrought iron bench that my father used quite often while he resided in Hell, I begin to run through the pros and cons of seeking out Desmond for help with my pregnancy. To be honest, I can't think of a good reason not to go to him. Jules is right. It is better to err on the side of caution and not take any chances with the welfare of my unborn child. Besides, it's not as if Desmond can harm me. He's just an angel, after all. If worse comes to worst, I can trap him down here in Hell with me until the birth of my son. Jules already told me that Desmond promised not to tell Ethan or the others if I visited him. From what I know of Desmond, he isn't one to tell lies just to get what he wants. However, I'm surprised he's still living in his residence in the down-world of Stratus. From what I understand, another Watcher, Brutus, is now emperor of Stratus since he married its empress, Kyna Halloran. You would think Desmond could find better accommodations in either the cloud city of Stratus or Cirrus.

I quickly make the logical decision and phase myself to Desmond's home in Stratus territory. As I stand on the stoop outside his front door, I'm vaguely aware of the people walking behind me on the city sidewalk at the bottom of the stairs to his home. I pay them no mind and open the door to Desmond's house without knocking first. I announce my arrival in his home by a quick shout out of his name as I close the door behind me.

I've never actually been inside his house before, but over the past few months, I've stood right outside his door trying to work up the courage to go inside and ask for his help. I know my sister and even that human, Jules, were just trying to give me some sound advice, and I have to admit that the story Jules told me about the loss of her own child has finally spurred me toward this moment.

Just as I click the door shut, I see Desmond phase in front of me.

His expression is a mixture of surprise, which is to be expected, and wonder at my out of the blue arrival in his home.

"Helena," he greets me in the native brogue of this part of the world, "I'm so glad you came to see me, lass. Are you having a problem with the baby? Is he all right?"

I turn to fully face Desmond as I place protective hands on my baby bump.

"I'm hoping you can tell me that. I want you to check him for me," I say, keeping my expression blank and giving nothing away about my worry. "I want you to make sure he's healthy."

"Of course," Desmond says, unable to hide his relief that I've finally come to him. "Please, follow me into the living room so we can get you settled."

I do as he directs and follow him into a modestly furnished sitting room to the left of the entryway. There isn't a great deal of furniture present, but what's there looks well used.

"Why in the world do you live like a pauper?" I have to ask Desmond. "You could have much nicer things than this considering who and what you are."

"Please, lie down here," Desmond instructs me as he uses his hand to indicate the Victorian style chaise lounge chair upholstered with a maroon and gold brocade material. "And to answer your question, I think the people here in the down-world would find it odd for me to have nicer things than this when most of them are still living in shacks made of pieced together scraps. You may not view my home as being much, but to most of the people in this territory, I live in a palace."

As I carefully lower myself onto the seat of the chair, I feel my son change positions inside me as if he knows we've finally come to seek help. Involuntarily, I inhale sharply from the pain I experience from his movements.

"Are you all right?" Desmond asks worriedly, automatically coming to my aid and resting a comforting hand on my right shoulder.

I shrug his hand off, not wanting to be touched by him.

"That's why I'm here, you imbecile," I reply tersely. "I need you to tell me if this pain is normal."

Desmond doesn't seem to take offense at my words. In fact, he chuckles at my show of temper.

"Well, you certainly haven't lost your spirit, so that's a good thing," he tells me. "Wait here just a moment. I need to go grab something."

Desmond phases away while I bring my legs up onto the chaise lounge to stretch them out. He returns quickly holding a small silver disk in his hands.

"I don't want to see him," I say adamantly, knowing the device Desmond is holding can project a hologram of my baby. "I only want you to check his vitals."

"But it would be better if we did both, Helena," Desmond argues.

"I said I don't want to see him!" I yell, causing the house to shake violently enough for it to sprinkle dust down on us from the movement of the second floor.

Desmond sighs in frustration, but he doesn't try to argue with me anymore. I see him press something on the underside of the silver disk in his hand before he lays it on top of my protruding belly.

Almost instantly, a series of readings hover over the disk giving us the information we need about my son's health. From what I can tell, almost everything looks normal.

"Hmm, odd," Desmond says as he looks at the readings. "Everything looks good, but I wonder why there is an increase in keratin levels."

"I was hoping you could tell me that," I say, grimacing as the baby moves once again, causing me to wince in pain.

"Helena," he says, bending down on one knee before me with an imploring expression on his face, "we need to look at the hologram of your baby. These numbers aren't telling me the whole story, and I think you've probably seen them before and understand that."

Of course I've seen these numbers before. It's not like doctors have a monopoly on health care devices. I've known about the high levels of keratin in my baby's system for quite some time. I just don't know why he has so much of it, and truth be known, I'm scared to find out the reason why.

I know from the thoughts of the War Angels who have entered my realm that they worry what my baby will come out looking like. I am neither human nor angel. I'm something else that not even God has classified, and since I'm so unique, that leads to the question of what my baby will look like. Will he look human, or will he end up being a physical mirror of the ugliness inside me? I haven't had the courage to find out, and I came here today hoping Desmond could take away my worries by seeing something in the vitals of my son that I might have missed over the past few months.

When my son moves again, I see Desmond place his uninvited hand against my stomach.

"Oh my," he says, his eyes opening wide in surprise as he feels the vibration associated with my son's movements. "What in the world ..."

"Get your hand off me," I say angrily, grabbing him by the wrist and pushing him away hard enough to knock him to the floor. "I didn't give you permission to touch me!"

"You came to me for help, Helena," Desmond says, standing back onto his feet. "Please, let me help you and your son. You know as well as I do that babies don't normally vibrate in the womb like that, and I think you came to me today to be your courage to finally look at him. It would be better if we both know what to expect during the delivery. The fewer surprises we have, the more prepared I will be to handle things."

"You mean to handle the monster that might come out of my body?" I question him curtly. "Don't stand there and try to pretend that you haven't at least considered the possibility that my son will simply be another creature of Hell. I know what you all have been thinking for the past few months."

"And apparently, you've been thinking the same thing too, lass, or you wouldn't be here right now asking for my help," he replies knowingly.

Eh. Angels and their god complexes. They think they know everything. In this case, Desmond is right, but I hate to admit that to him.

It would only foster his already inflated angelic ego. Yet he isn't quite like the other angels, especially Ethan. What a bloodthirsty curd that one is. He truly believes that cutting my son from my womb is the only course of action he has to ensure the safety of Cade's child. I know the sword he carries against his side is the one from alternate Earth. They all believe its blade will help destroy me one day. I hate to tell them that what they believe is a fool's fantasy, but given enough time, they'll figure that out on their own.

"The truth of the matter is," I begin to tell Desmond, "I don't know what he'll come out looking like. All I know is that for the first three months, I could barely keep any food down because I was nauseous all the time, and the strength of the vibration you just felt when he moves has grown along with him. It's getting so strong now, I fear he'll tear through my stomach when he's ready to be born."

"Then let's look at him and alleviate both of our worries."

"Or cause us all to have even worse nightmares," I say wearily, resting my head back on the curve of the small upholstered sofa and closing my eyes.

"I find it odd for you to say something like that, considering the fact that you designed creatures like the hellspawn and leviathans. What could possibly be so horrible about him that it would give you nightmares?"

"I designed those things to cause fear to those who reside in Hell," I say, opening my eyes and turning my head to look at Desmond. "I don't want my son to hate what I've made him into."

"He's not only your son, Helena. He's Cade's son too. And like any parent, he is half responsible for what your son becomes. I think you need to at least trust that his father gave him the best parts of himself."

I take in a deep breath because I know everything Desmond has said is true. I need to find out what's different about my son before he's born, so that I'm prepared for his birth. I still haven't decided if I will ask Desmond for his help when the time comes, but I haven't completely ruled out the possibility either. In the end, it doesn't really matter what my son looks like. I will love him all the same, and I will protect him to the best of my ability.

"Show me," I tell Desmond before I lose my nerve. "I've waited longer than I should have to find out."

Desmond reaches over and picks up the silver medical disk from my stomach to change its settings.

Once it's ready, he looks over at me and says, "I want you to know that whatever he looks like, I will love and protect him just as fiercely as his father would have. Cade was my friend, and all I want is for his son to have a happy and healthy life."

"Thank you for saying that."

"Are you ready to see him?" Desmond asks, willing to give me a little more time to compose myself, even though I can see how anxious he is to find out what my baby looks like.

I nod my head, letting him know I'm ready because my voice is failing me at the moment.

When Desmond places the silver disk back on top of my stomach, the holographic picture of my son appears above it.

I hear myself take in a deep, surprised breath. I raise a trembling hand up to my lips and stare at his image, unable to believe what I'm seeing.

"Oh, Helena ..." Desmond says, sounding as shocked as I feel. I look over to catch him smiling from ear to ear with joy. "He's beautiful."

I return my gaze to my son and begin to cry with joy because I know now that he has indeed inherited the best parts of his father and the best parts of me.

He is my child, and I will never let him go.

CHAPTER 13
(Return to Jules' Point of View)

After Helena phases away, I turn to Anna and anxiously ask, "Can you tell if she went to Desmond's house?"

Anna sighs disappointedly and shakes her head. "No, she didn't. She's in Hell."

I sigh too because I thought we were really persuasive in our arguments about her seeking Desmond's help.

"Maybe she just went there to think about what we said to her," I suggest because I can see how upset Anna is over the possibility that she failed in her mission. "I don't think Helena rushes into things. She still might decide to go to him later."

"I hope so," Anna replies, but she doesn't try to hide her despondency from me.

I look up at the white marble statue of Cade. I never met him in person, but if this is an accurate depiction of what he looked like while he lived on Earth, I can see why Helena was attracted to him. Anyone who says looks don't matter in a relationship is lying to him or herself. Sure, it's what's on the inside that counts in the long run, but initially, all you see is their outward appearance. There has to be a mutual physical attraction in order for the propagation of the species to occur naturally.

I notice that the marble pedestal the statue is standing on has

Cade's name engraved on it in a gold script. Right underneath his name are three words: warrior, friend, and father. Below those words is the sentence: "*He will be missed by all who were lucky enough to know him and even luckier to be loved by him.*"

"From what Helena said to you, it sounds like you can phase to Heaven," I say, looking away from the pedestal and back to Anna. "Is that right?"

Anna nods. "Yes, I can. It's an ability I inherited from one of my ancestors."

"Why do you think Cade doesn't want to speak with you?"

"I honestly don't have any idea," she replies, looking troubled by his reluctance to see her. "People tend to deal with grief in their own way. I suppose this is his way of coping with what happened."

"So does God visit you on a regular basis? You sounded like not seeing Him for a few months was uncommon."

"He only started visiting me when Malcolm and I found one another. I'm not sure why He hasn't been to see us lately. I'm sure He has His reasons though."

"I have to say, I wouldn't mind meeting Him one day. You know, without having to die first, that is."

Anna grins. "Well, if you stick around with us long enough, I'm sure you will." She tilts her head as she considers me for a moment. From the look of curiosity on her face, I know she wants to ask me a question.

"Go ahead and ask," I tell her. "What is it that you want to know about me?"

"Am I that obvious?" she inquires with a smile.

"Just a tad."

Anna doesn't ask me what she wants to know right away. I can only assume she's probably trying to figure out how to phrase her question without it coming out rudely.

"Do you mind me asking how you lost your son?" she finally says.

I go on to tell her basically what I told Helena the day before in my apartment about the accident Timothy and I were involved in.

"That's awful, Jules. I'm so sorry that happened to you," Anna sympathizes. "And I'm sorry you can't have any more children."

I shrug. "I've made my peace with that part of it. Maybe it just wasn't meant for me to have kids. I don't know."

"Do you mind me asking how your husband died?"

"I don't mind you asking," I say hesitantly, unsure how she will react to my next words, "but do you mind me not telling you?"

"Of course you don't have to tell me," she says graciously. "But I hope you will feel more comfortable with me in time and let me help you deal with the turmoil you seem to be in because of his death. I get the feeling you need someone to talk to about it. If I'm not that person, perhaps Ethan would be a good choice as a confidante. He cares enough about you to listen to the story and help you as much as he can."

"He's only known me for a day," I almost scoff, but I reign in my snarky side. Anna is only trying to give me helpful advice, and I can't refute the fact that there's something even I don't fully understand going on between Ethan and me.

"Sometimes fate decides the people we're supposed to care about," she tells me, sounding too wise for someone as young as she is. "I knew the moment I saw Malcolm that he was the man I was supposed to be with for the rest of my life."

"Love at first sight syndrome?" I ask, having heard of such a thing happening but never knowing anyone personally who had it happen to them.

"In a way," she tells me, looking hesitant to continue. "Have you ever heard of soul mates?"

"Actually Zane's wife, Verati, mentioned them to me yesterday. She told me I should ask Ethan about them, but, as you know, our dinner date ended abruptly last night, and we didn't get to talk much. Are you trying to tell me you and Malcolm fell instantly in love because you're soul mates?"

"More or less. We had our problems in the beginning like any other couple, but we quickly worked them out."

"So how do you find your soul mate? Dumb luck?"

Anna laughs. "I suppose you could think of it that way, but I would rather view it as divine intervention."

"I assume not everyone gets to meet their soul mate ..."

"That's right. Only a small percentage of us are lucky enough to find the match to our soul. I'm just thankful I happened to be one."

"So ..." I say, dragging out the word while I think of how to phrase my next question. "How exactly do you know when you've met your soul mate? Do the angels start singing in Heaven and alert you to their presence?"

"The Heavenly Host does sing loudly, but not quite loud enough to cross the veil between Heaven and Earth. Honestly, it varies from person to person. Those of us who possess angelic traits instantly know when we've met our soul mate. Pure humans, on the other hand, simply sense that there's something special about the other person. They tend to feel almost instantly comfortable and attracted to their soul mate for reasons they don't understand."

Well, that's certainly interesting information.

"And you said that angels instantly know when they've met their soul mate?" I ask, just to clarify.

"Yes."

The plot thickens.

"And if a certain angel met his soul mate," I ask, "would he tell that person about their connection?"

"Not necessarily," Anna replies with a great deal of caution. It's almost as if she wants to be careful not to tell me too much about this soul mate business.

"Why not?" I have to know.

"The easiest way for me to answer that question would be for me to tell you what Zane did when he first met Verati. Now, Zane knew instantly that Verati was his soul mate, but he didn't tell her until after he courted her and she agreed to be his wife."

"Why did he wait so long to tell her?"

"He wanted her to fall in love with him on her own, not because it was a predestined connection. There is a certain amount of free will that can come into play, especially when you're human. Just because two people are soul mates doesn't necessarily mean that they'll like everything about each other. One of them could slurp their soup the wrong way, or snort when they laugh, or tell bad jokes. There are numerous things that can get on your nerves enough to cause you not to want to spend the rest of your life married to the other person. From what I understand, that sort of situation happens very rarely, but it *can* happen. Sometimes soul mates simply remain best friends and never take it any further than that. Zane wanted to earn Verati's love and not let the fact that they're soul mates make up her mind for her. Does that make sense?"

I nod. "Yeah. It does actually. He just didn't want her to feel obligated to love him back."

"Precisely."

"Too bad I'm not part angel," I unintentionally muse out loud.

"Oh?" Anna questions me with a slight tilt of her head and an almost eager look on her face. "Why is that, Jules?"

I shrug, not really wanting to give her my answer but knowing I have to say something. Otherwise, I'm being rude, and I don't want to be rude to Anna.

"It would just make life a whole lot easier."

Anna seems to understand that I want to drop the subject. She doesn't push it. She simply holds out her hand to me.

"We should go back to Cirrus before Malcolm and Ethan come searching for us," she tells me.

"I don't want to lie to Ethan about this," I say adamantly. "You're not going to ask me to, are you?"

Anna shakes her head. "I would never ask you to lie on my behalf, Jules. Lies tend to lead to more problems than they solve."

I couldn't agree with her more.

I place my hand on Anna's, and she instantly phases us back to the veranda outside her quarters in the Cirrus palace.

As soon as we walk into the sitting room, I see Ethan pacing back and forth behind the couch while Malcolm and Lucas play with the babies on the floor.

Ethan sees us first and comes to an abrupt halt.

"Did the two of you enjoy your little *chat* with Helena?" he asks scathingly.

The anger I see on Ethan's face surprises me. I knew he would be upset, but he seems practically livid. His face is so red, I fear it might explode at any second.

"I believe it was a productive discussion," Anna answers, unflustered by Ethan's obvious rage and disappointment in her actions. "We encouraged her to go see Desmond. I'm not sure she will, but hopefully we gave her enough reasons to seek him out for his medical advice. I'm sure after she heard how Jules lost her own son that she'll reconsider not finding help of some sort."

The anger on Ethan's face almost instantly disappears after hearing Anna's words. He looks at me, and I don't shy away from his questioning gaze.

"You lost a child?" he questions me in a soft voice. He looks like he's sure he misheard Anna's words.

"I'm so sorry," Anna says as she looks over at me with an immense amount of regret. "I just assumed that if Helena knew the story, it was probably something you had already told Ethan."

"It's okay," I reassure her. "It's not exactly a secret."

"I'm sorry you lost your baby, Ms. Jules," Lucas tells me from his spot on the floor next to his father. His cherubic face shows how upset he is for me over my loss.

"It happened a long time ago," I tell him before forcing myself to look back at Ethan.

His gaze is averted as he stares at some unknown object on the floor a few feet away. He must sense me looking at him because he finally slides his gaze up and over to meet mine again. A strange silence settles over the room, suddenly making us all feel uncomfortable. I quickly think of something to say to break the unwanted tension.

"Before Helena left us," I tell him, "she told me to suggest that you check up on Xander. She made it sound like he's in some sort of trouble on Laed-i."

"Maybe I should go speak with him," Anna volunteers. "Sometimes, I'm the only one he'll listen to."

"Let me go there first to see if it's something I can handle," Ethan tells her. "If your intervention is needed, I'll let you know."

"Either way," Anna tells him, "keep me informed about what's going on and how much trouble he's gotten himself into this time."

Ethan nods his head in her direction as he walks over to me. "I'll gather what information I can and let you know what I discover." He looks at me and asks, "Would you like to accompany me to Laed-i?"

"Sure. As long as you don't think I'll get in the way."

"You won't," Ethan says confidently.

"Wait," Anna says to me, "I haven't given you your gold yet. We still owe you the half payment for your help with Helena."

"I hate to ask, but do you think you could give it to the Arcas Orphanage for me? I was going to give it to them anyway, and it would save me the hassle of arranging the donation to them."

Anna smiles. She seems pleased with my plan, but she's classy enough not to make a big deal out of it.

"I will have someone handle the details for you," she promises.

"Thank you."

"Oh," she says as if just remembering something else, "has Ethan had a chance to mention the royal introduction party we're having for the twins here tomorrow night?"

"Yes. He invited me and my family. I'm pretty sure we're all coming. I know my mom and I will be there, and usually my uncle ends up being my mom's date to social functions like that."

"Wonderful," Anna says with a pleased smile. "I look forward to seeing you all tomorrow then."

Ethan places his hand on my right shoulder and phases us away from Cirrus.

I expected him to take us directly to Laed-i to track down Xander, but instead, he phases us to the white gazebo on the planet where we attempted to have our first date. Everything has been cleared away from the inside of it, leaving it empty.

"I thought we were going to find Xander," I say, seeing no reason for us to be here.

"We will in a moment," he replies with a troubled frown on his face as he looks at me. "I just wanted to make sure you were all right first. I know you didn't want me to know about your son's death, and I wanted to make sure that the fact that I do know isn't bothering you."

"It's not that I didn't want you to know," I'm quick to correct him. "We just haven't had much time to talk about a lot of things from our past."

"Yet you found the time to confide in Helena about it," he points out, sounding confused on why I would tell his mortal enemy anything about my life, much less something so deeply personal.

"I only told her because I hoped it would convince her to seek medical attention when it's time for her son to be born. I don't habitually go around telling people about the darkest times in my life. If you want to know what happened, I am more than willing to tell you now."

"I would like to know, but only if you want to tell me. I don't want you to feel obligated to do it."

I glance over to the entrance of the gazebo, which faces the magenta ocean on this planet. It's daytime here, and the sun's reflection causes the water to shine like glass.

"Why don't we go over to the steps and sit down?" I suggest.

Without a word, Ethan follows me to the edge of the entrance, and we take a seat, allowing our feet to rest on the second step of the gazebo.

I go on to tell Ethan about the loss of my son, secretly hoping this is the last time I have to repeat the entire story to anyone. What I told Ethan is true. I don't go around telling my sad tale to anyone who will listen to it. In fact, Helena was the first person I ever told personally. My mother and uncle took care of telling the people we knew in town what happened. I just couldn't bring myself to talk about it. Then, when Timothy died, I completely shut people out of my life, except for my mom and uncle. I probably would have stayed away from them too, but they wouldn't let me be a shut-in. In fact, it was my uncle who first suggested I become a bounty hunter, even though he seems to regret his suggestion now because he thinks it's too dangerous. He knew me well enough to realize that I would be more likely to leave my apartment if I had a job to keep me busy. I'm grateful for my uncle's intervention because hunting down criminals on my own timetable has literally been a lifesaver. If I didn't have something worthwhile to do during my days, I would probably be spending them drinking, just like I do my nights. With that thought in mind, I realize last night was the first night in almost five years that I didn't need the added help of alcohol to fall asleep, just a man who made me feel safer than I've felt in a long time and a warm shoulder to snuggle against. The thought ends up being quite sobering.

After I finish my tale of the tragic events which led to my son's death, Ethan remains silent as he considers my story.

Finally, he says, "I can't imagine the emotional pain you've had to endure since then. How long afterwards did your husband die?"

"Exactly a year," I answer, unable to prevent myself from remembering the night I found Timothy's body. An unwanted picture of the scene I discovered in the cabin that night flashes through my mind. I shiver slightly, still remembering the bloodcurdling scream I heard come out of my mouth when I found him. It was in that moment that the first seed of guilt took root inside my heart and grew with each passing day.

"Exactly?" Ethan questions me, looking a little shocked and a lot confused by my answer.

As he considers the possibilities for such an unlikely coincidence, I can tell when he settles on the reason why.

"He killed himself," Ethan states without a tinge of questioning in his voice.

All I can do is nod because the words I need to say don't readily organize themselves within my mind as a coherent sentence. I want to tell Ethan exactly what happened and my role in Timothy's death, but I know once I say them, he may never look at me the same way again. I'm not sure I can handle that, but I do know that the longer I keep this a secret from him, the harder it will be for me to come clean about what I did.

I turn my gaze away from Ethan and stare out at the ocean, quietly studying the waves as they crash against the shoreline. I haven't personally told anyone besides my mother and uncle what I found inside the cabin that night. The police who came to handle the scene didn't need to ask me what happened either. It was obvious what Timothy had done, but what wasn't so clear was the reason behind his actions. Only I knew that, and only I could have saved him from himself.

"After the death of our son," I begin, keeping my gaze steady on the ocean, because if I don't, I might chicken out and not tell Ethan everything I need to, "Timothy and I drifted apart. I was told by the psychiatrist I saw later that the loss of a child can have one of two effects on a couple. They'll either become closer than they were before the incident because they use one another to lean on or they drift apart. Timothy and I ended up being the latter of those two options, but that was all my doing. I was so ... *angry* ... at him that I verbally abused him every day for a year and laid all the blame for our son's death on his shoulders. I honestly don't know why he even stayed with me. The only reason I've been able to come up with is that he didn't want me to be alone. I think he kept hoping I would eventually work through my anger and ultimately forgive him for what happened, but even now after everything, I can't seem to do that." I take in a deep breath because I know the worst part of the story is yet to come. "That night ... on the first anniversary of our son's death ... he left me a note in our apartment in town. Not the place I live in now. This one was a lot larger and nicer because we were preparing to start a family. The note asked me to come up to the cabin so he and I could talk and try to figure out what direction we wanted to take our relationship. I was livid when I read the note. I couldn't believe he wanted me to make that drive, on that night of all nights. But I did. I drove like a mad woman up that mountain, just so I could chew him out once I got there. As soon as I stepped inside the cabin, I could feel that something was wrong. I didn't see or hear Timothy, and I sensed an emptiness there that told me something bad had happened. I began to walk through the house calling out his name, even though I knew in my heart that he wouldn't be answering me back. I finally found him dangling with a noose around his neck from the railing on the second floor. He had a note that he had written to me safety-pinned to the front of his shirt."

I have to stop for a moment to catch my breath as I remember what Timothy's last words to me were.

"What did the note say?" Ethan asks, encouraging me to purge myself of a memory that's haunted me for five long years.

"He told me not to blame myself for what he did because he hadn't been able to forgive himself for our son's death either. He said he decided to end his life this way because it was his fault that our son choked to death trying to be born. By leaving the world in a similar fashion, Timothy said he hoped it would make me feel like justice had finally been served."

"He should have never written a letter like that to you," Ethan says, sounding angry at Timothy. "The only purpose it served was to make you feel guilt over a decision he alone made to end his life."

"But he was right," I say, finally working up the courage to force myself to look over at Ethan and make my confession. "A part of me did feel like justice had been served. But the more I thought about it, the more I realized that I might not have physically tied the noose around his neck, but my anger and harsh words led him to kill himself. I may have blamed him for our son's death, but we both made the decision to go to the cabin alone that night and home birth our child. Timothy's death was exclusively my fault. I pushed him to do it. I may not have consciously known it at the time, but I never gave him the opportunity to recover from the loss of our son. I focused all of my anger and pain on him because I couldn't figure out any other way to cope with the agony I felt. I killed him, Ethan. My *anger* and inability to forgive killed Timothy. I'm not sure what that says about me as a person, but it can't be good."

Ethan slowly shakes his head. "You didn't kill him, Jules, and I'm not just saying that to make you feel better about what happened. I don't think you will ever feel right about it no matter what I or anyone else says. But you need to realize that Timothy killed himself. Once a person makes the decision to end their own life, it's hard to talk them out of it."

"But I pushed him to commit suicide!" I argue, unwilling to shirk the role I played in my husband's death. "I told him a hundred times that I wished he had died in the accident instead of our son. How many times can a person hear that and not start to believe it's true? If I'm being honest, there were even times I wanted Timothy to die. I wanted him out of my home and out of my life forever."

"Then why didn't you ask him to leave?" he asks. "Why did you let him stay with you?"

The question brings me up short because I have never considered it before.

"I don't know," I say in a whisper, continuing to think about the reason I never asked Timothy to leave the apartment we shared. "I probably should have."

"I don't think you hated him as much as you think you did, or you wouldn't have taken his death so hard. There was probably a part of you that still loved him back then. Maybe subconsciously you hoped time would heal your pain and the two of you could eventually work back to where you were before the death of your son."

"I suppose it's possible," I say, considering Ethan's words. "At the time, all I could see was red whenever I looked at Timothy. I tried a dozen times to see him like I used to. We practically grew up together, you know."

"No, I didn't know that. Is he the boy in the photograph in your apartment?"

I nod. "Yeah. He was an orphan. In fact, he used to live in the orphanage that I'm donating money to. He used to always complain about having to wear hand-me-down clothing and shoes and never having a room of his own there. Maybe with the money I'm giving them, they can buy the kids their own clothes and do some construction to let them have their own rooms too."

"I'm sure you can set up the fund to go to those specific changes."

I nod. "Yeah. I'll see about doing that."

"So apparently, the two of you knew each other for years before you married one another."

"We were best friends all through elementary school, and then when our hormones kicked in, we decided friendship wasn't the only thing we were good at with one another. We ended up getting married right out of high school, but we put off having children until we were both set up in our careers. There was a time I couldn't even imagine living without Timothy in my life. Now, all I feel is guilt when I think about him. That's the reason I drink so much."

"But it doesn't seem like drinking makes you feel less guilty."

"No. It doesn't. It only makes me forget for a little while what it is I feel so guilty about. I don't think I can ever forgive myself for what happened to him."

"If you can't forgive yourself, then you need to find a way to live with the guilt better," Ethan tells me. "I understand what it feels like to live with the burden of killing someone. Even though I don't believe you led Timothy to kill himself, it's obvious you do, and I would never try to convince you otherwise. Only you can absolve yourself, and if you can't do that, you need to channel your guilt into a more worthwhile pursuit than drinking. You need to find a purpose for your life again that will give it meaning."

"How am I supposed to do that? It's not like I can just walk downtown into a store called Redemptions R' Us."

Ethan cracks a grin at my attempt at humor, even though I'm partially serious.

"I think you need to keep your eyes open for a way to find meaning in your life again. Sometimes opportunities present themselves when you least expect them to."

"I think it would take a miracle for that to happen to me."

"Miracles can happen," he assures me.

"I guess you would be more of an expert on that subject than me, since you're an angel."

"I don't know if I'm an expert, but I do know they've been known to occur from time to time. Just keep your faith and trust the path God has set you on."

Ethan's suggestion sounds easier said than done, but it's not like he's advising me to make any extra effort. He seems to believe that something will spontaneously occur in my life to help me cope with my guilt better.

Ethan stands and holds a hand out to help me back onto my feet.

"Why don't we go see what trouble Xander has gotten himself into?" he suggests. "It might help take your mind off things for a while."

I place my hand into his and let him help me stand up.

"Are you still mad at me for going with Anna to talk to Helena?" I ask.

"No," he answers. "I just wish I had been told what was going on instead of learning about it after the fact."

"Would you have insisted on going with us?"

"Yes," he answers, "and I know that's the reason Anna went

without letting me know what she was doing. I understand her reasoning. I just didn't appreciate being left out of the loop."

"If there's ever a next time," I say, "I'll make sure you're kept in the loop."

"I would be grateful for that," he says with a small smile.

Ethan doesn't let go of the hand he still holds. In fact, he intertwines our fingers, making it feel like the most natural way for us to phase together.

"Are you ready to go to Laed-i?" he asks.

I nod.

Just before we phase, I realize the heaviness I've felt inside my heart since the night I found Timothy is a lot lighter now. Sharing the reason why I drown my guilt in alcohol has been more therapeutic than I thought it would be. Perhaps I should have talked it out with someone a long time ago, but then I realize that the reason it worked is because I shared my secret with Ethan. If I had told anyone else, I don't believe I would feel the same way.

I squeeze his hand a little tighter, knowing now that I want him to be an integral part of my life. I'm not sure if he's my soul mate or not, but I do know we're building a connection to one another unlike any other that I've ever experienced, and I have no intention of squandering an opportunity that God Himself might be giving me.

CHAPTER 14

For some reason, I expected Ethan to phase us to either Xander's home on Laed-i or at least Zane and Verati's house. Instead, he phases directly inside an establishment that looks strangely similar to Grace House. We're standing beside a bar where people are yelling out drink orders to a harried bartender working the counter. Bottles filled with colorful liquids line the shelves of the glass wall behind him. The translucent wall provides a clear view of a bright blue sky and white fluffy clouds in the distance. I immediately direct my gaze to the floor I'm standing on and see nothing but the white of clouds. As I let my gaze travel around the structure we're standing in, I soon realize that it's floating in midair.

A chiming noise causes me to look up to where the ceiling should be but isn't. I had expected to see a glass roof to match the walls and floor, but instead all I see is open sky. Dozens of dancing couples are floating in the air above us enclosed in what looks like translucent bubbles. Each bubble emits a particular color. When one bubble touches another, the color of each one changes to a new color.

I look back at the room and see that there is a casino type area just past a normal, and very crowded, dance floor.

"Come on," Ethan shouts to me over the loud music as he gently tugs on the hand he still holds. "If Xander isn't here at the bar, he's probably at one of the gambling tables in the back."

Ethan leads me through the crowd of people toward the opposite side of the structure. I notice that the farther back we go, the quieter the music becomes. It's almost like there's an invisible dampening field causing the music to fade naturally. Once we reach the first set of gambling tables, I can just barely hear the music anymore. Everyone in the back seems to be playing the same game. A total of four people are sitting around each of the twenty tables in the room. On these tables, they're playing some sort of card game.

"There he is," Ethan says, spotting Xander easily since he's the most vocal of the bunch in the room.

It's easy to tell that Xander is drunk. His eyes are bloodshot, and he's singing a song woefully out of tune. I'm not sure if the bad singing is part of his strategy to distract the people he's playing with and get them off their game, or if he's just an obnoxious drunk.

Ethan doesn't let go of my hand until we're standing next to his wayward angel's table. As soon as we get there, he reaches down with both hands and grabs Xander by the front of his jacket to lift him out of the chair he was sitting in.

"What is wrong with you, Xander?" Ethan snarls, openly showing his anger and disappointment in his fellow angel. "I thought you said you were going to change your ways after what happened in Hell."

Xander looks at Ethan with unadulterated disdain. I feel sure he wouldn't normally let his emotions show so blatantly, but he reeks of alcohol, and since he's an angel, I know how much of the stuff he has to drink in order to become this drunk.

"The high and mighty Ethan Knight has come to save the day yet again," Xander says contemptuously. "Don't you ever get sick and tired of being so damn perfect, Ethan? Not all of us can be."

"I don't expect you to be perfect," Ethan growls. "But I do expect you to do your job here and stay out of trouble. What exactly have you gotten yourself into this time, Xander?"

"Perhaps I can answer that question for your inebriated friend," a strange little man says as he shuffles toward us from the other side of the room.

As I watch his progress down the aisle between the gaming tables, I'm not sure if there's something physically wrong with his legs or if the way he's walking is an odd personal choice. My hunch tells me it's the latter explanation. I'm just not sure why. Other than that, he looks pretty normal. He's wearing a white tunic dress over a plain black shirt. He has the same light brown skin that most of the people in the room have, so I can only assume he's a native to this planet. His hair is jet black—again the same as pretty much everyone else inside the nightclub. His face is a little on the weaselly side though, and I never trust a person with pinched features like him. They're always up to no good, and this man is definitely not an exception to that rule.

Ethan sets Xander back on his feet, but he's too wobbly to stay upright for very long. He ends up falling back onto his chair, which is the safest place for him to be at the moment. It keeps him a safe distance away from Ethan and allows gravity to work in his favor, not against him.

"And who are you?" Ethan asks curtly, looking the man up and down with open wariness.

"I am King Manas' royal treasurer, Sir Uwe Hunya, at your service," he says, bending at the waist slightly to Ethan in mock humbleness because humility is certainly not written on Uwe's face. He's as arrogant as they come because he believes he has power over the situation. And maybe he does. I have no way of knowing until he explains what's going on with Xander.

"What kind of trouble is Xander in, and why are you here?" Ethan asks, sounding suspicious of the other man's presence.

"I'm here to settle your friend's debt to the king," Uwe says with a grin that looks disarming and almost innocent, but I sense an ulterior motive to his presence here at this exact time.

"How much does he owe to the king?" Ethan asks cautiously.

Uwe pulls out a small black notebook from the folds of his outfit and flips through a few pages until he comes to the one he's looking for.

"Ah, here it is," he says with a satisfied grin. "Your friend owes the king twenty million M coins."

"And just how many bars of gold would that translate into?" Ethan asks, bracing himself for the answer.

"Well, let's see," Uwe says as his eyes wander skyward and he tilts his head slightly while he calculates the rate of conversion. "I would say that would come to twenty standard gold bars."

Ethan sighs. "I can get that for you, but I'll need about an hour to gather it together."

"Oh," Uwe says, waving a hand at Ethan like he's said the funniest thing, "no need. The debt has already been settled."

"By who?" both Xander and Ethan ask at the same time, but not in the same voice. Xander sounds surprised while Ethan remains cautious of such good fortune.

"By your friend, of course," Uwe says with a smile. "She came to see the king personally and convinced him to agree to the trade instead."

"Trade?" Ethan asks in surprise. "Who was this woman, and what did she trade to the king?"

"Something quite rare and beautiful that we do not naturally possess on this planet," Uwe replies without answering the first question. Whatever was given must be highly prized on this world to cover such a hefty debt.

Before I can react, and before Ethan or Xander understand what's happening, Uwe clamps one of his hands on my arm nearest to him. Within a millisecond, I find myself trapped inside one of the translucent bubbles I saw the dancers in earlier with my captor. We zoom high into the sky, leaving the floating casino far behind within seconds.

"What are you doing?" I scream to Uwe as the ball we're in hurtles through the air with the pair of us completely weightless inside. I wrench my arm out of his hold and glare at him scathingly.

Uwe holds up his hands as if he's innocent of any wrongdoing.

"I am only making sure the king receives his payment for your friend's debt. Nothing more, young lady," he protests crossly.

"Payment?" I yell, just as all the pieces fall together within my mind, revealing Helena's true motive for telling me to urge Ethan back to this planet. "That bitch!"

"Well, I'm not sure what that word means on your world," Uwe says snottily, "but I assume it's not a compliment."

"No, it sure the hell isn't, you sniveling kidnapper," I reply unable to hold in my anger.

Uwe lengthens his neck somewhat indignantly. "I resent that

remark, young lady. I am merely adhering to the rules of barter. The king graciously accepted to take you for the remaining years of your life as payment for your friend's debt. If you ask me, you should be grateful for his generosity. He was well within his rights to execute your friend. Ever since those earthlings traveled here, they've been a nuisance to the king's plans. Frankly, I'm surprised he hasn't already killed them for their insolence."

Earthlings? From the way Uwe just talked about Xander and Zane, it sounds like he doesn't know they're angels.

"Have you ever been to Earth?" I ask, curious to know if the inhabitants of this planet have the ability to travel across galaxies.

"We have not developed the technology required to travel so far," Uwe replies, not sounding so arrogant now that he has to admit that his planet is behind Earth's science. But it does tell me that he and his king don't know that the 'earthlings' aren't using technology to travel. It appears that they don't know my friends can phase.

"So basically, you're telling me that your people aren't as smart as the people on Earth," I say, just to rile Uwe up because he needs to be taken down a notch or two.

Uwe narrows his eyes on me. "You are *not* a nice person, and I will report your insubordination to the king himself!"

"Was your threat supposed to scare me?" I ask him with open amusement. "I hate to tell you, but my friends won't just stand idly by and let your king keep me. They'll come for me, and when they do, I would advise that you find a deep dark corner to hide in until it's all over."

Uwe lifts his nose in the air as if he believes I'm bluffing, but he doesn't say anything else to me for the remainder of our journey.

It seems like it takes forever for us to finally begin our descent out of the sky and back toward the ground. Once we've passed through the cloud layer, I see an island, at least I think it's an island at first. The closer we get to it, the more details I'm able to make out. I soon realize it's a fortress built in the middle of a vast blue ocean. A thick wall of rough-hewn black stone surrounds a palace made of a polished version of the same stone. It's beautiful in its darkness, but I can't say it's very welcoming. Then again, I remember what Ethan and the others said about the king of this world. He is basically destroying his own planet to gain personal wealth. The plan seems a bit shortsighted on his part, but then again, egomaniacs aren't usually the smartest bunch in a crowd.

The bubble Uwe and I are traveling inside of decelerates to a point where we're hardly moving at all. It hovers over the center courtyard within the palace before making a gradual descent to solid ground.

"Has Zane or Xander ever been here before?" I ask Uwe, praying that at least one War Angel has a phase point inside the palace to make my rescue easy.

"Absolutely not!" Uwe tells me haughtily. "The king would never permit such riffraff to enter his fortress."

Well, so much for plan A. Hopefully, Ethan and the others come up with a plan B quickly. Since the king's palace is in the middle of an ocean, there's virtually no fleeing it on foot—not unless I can figure out how these bubble things work or happen to come across a submersible somewhere. Considering the choppy, shark-infested waters I saw, escape by boat is out of the question.

After we land, the bubble surrounding us suddenly disappears. I suppose I should have paid more attention to what Uwe was doing before we touched down. He maneuvered his body upright, so that when the bubble disintegrated, he would land firmly on his feet. Unfortunately, I didn't have such a graceful landing. I end up falling directly onto the grass below us back first, which jars the air right out of my lungs.

"Oh, sorry," Uwe says as he looks down at me with a slightly sadistic smile on his face. "I guess I should have warned you about the landing."

I hear a small group of booted footsteps run in our direction. Uwe looks up toward the noise and says, "Take her to the consort chambers and inform Lady Maya that the king's latest addition to his collection has arrived and needs to be prepared."

Just as I sit up on the grass, but before I have a chance to ask Uwe (the wannabe tyrant) what kind of "collection" he's talking about, I feel two sets of hands grab my arms and snatch me up off the ground rather roughly. They turn me around and drag me into the palace. When I look at my captors, I see faceless men. It's not that they don't have faces exactly, but their bodies are covered from head to toe in some sort of stretchy black cloth. They're wearing long white dress type clothing, similar in style to Uwe's outfit, except theirs are chalk white and nondescript.

I attempt to struggle out of their grasps, but they simply refuse to let me go. In fact, their grips tighten on my arms with superhuman strength. I begin to wonder if the two people dragging me through the palace are actually androids of some type and not men.

Finally, my captors stop when we reach a white marble door in the hallway we're in. One of my escorts holds out a hand and pushes the door open. Once inside the room, they shove me farther into it with such force I end up sprawled onto the white marble floor. By the time I turn around, the door is closed and the creatures who brought me here are nowhere to be seen. I immediately stand to my feet and run over to the door, trying to find a way out. Since there's no knob, I try to push it open, but it doesn't budge. I look around the room to search for a different exit. I see another door—one with a knob this time—and run toward it.

When I enter the room, I discover it's simply a windowless bathroom.

"Great." I sigh, resigned to the fact that I'm going to have to wait for the rescue party Ethan is sure to bring. All I need to do is stay alive until they come. I can do that. At least I hope I can.

Uwe said I was to be a part of the king's collection. I hope it's a live collection and not one where he intends to hunt me for sport and mount my head on his wall. I also remember Uwe telling the creatures to take me to the consort chambers. I'm not sure if "consort" means the same thing on this world as it does mine, but I hope it doesn't. Hopefully, this Lady Maya who is supposed to come to my room will fill me in on the details of my captivity.

I look around the bedroom to see if there's anything here that can be used as a weapon. I don't see much except a large bed with black covers and two chairs directly across from it. The positioning of the chairs seems odd to me. It's almost as if they're there for the people who sit in them to view what happens on the bed. The thought sends a chill down my spine, causing me to shiver involuntarily, and I continue to look for anything I can use to defend myself with. My search is cut short, however, when a tall, statuesque dark skinned, black haired woman opens the door and walks into the room. She's physically beautiful, but the arrogant expression on her face makes her ugly to me. She's wearing a long sleeved black dress that clings to her body, showing its perfect proportions.

"Hello," she says, looking me up and down. From the disappointed look on her face, I can tell I'm not meeting a certain physical standard she was expecting me to. "I am Lady Maya. I'm here to prepare you to meet King Manas."

"What if I refuse to meet the king?" I ask, folding my arms across my chest in open defiance.

Lady Maya smiles, but it's not the sort of smile you give when you're being friendly. It's more of an indulgent one—the kind you bestow when you feel as though you're being forced to discuss something important with an idiot.

"Refusing to meet with the king would not be in your best interest, I'm afraid. He may prize your yellow hair and pale skin, but being rebuffed by someone as low as you can only lead to one action from him: death. Now, if you want to survive tonight, I suggest you listen to me very carefully and do exactly what I tell you to do."

"What's happening tonight?" I ask. "And what's so dangerous about it?"

"It's dangerous, because if you don't do what the king wants, he will kill you."

"What's happening tonight?" I ask again, since she didn't answer the question the first time.

"Do you want to live or not?" she questions me tersely, obviously losing her patience with me. "If the answer is yes, then stop asking me so many questions and just do as I tell you."

I do want to live. I want to live long enough for Ethan to find me and take me back home.

I lower my arms back to my sides and ask, "What is it that you want me to do?"

Lady Maya's instructions are simple at first. She asks me to go into the bathroom and bathe, then return to the bedroom so I can be properly groomed to meet the king.

I quickly take a shower, and while I'm towel drying myself, Lady Maya walks into the bathroom without giving me the common courtesy of knocking on the door first.

I quickly cover my nakedness up with my towel and yell, "You're supposed to knock before you come into a room where someone is most likely naked!"

"Trust me," she replies, holding out the thick white robe she has in her hands, "there is nothing about your body that interests me in the slightest. For your sake, I hope the king finds you more appealing than I do."

"Don't ever try to become a motivational speaker," I advise her as I step out of the shower and slip into the robe she's holding out for me. "You're terrible at it."

"I'm not here to motivate you," she says snidely. "I'm only here to do my king's bidding and prepare you for tonight."

Lady Maya turns on her heels and exits the room with me trailing behind her like a lost puppy dog. I hate relying on someone as patronizing as her, but considering Uwe's behavior, I start to believe everyone on this planet—with the exception of Zane's wife—is full of themselves. Or perhaps it's only those who deal with the king on a daily basis, but I don't plan to stick around long enough to find out.

I may not like Lady Maya, but she is extremely proficient when it comes to personal grooming. She styles my hair in an intricate up-do and even incorporates a gold mesh fabric throughout the braid, leaving enough on top to fan out for dramatic effect. The makeup she uses is silky smooth and weightless. She tells me that no matter how much I rub my face with my hands, the makeup won't smudge or come off. The only way to remove it is to use water and soap.

"Considering how you look without it on, I would advise you to never wash your face again," she says haughtily.

I let her remark slide because I could probably look like Anna Devereaux and Lady Maya would find fault with my looks. When she orders me to disrobe in front of her, that's where I draw the line.

"If you just show me what I need to put on," I tell her, "I can dress myself."

"Dressing you was not my primary reason for asking you to take the robe off," she says in a huff. "I need to make sure you are properly groomed ... in all areas of your body."

I begin to laugh harshly. "Oh, hell no. That's not happening. And I swear to the good Lord above that if you even attempt to 'groom' me anymore, I will break both of your arms, and possibly a leg, if you push me too far."

Lady Maya lets out an irritated sigh. "Very well, but if the king is disappointed in your appearance, you will be the one who suffers the consequences, not me."

"I can pretty much guarantee you that your king won't be seeing me naked tonight."

She doesn't look convinced, but neither does she try to argue with me anymore. Lady Maya walks over to a closet and pulls out a dress that's a lot tamer than I expected to be given. Considering everything, I thought she would make me wear something that showed a lot more flesh. The crop top is made out of a sheer fabric, but most of it is covered with crystal beads stitched in a lace pattern that covers all my important parts adequately. The plain white skirt is long and has the same crystals as the top stitched onto the waistband to give the appearance of a decorative belt. There is a long slit in the front, but the material is free-flowing, and the slit probably isn't noticeable unless I'm walking. Lady Maya hands me some matching shoes and then leaves my room without even saying a good-bye.

"Good riddance," I mutter after she's gone.

Considering how rude the people on this planet have been so far, I don't see why Ethan stationed Zane and Xander here to save it. Though, I'm not sure Xander is all that interested in protecting it. If he was, it seems like he wouldn't be spending his time wagering money he doesn't have on card games and booze.

I have no idea what else is expected of me next or when someone will be coming to escort me to the king. I decide to take the extra time I have to fashion a holster for my tracking device. I don't dare leave it in the room, so I rip out the elastic in my bra and use it to strap the tracker to my right thigh. As long as the king doesn't get frisky, I should be able to hide it there safely. However, I am a bit worried now that the king believes he owns me. From what Uwe and Lady Maya have said to me so far, I am supposedly the king's property. I hate to inform King Manas, but no one owns me, especially not a piece of scum like him who is pillaging his own planet for personal gain.

About an hour after Lady Maya left, the door to my room opens and the two faceless guards from before stand in the doorway. They don't move or say anything, just stare at me as if I should know I need to follow them. I rise from my seat on the bed and walk out of my room. One guard walks in front of me and one walks behind me, presumably to make sure I don't try to run away. I would be a fool to say that I'm not scared about what's going to happen next.

My only consolation is that I know I have a guardian angel watching over me, and that angel's name is Ethan Knight.

CHAPTER 15

My irritatingly silent escorts walk me through the halls of the palace. We only pass a few people on the way to wherever it is we're going, but those few stare at me like I'm a freak of nature. I see them whisper to each other and shake their heads in dismay. I'm really starting to get a complex now. I don't think I am ugly, but from the looks these people are giving me, I must look hideous to them. Is it my pale skin? Blonde hair? Both? I'm not really sure, which makes me question why the king willingly accepted me in Helena's barter.

Once we reach a set of shiny gold doors, I can only assume King Manas is in the room that lays behind them. Only an obnoxious person would make doors out of pure gold, and from what I've been told so far, the king is quite full of himself.

My escorts each push one of the doors inward, allowing me entry into the room. The first thing I notice is that the walls of the room are white with gold trim and numerous gold pillars placed randomly inside. There are possibly two hundred people within the interior standing on either side of the entrance dressed in colorful clothing. A plush red carpet runs from the entrance to the center of the room where a man and a woman sit on a golden platform that is built about a foot off the floor. They're sitting on red pillows around a short square black marble table. The only things present on top of the table are two golden goblets and what looks like a gold tea kettle encrusted with rubies and emeralds.

The man is obviously King Manas because he's wearing a gold bejeweled crown on his head. I hate to admit that his physical appearance is handsome, but it doesn't make him in the least bit appealing to me since I know his insides are filled with hatred and selfishness. He has shoulder-length curly dark hair, and the lower half of his face is covered with a mustache and a well-trimmed goatee. His eyes are dark brown, and his skin is just as tan as those gathered in the room. He's dressed in silky looking gold and maroon robes, which accentuate his broad shoulders and trim physique. There is a pleased smile playing at the corners of his mouth as he watches me stand in the entrance.

"Come!" he beckons with a wave of his hand in my direction. "Come sit with us, Julia Grace."

Interesting that he knows my name, but not exactly unexpected. I'm sure Helena gave him as much information as she could about me when she bartered my freedom to him.

As I walk closer to the platform the king is sitting on, I can feel the curious and disapproving stares of all those around me. I've never enjoyed being the center of attention, but in this case, it's not like I have anywhere to hide. I don't even have an ally in this room to lean on for support to face what's to come next. If I knew what to expect, I don't believe I would feel so uncomfortable, but no one has told me what the king intends to do now that he owns me. Lady Maya seemed to imply that the king might want to have sex with me, but even that wasn't confirmed.

When I reach the table, the king pats a red pillow next to him, indicating that I should sit down beside him. I carefully do what he wants, making sure the tracking device strapped to my thigh stays well-hidden as I sit. I allow myself a moment to consider the woman sitting on the other side of the king. She's dressed in an outfit similar to mine, but hers is black. I find it strange that we're dressed in identical dresses with only the color being the primary difference.

The woman looks despondent, but the small crown on her head seems to indicate that she's probably Manas' queen. I can only imagine how horrible it must be to live as his wife. She's young though, maybe close to twenty, so they probably haven't been married for very long.

"Tell me, Julia Grace," the king says as he studies every aspect of my face, "how do you like my palace?"

"It's stark," I reply, seeing no need to lie. "Black really isn't my favorite color."

The king smiles, but his eyes never light up to match the false expression.

"Black can hide many things," he tells me, reaching over and taking hold of the handle on the tea kettle. He cautiously pours the steaming liquid from the pot into the golden goblet sitting in front of me. He then fills his own goblet to near the rim before setting the kettle back in its original spot.

"Please," he says to me, "let us toast your arrival to my home and into the hearts of those present here today to share in our first joining."

Manas raises his goblet and holds out his arm to me as if he expects me to twine my arm around his as we make whatever absurd toast this is supposed to be. I pick up my goblet, but hesitate. When you're in the midst of the enemy, it's never a good idea to drink something that they have given you. Yet I have a feeling that if I don't do what he wants, this pretense he has going on that he's a benevolent host might end, and without knowing when or if Ethan and the others will be coming for me anytime soon, I need to come up with a plan that will delay Manas' wrath.

I twine my arm around the king's and bring the goblet up to my lips, but I don't take a mouthful of the hot liquid. Instead, I pretend to take a sip and then quickly place the goblet back down on the table, hoping he doesn't expect me to drink any more of the tea.

As soon as the king slams his own goblet back onto the table, the crowd erupts in a show of jubilation. The king stands from his pillow, raising his arms high into the air as he announces, "I am the first king of Laed-i to ever take a yellow haired woman to be his wife!"

"You're what?" I say in surprise and perhaps a little too loudly.

The king looks down at me, and before I know it, he backhands me across the right cheek, causing me to lose my balance and fall backwards off my pillow and onto the platform.

"Never," Manas says as he continues to look down at me, "raise your voice above a whisper in my presence, wife. You should feel lucky to have me as your husband. Our children will become the rulers of this land, and with your yellow hair, they will be unique among our people."

I get the feeling that now isn't the time to tell the king that I'm not physically equipped to bear his or, for that matter, anyone else's children. I'm sure he would simply kill me where I lie and move on to the next woman who would be his queen.

As I sit back upright, I notice the woman in the black dress take the small crown off her head and place it onto the table in front of her. She then leans to her left slightly to pick something up that is laying on the platform beside her. In the time it takes me to blink, the old queen stabs herself in the gut and twists the knife to make sure the job is done right. I hear myself scream the word "no" while those at the gathering all cheer the untimely death of the woman. Her body slumps to the floor in a lifeless heap, and my two faceless guards walk onto the platform and haul her body away like it's a piece of trash that needs to be discarded.

I sit where I am and watch the guards drag her corpse from the room. I'm left feeling completely bereft of hope about my situation and confused over why the people of this world are so heartless and bloodthirsty. How will I ever find anyone among them to help me?

And then, my prayer is answered.

Quite nosily, the gold double doors of the room are pushed open hard enough to make them bang against the walls on either side. Everyone present, including me, looks toward the entrance and sees a sight that would make most mere mortals drop to their knees. Empress Anna Devereaux stands tall and proud on the threshold of the room as she stares straight at King Manas. She's wearing a white gown befitting someone of her station, adorned with diamonds from top to bottom. The gold and blue sapphire crown on her head glistens in the light of the room, and I hear most of the people present gasp in awe of the empress. I'm sure none of them have ever seen anyone like her. It's not only Anna's physical beauty that's intimidating, but the expression of fierce determination on her face would make anyone quake in their shoes if it was directed at them. I notice King Manas shuffle his feet slightly as he watches Anna stride confidently into the room. While everyone else is mesmerized by the empress, my eyes are drawn to Ethan, Xander, and Zane who are following closely behind their earthly commander, dressed in their black leather War Angel uniforms.

Ethan's gaze remains steadily on me, as if he's checking to make sure I'm physically unharmed. I see his eyes narrow slightly in anger and can only assume the king's slap has left a mark on my face. Unconsciously, I lift a hand to cradle my wounded cheek, which only seems to inflame Ethan's anger even more.

Once Anna is standing in front of the platform, her War Angels remain behind her in a defensive line to guard her back.

"Empress Anna Deveraux from Earth, I presume," Manas says disdainfully.

"King Manas of Laed-i," Anna begins in a commanding voice, "you are holding a dear friend of mine captive. I demand that you release her into my custody at once!"

The king folds his arms over his chest and spreads his feet slightly apart to take a more defensive stance.

"I'm not quite sure how things work in your world, but once a bargain is made on this planet, it cannot be broken by either party. We rely on honor here, Empress Anna. Besides, Julia is my wife now and not even you have the authority to dissolve a marriage."

"He tricked me into marrying him," I quickly inform my rescuers before they get the wrong impression. "I just thought we were having tea, not a wedding ceremony."

"I'm not sure how it works in this world," Anna says to the king, using his own phrase against him, "but a real man doesn't have to trick a woman into marrying him."

"Are you questioning my virility?" Manas roars. "I can show you just how virile I am if you desire a personal demonstration, Empress."

I hear the sound of a sword being drawn and see Ethan has pulled his blade from its scabbard on his hip. When he takes a threatening step toward Manas, Anna holds out a hand to block his way.

"Stand down, Ethan," Anna tells him in a whisper. "Let me handle this."

Reluctantly, Ethan takes a step back and sheaths his sword.

"What obedient little puppies you have following you around," Manas says as he looks at the three War Angels with contempt. "Do they do tricks too?"

A few people in the crowd laugh, but their laughter stops as soon as Anna casts her withering glare in their direction.

Anna quickly returns her attention to the king and says, "I've heard that you take pride in your skill as a warrior and that you tend to enjoy games if the stakes are high enough."

This seems to pique Manas' interest. "Are you suggesting that we play a game to see who wins my queen? Why should I wager her when I already own her?"

"I'm saying that we should have a duel to see who is better with a sword," Anna tells him, "and that the stakes shouldn't be just for one person, but for each of our planets."

A collective gasp can be heard in the room, followed by excited, quiet whispers.

"Are you saying that you will put up the whole of Earth on the outcome of a single duel?" the king questions, sounding as if he's sure he heard her wrong.

Anna lifts her right hand, palm up. A holographic picture of Earth from space suddenly appears hovering over her hand as she says, "Earth is a planet plentiful with natural resources. We also control quite a large number of outworld colonies on neighboring planets. Not only would you be able to add all of this to your own kingdom, but you would also gain the technology we possess to travel to distant galaxies."

"And you're wagering your entire world just because I took one woman?" King Manas says incredulously. "Far be it from me to point out the mistake you just made. I accept your challenge, and I accept the wager of my planet against yours. However, what I will not do is fight a woman. There is no honor in beating someone so frail."

"I assure you," Anna says fiercely, "I am the best fighter on Earth."

"You are an empress. Of course your subjects let you believe such a ludicrous fantasy," the king scoffs. "If you truly want this duel to happen, I suggest you bring me someone worthy enough for me to fight."

"I'll do it," Ethan is quick to volunteer. "Let me fight the duel for you, Empress."

Anna looks over at Ethan and nods her head, agreeing to allow him to take her place in the challenge.

"Then tomorrow we duel!" Manas announces excitedly. "But tonight is my wedding night, and I plan to take advantage of my fair haired bride while I can."

"Go right ahead," Anna says, surprising not only me but also Ethan.

"Anna ..." he says in disbelief.

I see Anna wink at Ethan, but I'm not sure anyone else was paying close enough attention to her subtle reassurance to him.

When she turns her attention back to the king, she continues, "Our scientists have proven that sex before a fight can weaken a man's stamina and reflexes. That's why many of my ancestors would hire whores to enter the camps of their enemies on the eve of a battle. It made their adversaries weak and ensured a swift and satisfying victory. So, be my guest. Have your way with your new wife because it will make it all the easier for Ethan to beat you tomorrow so I can claim this planet as an extension of Earth's domain."

Manas doesn't say anything as he contemplates Anna's words of caution. He realizes that Earth's scientific knowledge far surpasses what the scientists of his own planet know. If he doesn't at least consider what she's said, he would be a fool of the highest order, and I can't believe even he would be stupid enough to take a chance on losing his planet for one night of sex.

"Fine," Manas says. "I will forgo my husbandly duties this night and meet with your man in the arena tomorrow at noon. If you don't show up, you forfeit the game, and I still win."

"Oh, we'll be there," Anna says with a beguiling smile. "And we'll finally be able to rid Laed-i of the tyrant who rules it. There is one other thing though," Anna looks over at me for the first time, "I need to have your word that your new queen will be cared for until the end of the duel. I can see your handiwork all over her face," Anna says angrily. "I need your assurance that she won't be harmed while she remains in your care. If I see that she is hurt any more than she already is by tomorrow, you forfeit the duel and hand over your planet to me willingly. Those are my conditions."

"She will not be harmed," Manas promises, sounding bored by what he seems to consider an unnecessary threat by Anna. "You have my word."

"Then we will see you at noon in your arena," Anna says before turning her back on Manas and walking out of the room without even a backwards glance in my direction. Xander, Zane, and even Ethan turn sharply on their heels and follow her out. I thought at least Ethan would give me some encouraging words or even a smile before they left. Perhaps they thought showing me any more favoritism would incense Manas to violence. I'm not sure, but I am disappointed.

The king turns to face me.

"I suppose our first night together will have to wait," he tells me as his gaze travels the length of me. "Go back to your chambers for now, and I will call on you when I'm ready to bed you."

Barbaric much?

"Can I make a request?" I ask him, seeing no reason not to ask for what I want. All he can do is say no because Anna has already laid down the law about hitting me any more before the duel.

"What is it that you want?" he asks gruffly.

"Can I attend the duel? I would like to watch it for myself since it will be determining my fate."

"You can come watch me kill your friend, if you wish," Manas says off-handedly.

"Kill?" I question him. "I didn't hear the empress say that the duel was to be to the death."

"Neither did I," Manas grins cruelly. "I'm sure she'll mourn the demise of her champion just like she'll mourn the loss of her planet."

"Are you at least going to tell them that the duel is to be to the death?" I ask.

"I'm sure they'll be able to figure it out on their own once it starts." Manas looks toward the entrance and yells, "Guards!"

My two faceless guardians come running up to the platform and bow before their king.

"Take your new queen back to her chambers," the king orders. "I will instruct Lady Maya to watch over her tonight, but no one else is allowed inside her room. Is that understood?"

The guards bow again to their king, silently letting him know that they understand his instructions.

Before they can reach me, I stand on my own because I don't particularly want them to touch me again. All I need is to be dragged out of the room by them like I was from the courtyard. We exit the room just like we entered it—with one guard in front leading the way and one guard following to prevent me from escaping.

"Sweet dreams, Julia Manas," the king calls out, reminding me that I am now his wife, at least according to the laws of this world. As far as I'm concerned, I didn't sign anything, so this so-called marriage is a complete sham. I have to wonder how many "wives" the king has had over the years. Uwe did mention that I would become a part of the king's collection. If he collects wives, that has to mean that he has had at least two, more than likely more. I pity the women who came before me and wonder if they had to commit suicide like the previous queen did tonight in order to make way for a new queen to take their place. I don't want to die, but if something unforeseen happens and Ethan loses the duel, I would rather be dead than let Manas touch any part of my body. He doesn't seem like a man who would care much about a woman's needs. I'm sure he's as selfish in bed as he is to the people of this world.

Once we reach my quarters and the door to my room is closed behind me, I breathe out a sigh of relief.

"I'm so sorry, Jules," I hear Ethan say from the doorway of the bathroom, presumably where he was hiding until the guards left.

We walk toward each other, and I soon find myself wrapped in his arms. I needed this. I needed to feel the warmth of his embrace to be reassured that everything will be all right.

"How did you know this was my room?" I ask him.

"Verati knew the basic layout of the palace. She told me this was more than likely where the king would be keeping you."

"Can you phase me out of here?" I ask him, holding him even more fiercely to me.

When Ethan doesn't answer, I pull back slightly and look into his troubled eyes.

"I wish I could," he says with a great deal of regret. "But Anna wants to use this duel to not only set you free but to set the people of this world free from Manas' control. You should be perfectly safe here until after the duel."

"He plans to kill you. So don't go into this fight thinking he will fight fair," I warn Ethan, not in the least bit angry about his reason for not phasing out of here immediately. I agree that if Anna and Ethan can force Manas off the throne in such a way that his people will readily accept a regime change, they should take advantage of the opportunity.

Ethan raises his left hand and cups my right cheek where Manas hit me.

"I would be within my rights to kill him for doing this to you," Ethan says in a low, menacing voice. "I can't believe Helena put you in this position in the first place. It just gives me another reason to hate her."

I don't want to admit it to Ethan, but I feel kind of hurt that Helena would use me as a pawn in her game with him and Anna. Or maybe she did it to distract Ethan in order to keep him off her trail for a little while. Speaking of Helena ...

I take a step back from Ethan and slide my right leg through the slit of my skirt. It doesn't take me long to pull the tracking device off my thigh and hand it over to Ethan.

"I want you to have this," I tell him. "I don't want Manas to take it away from me, or worse, destroy it. It'll be safer with you."

Ethan tucks the device inside a pocket of his leather jacket. "Are you kicking me out of your room so soon?"

"I don't want to," I say regretfully, "but Manas is sending someone to keep an eye on me until the duel. I talked him into letting me attend it, so I'll see you again in the arena tomorrow."

"That's where Anna and the others are right now. They asked one of the guards to show them where the arena is located, and I made up an excuse that I needed to prepare our shuttle for departure. Do you hate me for leaving you here?" he asks. "I'll take you away, if that's what you want. I'll go against Anna's orders and phase you anywhere you want to go. You're only in this mess because of me."

"No, I'm in this mess because of Helena," I remind him. "And I honestly think she just did it to make you stop looking for her for a while. I'm sure the pregnancy is taking a toll on her, and she just wants to rest since she's so close to giving birth."

"I have to find her before the baby is born, Jules," he says desperately. "I can't let her keep him."

I don't want to argue about this with Ethan again, so I just wrap my arms around him one last time.

"You need to go," I tell him, squeezing him around the waist in a direct contradiction of my words.

I feel him kiss the top of my head. "He won't hurt you. He knows Anna would take this planet in a heartbeat if he breaks the rules of their deal."

"I'm sure we can at least count on his greed to keep him honest."

Ethan hugs me tightly one more time before letting me go. Reluctantly, I do the same and even manage to force myself to take a step back.

"All you have to do is make it through tonight," Ethan tells me. "I wish I could give you one of the communicators they use on this world in case you have a problem so you could call Zane, but Manas has a force field up that prevents digital signals from coming in or going out of this fortress."

"How did the four of you even get here?" I ask. "This place is out in the middle of nowhere, and Uwe told me that neither Xander nor Zane have ever been here."

"After we told Anna what was happening, we took one of the pods from Cirrus, phased it to this world, and flew it here. Zane and Xander knew where the palace was. They've just never had a reason to come here before now. I told Anna I couldn't leave here without making sure that you're all right."

"I'm glad you came," I tell Ethan, reaching out to take hold of his hand with mine. "I prayed that you would. Maybe prayer really does work."

Ethan squeezes my hand as a tender look comes into his eyes. He pulls me in closer to him until our bodies touch. I watch expectantly as he lowers his head, making me think that he's about to kiss me on the lips. Instead, he turns his head at the last possible moment and kisses the cheek Manas hit.

"I'll make him pay for doing this to you," Ethan promises, kissing the cheek again but a little bit closer to the corner of my mouth this time.

"Do you always tease your women this unmercifully?" I ask him breathlessly, hoping he gives me a third kiss that will actually land on my lips.

"I don't normally tease," he whispers, "but I like knowing that you want me to kiss you."

"Am I that obvious?"

"Your breathing is a little faster, and there's a rosy flush across the top of your cheeks that I find beautiful. Do you really want me to kiss you, Julia Grace, or do you find the anticipation of such a kiss to be more enjoyable?"

Unfortunately, I don't get to answer that question, because before I know it, Ethan is gone and Lady Maya is walking into the room.

I sigh in disappointment. A part of me wishes I could have answered Ethan's questions, and a part of me is glad he left when he did. Otherwise, our first kiss would have happened in Manas' fortress, and that's not really how I want to remember such a life-altering event.

All in all, Lady Maya's arrival was fortuitous because I can now look forward to a first kiss with Ethan knowing that he wants it as much as I do.

CHAPTER 16

I never knew a person could be so meticulous about their personal hygiene regimen. Lady Maya ends up spending most of the night preening herself in the bathroom. I'm not completely sure what all she ended up doing to herself while she was in there, and I feel certain I don't want to know. When she comes back out into the bedroom, I don't see much of a difference in her appearance. She quickly declares that the bed is hers for the night and that I should make myself comfortable in one of the two chairs in the room.

"I thought *I* was the queen," I protest. "Doesn't that mean I should automatically get the bed?"

"Being called a queen here doesn't mean the same thing as it does on other worlds," she quickly informs me. "The title should actually be royal concubine, because until you give the king a son, that's basically all you are."

I plop down onto one of the chairs, finding the hard plastic quite ungiving.

"Seems weird to have these chairs here. Is there a reason why they're facing the bed?" I ask, as I watch her bury herself underneath the black covers and fluff her pillow.

"They're for the royal observers to sit and record each of your sessions with the king while you try to produce an heir."

"You have got to be kidding me ..." is the only response I can come up with, because what she just said is absolutely ludicrous.

"I am not ... kidding ... as you call it," she tells me haughtily. "How else will they know each time the king fertilizes you and when to expect a positive result?"

All I can do is shiver in revulsion and thank my lucky stars that this will be the one and only night I have to stay in King Manas' palace. I begin to wonder if the people of this planet are even worth rescuing, but then I remember Verati, Zane's wife. She's a native of this world and one of the kindest people I've ever met. It has to only be the privileged on this planet who are so arrogant. It makes me ponder who Anna will place on the throne after King Manas loses the duel. Whoever it is, I pity them.

By the time morning rolls around and Lady Maya has prepared herself for the day's events, she sets to work on me. I don't need much done. The makeup she put on me yesterday is still on my face, looking flawless. All she does is take my hair out of the braid and allow it to flow naturally around my shoulders. She gives me a dress made from a peach-colored, chiffon-like material to wear to the duel. It's a pretty halter top style dress with a long full skirt. After I'm ready, I ask Lady Maya for something to eat.

"I'm afraid you can't have anything until after the consummation of your marriage to the king," she tells me, obviously gaining a small bit of pleasure from denying me food.

"And why is that?" I ask since the monster that needs to be fed in my belly demands to know.

"It's simply tradition," she replies. "Normally after the king takes a new wife, there is a royal feast afterwards. Since your friends interrupted the festivities with their nonsense, the feast has been postponed until after the king has won the duel."

"Exactly how many wives has the king had?" I ask. If the feast is a "tradition," that must mean it's happened multiple times.

"You are his tenth wife," Lady Maya informs me.

"And how many children does the king have from these ten wives?"

Lady Maya looks nervous all of a sudden, and I'm not certain she'll answer my question.

Finally, she does.

"The king has no heirs yet. We are all hoping that you will be the one who breaks the chain of his disappointments."

I don't dare say it out loud, but if Manas hasn't been able to father a child after bedding ten wives, odds are it wasn't the fault of the females he chose. Sounds to me like the king is shooting blanks and no one here has the guts to tell him that.

"I guess we'll see," I reply, just to appease Lady Maya, because I know I won't have to worry about Manas for very much longer.

When the time comes for us to go to the arena, my ever-faithful faceless guards show up at the door to escort us there.

"I have to know," I say to Lady Maya as we walk down a hallway of the palace, "are there real men under those black body suits or are they androids?"

"Oh, they're real enough," she tells me. "Each of them was caught trying to help one of the king's wives escape the palace, and each of them lost what makes them a man and the skin that was covering their faces."

I gasp in horror, suddenly feeling pity for my captors instead of dislike. I guess what they say is true about not judging people by the way they look. I just assumed they were mindless drones that King Manas controlled, which is partially true, I guess, but they were once men of honor who tried to do the right thing for past queens. I suppose Manas decided that death was too swift a punishment for them. Instead of mercifully ending their lives, he kept them around as a reminder of what happens to people who try to defy the king.

After what seems like forever, we finally reach the arena on the far side of the palace. The arena is a semi-circle made of the same black stone that the palace is constructed out of. It faces a sandy beach area where the fight will presumably be taking place. Our guards escort Lady Maya and me to the king's box, which is at the center of the semi-circular structure. Manas sits on a large gold throne, wearing only a pair of brown leather pants and strips of the same leather wrapped around his wrists as arm guards. A large broad sword made from some sort of black metal lays across his thighs.

"I hope you aren't too attached to the man I will be killing today,"

Manas says to me, keeping his gaze on the horizon like he's watching something in particular.

Thunder rumbles through the air like a harbinger of death. I look out across the water and see the dark clouds of a thunderstorm rolling in. Do duels get canceled because of bad weather? I definitely hope not. I wish I had asked Ethan if he can even die. I know the bodies of my mother and uncle can die, but if they wish to, they can move their souls into new bodies and live forever that way. Though, they're rebellion angels. I'm not sure the same rules apply to War Angels. Besides, I quite like the body Ethan has now. I would hate to see him lose it.

I look around the arena, but I don't see Ethan or Anna anywhere.

"Is it noon yet?" I ask Manas.

"They have one minute to get here," he tells me, sounding pleased that they haven't shown up yet. "Unfortunately for you, it appears that your friends are weak and intend to forfeit the duel."

"They're not quitters," I defend them. "If they're late, it's for a good reason."

Just as Manas is about to make a retort, a collective gasp can be heard from the gathered crowd. I return my gaze to the center of the arena and now see Ethan, Anna, Xander, Zane, and Verati standing on the sand looking like they just came from a bloody battle. Obviously, they've decided not to hide their ability to phase from the king any longer. All of them, except for a frightened looking Verati, have their weapons drawn. In what remains of the light despite the oncoming storm, their blades glisten with fresh blood. I notice that Anna has a streak of crimson marring her otherwise pristine white gown like a gruesome sash.

Even though they all look angry, it's the rage I see within Ethan's eyes that scares me the most. He looks like a man on the verge of losing his self-control as he stares hard at King Manas.

"Your men are dead, Manas!" Anna calls out across the distance between them. "What kind of ruler orders his minions to kill his opponents so he doesn't have to fight a duel?"

"A smart one!" Manas replies snidely, showing no shame in trying to cheat his way to victory. "Frankly, I'm surprised any of you made it out alive."

"There was a pregnant woman in that house, Manas!" Ethan rages. "Your men could have killed her trying to get to me and my empress."

"Casualties of war are to be expected," the king replies, sounding bored. "Now, are you ready to fight me, boy, or do you intend to keep standing there whining?"

I hear a few surprised gasps after King Manas' taunt, but all it does is make Ethan look even more determined to teach the king a lesson in humility.

"I'm ready whenever you are, you coward," Ethan taunts back while Anna, Xander, Zane, and Verati use a set of stairs on the left end of the semi-circle to watch the fight from a better vantage point.

The king grips the hilt of his sword and rises from his seat. He eagerly bounds down the steps from his throne to the sand just as the first few raindrops begin to fall.

"The gods are weeping over your imminent demise!" Manas goads him as he twirls his sword in his hand in front of Ethan.

"There is only one true God," Ethan informs him, "and unfortunately for you, He isn't on your side in this fight."

Manas raises his sword and grips the hilt even tighter with both of his hands.

"I guess we'll see about that," the king says before he lets out a guttural war cry and runs toward Ethan.

Ethan charges forward across the sand as well and easily blocks the king's first swing, twisting his sword downward and pushing Manas back a few steps.

"You fight like a child still learning," Ethan informs the king, earning him a few chuckles from the crowd. "I know a seven-year-old in Cirrus who has better control of himself when he fights than you do."

Manas lets out another war cry and attempts to rush Ethan with his sword held out in front of him and his shoulders hunched slightly as he prepares to barrel Ethan over with his maneuver. Even I can tell it's a bad move.

Just before Manas reaches him, I watch as Ethan quickly takes a step to the left, leaving nothing but empty air for the king to tackle. Manas' own momentum causes him to go sprawling across the sand face down, earning him quite a few laughs from his once loyal followers.

"I would advise you to forfeit this duel before you lose more than your planet because of your own stupidity," Ethan warns him as he turns to watch Manas pick himself up from the sand.

Manas uses his sword like an old man uses a cane to get up off the ground. He doesn't even bother to dust himself off before he attempts to charge Ethan again. I just shake my head in dismay over the king's inability to control himself. It seems to me that no one bothered to tell Manas that he's a horrible swordsman. I presume his instructors allowed him to believe he was good, just like the people here let him believe that it was his wives who were barren and not the fact that he is more than likely sterile. In a way, I feel sorry for Manas because it doesn't seem like anyone has been honest with him his entire life. They've allowed him to believe he's better than he is at a lot of things.

Ethan easily blocks Manas' next strike and seems to play with him a bit as they exchange blows. While their duel continues, thunder rolls through the arena, causing the floor beneath me to vibrate with the force of its strength. Anna, Xander, Zane, and Verati make their way toward me and stand in a protective semi-circle around my back as we all watch the fight together. The rain begins to come down in sheets, making it difficult to see the battle between Ethan and the king. Although I guess it's not exactly a battle as much as it is a lesson on proper swordplay. Manas seems to be struggling as his sword swings become weaker and less exact while Ethan stands strong and looks almost bored by it all. When the rain diminishes in strength, allowing all in the arena to have a clear view of what's happening, Ethan seems to decide that he's toyed with Manas long enough. In three quick and strong moves of his sword, Ethan disarms the king of his weapon, sending it sailing into the air and landing a few feet away. With one mighty kick to his mid-section, Ethan sends Manas flying through the air until he lands on his back, causing the other man to grunt from the force of the impact.

Before Manas can catch his breath or even think about sitting up, Ethan stands over him and places the tip of his sword against the king's throat.

"Do you yield?" Ethan asks, loud enough for everyone in the arena to hear his question.

"I will never yield to someone as lowly as you!" Manas shouts, literally foaming at the mouth like a rabid dog. "You'll have to kill me if you want my planet, because I'll never hand it over to Earth scum like you!"

"I don't want to kill you," Ethan tells him. "And whether or not you verbally yield doesn't really matter. You've already lost this duel. You're unarmed and at my mercy." Ethan pushes the tip of his sword far enough to make a small cut. As Manas' skin is gradually stained red with his own blood, Ethan tells him, "By the laws of this world concerning duels, when a combatant is disarmed and first blood is drawn, the duel is over and the victor is granted the spoils agreed upon." Ethan looks up, keeping his blade against Manas' throat as he scans the gathering of people. "Who here agrees that King Manas has lost this duel?"

Practically the whole group present begin to cheer. I can't tell if they're trying to suck up to Ethan because they presume he will be the next king, or if they're finally showing their contempt for the old regime and truly welcome the change dethroning Manas will surely bring to this world. Either way, no one in the arena—with the exception of Lady Maya who is strangely mute—seems to disagree with Ethan's assessment of the situation.

Ethan looks down at Manas and says, "I officially call an end to this duel and hereby take your planet and your wife as the wager owed to Empress Anna of Earth. I would strongly advise you to take what belongings you can and find another planet to live on."

Ethan withdraws his sword from Manas' throat and turns away from him to head toward the center stairs of the arena leading to me.

Just as lightning strikes the sky over the ocean, I see Manas quickly stand to his feet and grab his sword from off the sand. Like a man who has nothing to lose, he rushes toward Ethan silently, possibly hoping to catch him off guard and run him through with his blade. Just as I'm about to scream Ethan's name to warn him of the imminent attack, I see Ethan tilt his head slightly as if he hears Manas' approach. Ethan's eyes raise up to look at me as he lifts his sword. In the split second that our gazes meet, I see a mixture of emotions play across Ethan's face. He's determined to end this fight, but he also seems to regret doing what he knows must be done.

With the hilt of his broad sword gripped in both hands, Manas leaps into the air toward Ethan's back with the tip of his blade in a downward angle. While the king is still in midair, the sword Ethan is holding bursts into blue flames as he whips around and slashes Manas across the gut. In the same sweep of his blade, he continues the gash from gut to sternum.

Manas falls to the wet sand with the heavy weight of a dead man. As his blood stains the ground around him, the crowd erupts into cheers to celebrate the king's fall. I'm not sure what to think about their reaction. Perhaps the tyrannical way Manas ruled his people severed any feelings they may have had for their king, or they're simply a bloodthirsty lot. I'm not sure. Either way, it seems sad to know that no one here mourns his passing. If their reaction is any indication, they welcome it with open arms, even though they have no way of knowing if Anna will be any kinder of a ruler. She will, of course, but no one here knows that for a fact. They seem to be of the consensus that anyone is better than Manas.

Ethan doesn't turn around to face me. He simply remains standing beside Manas' corpse, looking down at it. The blue flames on his sword slowly fade away as Zane and Xander walk down the steps to go to their commander to see what he needs. I see Ethan lift his head and tell Zane something. Zane nods in understanding and begins to walk back up the stairs to me, Anna, and Verati.

"Ethan asked me to take you home, Jules," Zane tells me, looking slightly uncomfortable before he says his next words. "He says he doesn't want to see you right now."

I feel as though someone has just stabbed me in the heart.

"Why?" I ask, hoping for an explanation that makes sense.

Zane begins to shake his head. "He didn't say. He just asked me to take you home. I'm sure he'll explain things to you later."

Anna turns to me. "He just needs some time to recover," she assures me. "Ending a man's life, even if he's one like Manas, takes a toll on the one who delivered the killing blow. I'm sure he'll come to you once he's processed everything. Just have a little patience with him."

I nod. "I understand and that makes sense, but tell him for me that I'll be waiting in my apartment for him when he's ready to talk."

"I'll let him know," Anna promises with a gracious smile.

She turns her head away from me and looks back at Ethan with a worried frown. I sense a small bit of regret from her for making Ethan fight Manas, but we all know the king needed to be taken off the throne. It was his own arrogant stupidity and dishonorable act that led to his death. If he had simply accepted defeat graciously, he would still be alive now. Yet he chose to attack Ethan from behind like a coward. As far as I'm concerned, he deserved to be gutted like the pig he was.

"I'll be right back," Zane tells his wife, placing a hand on my shoulder and phasing me back to Sierra.

I soon find myself standing right outside Grace House.

"I'm sorry I can't get you any closer to your place," Zane apologizes. "I'm not even sure where it is."

"That's okay," I tell him. "It's not far from here. I can walk there."

"I'm glad we finally got you out of the palace. I thought Ethan was going to go crazy when Anna told him we had to leave you there. He definitely wasn't happy about that order. He argued that we should just grab you and go, but Anna felt that it was important to take the opportunity we were given to win Laed-i and free its people from Manas' hold over them."

"I understand," I say. "Anna was right to do what she did."

"She basically told Ethan that you could hold your own against Manas if it came to that."

I let out a short laugh. "Well, I'm glad she had so much faith in me."

"Ethan did too, but you know, he still didn't like leaving you there."

"How many men did Manas send to your house?" I ask. "At least I'm assuming they attacked your house since Verati was involved."

"Yes, they came to my house. We're going to have quite a bit to clean up there later. I might have to call in some of my brothers to come help with the pile of bodies. I think Manas wanted to make sure none of us survived, so he sent about a hundred men to get the job done."

"Wait a minute," I say, feeling sure that I heard the wrong number, "are you telling me that the four of you took on a hundred of Manas' guards and won?"

Zane grins. "To be honest, it really wasn't a fair fight. He should have sent more men."

I have to chuckle at that remark, which earns me a smile from Zane, but my thoughts quickly take me back to Ethan.

"He'll come to you when he's ready," Zane says.

"Am I that transparent?" I ask, feeling somewhat embarrassed and wondering when my thoughts began writing themselves on my face.

"Caring about someone else isn't a bad thing, Jules. In fact, it's one of the best things about being alive."

I know he's right, but it's been so long since I cared about someone who wasn't my mother or uncle. I haven't let myself feel much of anything in the past five years. I've allowed myself the privilege of wallowing in self-pity for so long it feels strange to be thinking about someone else's needs before my own. Maybe it's a sign that I'm finally ready to let go of my past and find a better way to live what remains of my life. Yet there's one thing I have to tell Ethan before things between us reach a point of no return. I have to tell him that I'm unable to have children. I know from my mother that God's plan for the War Angels He sent from Heaven is to progress humanity to their next level of evolution. Considering that fact, Ethan may change his mind about getting involved with me because I would be preventing him from accomplishing one of his primary objectives.

"Why don't you go home and get some rest?" Zane suggests. "You've been through a lot the last couple of days."

With the mention of rest, I realize that I'm exhausted. Trying to sleep in that chair last night was nearly impossible, and now I'm feeling the aftereffects from all the excitement from the duel.

"I think that's a good idea, and you need to get back to that beautiful wife of yours."

Zane grins at the mention of Verati. "She and I will probably be busy for a while. I'm sure Manas' death will cause a lot of fallout that will need to be handled. Anna said she would help as much as she can, but Verati and I have personally dealt with the aristocracy there and know how to deal with them."

"Will Anna take the throne on Laed-i, or hand that responsibility over to someone else?"

"She hasn't really said anything about that to us yet, but I'm sure she has a plan in mind. I don't think she'll let the throne go unoccupied for very long. The people on that planet need someone to follow. They're not very adept at thinking for themselves, as you might have noticed. I think that's because Manas' family has ruled them for so long that the people there have forgotten what it's like to make choices about their own lives. I know the first thing that we have to do is slow mining on the planet, if not stop it completely. Manas has already harvested over seventy percent of its natural resources. If the planet has any hope of surviving, we have to let it heal, especially the vegetation, or Laed-i will end up being a barren rock hurtling through space."

"Don't let Verati overexert herself," I say. "That little baby growing inside her will be using up a lot of her energy, especially when she gets closer to giving birth. Make sure she gets plenty of rest."

Zane smiles. "It's not me you'll have to worry about. Verati thinks she can do the work of a hundred women. Maybe you can talk to her at the party for the twins this evening and convince her to take it easy."

"I'll certainly try," I promise.

"Good," he replies with a small nod of his head. "I'll see you later, Jules. Go get some rest."

Zane phases away, and I turn to start walking down the street toward my apartment building.

Once I'm inside my home, I feel the weight of the past day land on me like a ton of bricks and don't even make it into my bedroom. I simply slip off my sandals and plop down on my couch, hugging one of the throw pillows. Within a few seconds, I'm sound asleep.

I'm not sure how long I nap, but I'm suddenly awoken by the consecutive slamming of the cabinet doors in the kitchen. My mother is always bringing me groceries, so I assume that's who's making so much noise.

"Mom," I moan loudly, placing the pillow my head was resting on over my ears to block out the sound of her racket, "I'm trying to sleep!"

"Well, instead of sleeping, you should be out shopping for some food," I hear Helena chastise me from the kitchen, which immediately causes me to sit up straight on the couch.

"Helena?" I call out, convinced my tired brain is confusing my mother's voice for Helena's.

Helena steps out past the wall of the kitchen and stands beside the dinette. So unless I'm hallucinating, she actually is in my home again. She has a glass jar of peanut butter in one hand and a silver spoon in the other.

"Honestly, Jules, it's no wonder you're so skinny considering the paltry amount of food you keep in your home. You don't even have anything to offer your guests when they visit."

"Guests are usually invited, and I don't remember inviting you," I grumble tiredly.

"Trust me," she says as she walks into the living room and sits down in the chair across from me, "I would much rather be somewhere else right now, but that decision was taken out of my hands."

Helena rests the jar of peanut butter on her protruding belly like it's a small table and proceeds to take a large scoop of it out with her spoon.

"What do you mean by that?" I ask. "Who made the decision that you should come here?"

Helena doesn't answer right away, and I know it will take a little while longer before she's able to, considering how large a spoonful of peanut butter she just placed inside her mouth. I watch her jaw muscles move as she works the sugary spread down her throat. Once her mouth is clear, she looks back at me.

"My son brought me here and won't let me leave yet. I'm just not sure why," she tells me, sounding mystified by her unborn baby's actions.

"Your son brought you here?" I have to ask, finding this an odd turn of events. "How exactly is that possible?"

"The little angel has hijacked my powers for his own needs," she tells me as she reinserts the spoon into the jar and pulls out another large portion of the spread to eat. "I just don't know why he brought me to you."

"Maybe he knows you need to apologize to me," I tell her irately. "How could you pawn me off to King Manas to pay for Xander's gambling debt? What did I ever do to you to deserve that?"

Helena narrows her eyes on me and says, "Nothing that I know of, but since you're a bounty hunter, I can only assume that you're working with Ethan to find a way to take my baby away from me. I've seen my son now, and I can tell you for a fact that there's no way I'm going to let him go. You'll have to find a way to kill me first, and I can assure you that even that won't be enough."

I sit up straighter in my seat. "So you did go to Desmond to let him check the baby?" I ask excitedly, forgetting about what happened on Laed-i for now. "Is the baby okay?"

Helena grins. "He's more than okay. He's perfect."

"Then why have you been having so much trouble with the pregnancy?"

"It was nothing to worry about," she says off-handedly. "Everything I was experiencing was completely natural."

I breathe a small sigh of relief. "That's wonderful," I tell her. "I'm so glad you went to see Desmond. Have you decided if you will let him be present for the delivery?"

"No. I haven't made a decision about that yet," she says right before placing another spoonful of peanut butter into her mouth. Once she's swallowed her second helping, she declares, "This stuff is delicious! I can't believe I've never tried it before now."

I suddenly have a surreal moment when I realize Hell is sitting in my living room eating up all of my peanut butter.

"So, tell me, Jules," she says, as she dips the spoon in the jar a third time, "what happened on Laed-i with King Manas? Since you're here and not there, I can only assume something interesting transpired."

"I'll tell you, but you have to tell me something first," I try to bargain.

Helena raises a dubious eyebrow as she considers me. I have a moment of trepidation when I wonder if she's thinking about killing me for my insolence. It's not the first time she's looked at me in such a way, and before now, I didn't care what she did to me. Now, I do. It doesn't take a genius to figure out what's made the difference or, in this case, who. I have something in my life now that I don't want to lose. I need to know where things are going with Ethan, and I want to experience the sensation of falling in love with him. We're at the very beginning of what could end up being a lifetime together, and I want to know if that's where we're headed. For so long, I've felt dead inside. Now, I feel a glimmer of hope that my life could be changing for the better. I don't want to let that spark die. I want it to ignite into a flame and drive away all of my loneliness and self-loathing.

"I'm sure you've probably already figured it out by now," she says with a small shrug. "I wanted to keep Ethan busy for a while, and the best way to do that was to put your life in danger."

"And if I had died?" I ask, deeming her reason as purely self-serving, but I'm not sure why I find that so surprising since I know exactly who and what she is.

"I could sit here and tell you that I would have mourned your death, but obviously, that would be a lie. I do have a modicum of respect for you, so I won't tell you that. I will say that I'm pleased to see that you didn't die, because I know now how much Ethan truly does care for you. Are you his soul mate by any chance?"

"I have no idea," I tell her. It's the truth, but I get the feeling that even if I knew the answer to her question that I shouldn't tell her. She would probably find a way to use the information against Ethan. She already used me once to distract him. It's quite possible she could try to use my safety against Ethan again in order to stop him from taking her baby.

"Interesting," she says before sucking on her spoon to pull off the remainder of the peanut butter. She lifts the jar from her belly to look inside it. Then she lowers it and looks over at me. "I don't suppose you have some more of this hidden somewhere. I don't recall seeing another jar of it in your cabinets."

"Sorry. That's all I have, and now I have none because you ate it all."

Helena drops the spoon in the jar, causing the metal to clang against the glass.

"Why is it that you're here alone, Jules? I thought Ethan would stay glued to your side after being held captive by Manas."

"I think he needed some alone time," I say. "After he killed Manas, he asked Zane to take me home."

"He didn't even bring you here himself?" Helena asks. She seems to find this development troubling.

"I honestly don't know why he didn't. I mean, I get it that taking a man's life is a big deal ..."

"Not for a War Angel," Helena interrupts. "No, there's another reason, but I'm not sure what it is."

She stands from the chair she was sitting in and waves a hand, motioning for me to stand up as well. I do it, but only because I want to know what she's up to.

"I think you should go see what's wrong with lover boy," she announces, setting the empty jar of peanut butter down on the glass coffee table. "Come closer and I'll take you to him."

I slowly shake my head. "I don't think that's a good idea. If he wanted me with him, he would have asked me to stay."

"Between the two of us, who has the most experience with angels and the inner workings of their guilt complexes? Trust me, he wants you with him. He's just too stubborn to admit it. If you go to Ethan, it'll show him that you care. Right now, he needs someone to listen to him so he can bare his soul. And if you happen to be his soul mate, there's no one else he'll open up to as readily as you. If I were in your shoes, I would ask him if he's your soul mate. I mean, isn't that something you should know?"

"What if I'm not?" I ask, considering this a real possibility.

What if I'm not Ethan's soul mate, and he finds out that I can't have children? Would that be enough to make him dismiss what we have growing between us and wait for his soul mate to show up, hoping she's able to bear his children? Just the thought of that scenario makes me nauseous, and I seriously consider not taking Helena up on her offer.

"Do you know where he is right now?" I ask her.

"I assume he's gone back to Cirrus. I can take you to where I think he will be there, and if he isn't, I'm sure you can find someone in the palace who can take you to him."

"What you're offering to do seems a little too kind for you," I say cautiously. "What advantage do you get for taking me to him?"

Helena smiles. "You learn quickly. I like that about you. I advise you not to worry about what I'm up to. Whether I take you to him or not, it won't stop me from doing what needs to be done."

"So you *are* planning something," I say knowingly.

"When am I not?" Helena asks in exasperation with a roll of her eyes. "Do you want to go to Ethan or not, Jules? Your window of opportunity is closing fast here."

Against my better judgment, I put a little faith in Helena and walk over to her. She places one hand on my arm and one on her belly.

"Are you planning to let me go where I want to this time, little one?" she asks her baby bump, making me wonder if she can speak to her son telepathically or if she's just being rhetorical.

Apparently, her son does grant her access to her powers because we phase into a fancy looking hallway, right outside a white door.

"This is Ethan's room," Helena tells me. "Good luck."

She phases away before I can say anything in reply.

I stare at the door, trying to work up my nerve to knock. This could be the moment Ethan decides I'm not really the woman he wants. And who knows? Maybe he never imagined us in a serious relationship. He could just want someone to spend time with while he waits for his soul mate to magically appear. Either way, I need to know where he stands, and he needs to know that I'm unable to have children.

With my heart pounding double-time inside my chest, I raise my right hand and lightly tap on the door to discover which path my life will take.

CHAPTER 17

I don't have to wait for very long before the door is opened. Ethan stands on the other side of the doorway still shirtless and wearing the black leather pants and boots he wore to the duel. When he looks into my eyes, all I see is a blank slate. He's showing zero emotion to me, and I don't like that at all.

"Can I come in?" I ask him, not particularly wanting to have our talk while standing out in the hallway.

Without a word, he steps aside to give me enough room to enter. After I'm inside, he closes the door behind me with a soft click. As I let my eyes wander around the room, I immediately notice how stark it is. The basic architecture is the same as the rest of the palace with its golden beige walls and white trim, but there's barely any furniture except for a simple bed that lacks even a headboard and a small writing desk and chair up against the wall directly across from the bed. There is one large window on the wall opposite from the doorway that looks out over Cirrus, but it has no curtains or other decorations around it.

The only spot of color in the room is a single orange flower in a dainty glass vase on top of the writing desk.

Ethan must notice me staring at the bloom because he says, "Anna has been trying to teach me about all of the flowers found on Earth. She has the maids bring me a new one each day."

"What's that one called?"

"A daylily."

I turn to face Ethan fully because I didn't come to talk about flowers. I came to ask him something, and that's exactly what I intend to do.

"I guess I could beat around the bush and make small talk with you," I say, "but I'm really not that kind of woman. When I want to know something important from a friend, I just ask."

"Are we friends, Jules?" Ethan inquires, still maintaining his guarded expression.

"I would like to think so," I answer, feeling nervous now that I've set the stage to ask my question to Ethan. A part of me wants to know the answer and a part of me fears that I'll be given a reply I don't want to hear.

"Then ask your question, and I'll do my best to answer it," he says reasonably enough.

"Does anything faze you?" I say, finding it troubling how calm he is about me just showing up on his doorstep unannounced.

Ethan looks confused. "You came all the way here to ask me that?"

I shake my head. "No. That's not the question I want to ask you. I was just wondering how you can look so unruffled all the time, except when you're mad of course. Then you make everyone around you quake in their shoes."

Ethan takes a step forward and reaches out to touch my arm. Gently, he glides it down the soft skin, past the elbow, until he has my hand in his. Slowly, he brings it up to his bare chest and places the palm of my hand over his heart. I'm slightly startled by how hard and quick the beating of his heart is underneath my hand.

"Do all War Angels have heartbeats like this?" I ask in a whisper as I look into his eyes, waiting for the answer.

"No, it's not common," he tells me. "And my heart doesn't beat this fast all the time. Just when I'm with you."

I can't help but smile at that remark because it makes me happy. I'm not ashamed to admit that I like affecting Ethan physically. It at least shows he cares, and I feel less awkward about asking my next question.

"Am I your soul mate, Ethan?" I ask him.

"Yes," he replies readily, as he watches for my reaction to the news.

The smile on my face simply grows wider, which earns me a smile from Ethan in return. Then I remember what else it is that I need to say and my smile fades.

"What's wrong?" he asks. "Why did you stop smiling?"

Reluctantly, I take my hand off of Ethan's chest and clasp it with my other one as I begin to rub their heels together nervously.

"I have to tell you something about me before we take this any further," I say, swallowing hard to work up the courage to continue. The next words out of my mouth might tear down everything Ethan feels for me right now, and I'm not sure I'm ready to do that. But my conscience is screaming to me that he deserves to know the truth about me before we take things any further.

"Jules," he says, reaching out to grab ahold of my right arm. "What's wrong? You can tell me anything."

"I can't have children," I blurt out, feeling on the verge of tears because I don't see how he can want to be with me now. "I know one of the reasons God sent you and your men to Earth is so you can take humanity to the next step of our evolution, and if you stay with me, you'll never have a child of your own. I'm all you'll get." I shrug my shoulders slightly because I don't know if I'm enough for Ethan to turn his back on such a large part of his mission.

Ethan tugs on my arm, urging me closer. Once I'm against him, he loosely wraps his arms around my waist to ensure that I stay put.

"I already assumed you couldn't have any more children after you told me about the accident," he reveals.

"And it doesn't bother you?" I ask, finding it hard to believe. I know the facts of my situation trouble me a great deal. I've always wanted children, and now that I can't have any, I feel like a part of me is missing. I feel broken inside, and it might be foolish, but I'm not sure I'll ever feel whole again.

"I would have loved to have children with you, Jules, and I do regret that we won't have a tiny Jules running around our legs one day, but you're all I need to find happiness on Earth."

"But what about your God-given mission?" I ask. "Won't He be upset with you for abandoning it to be with me?"

Ethan grins. "No, He won't be upset. In fact, I believe He'll be overjoyed that we found each other. Most people don't get to meet their soul mates, but He seems to be rather lenient about it when it comes to his angels. So many of us who have been sent to Earth have met the matches to our souls. I don't know if it's His way of helping us heal from what happened during the War in Heaven, or if He knows we need to meet certain people during our lives to help us carry out a much larger agenda He has in mind. All I know is that you are the only person in this universe I will ever feel this way about."

"I'm sorry you drew the short straw," I tell him, which simply earns me a look of bewilderment from Ethan. "It means you were unlucky by having me be your soul mate."

Ethan looks even more puzzled. "Why in the world would you think that?"

"I'm damaged goods any way you look at it, Ethan. Let's face it. I'm not good enough for you."

"That's ridiculous, Jules," he says almost angrily. "Why would that thought even enter your mind?"

"Because it's true," I say, pulling myself out of his embrace. "My life is dark, Ethan, and I know I only have myself to blame for that. I allow things to affect me more than they should, and I'm prone to wallow in my own self-pity."

Ethan grins slightly, like I just said something that amused him.

"What's so damn funny about that?" I ask, not liking being laughed at for my honesty.

"We're more alike than you seem to think," Ethan informs me. "Do you know why I asked Zane to take you home instead of phasing you there myself?"

"No," I admit. "But I was wondering why. You wouldn't even look at me after the duel was over."

"I was built to kill, Jules," he tells me. "And today, I killed someone right in front of you."

"King Manas didn't give you much of a choice," I reason. "He was attacking you from behind. What else were you supposed to do? Let him stab you in the back?"

"I didn't have to kill him," Ethan tells me, looking conflicted by the decision he made. "I could have just wounded him enough to prevent him from getting off the ground again."

"You and I both know that Manas would have ended up causing more problems on Laed-i. He had to be taken out of the equation, and you did what needed to be done, Ethan. You shouldn't feel ashamed of that. Did you honestly believe that I would think less of you because you decided to end a needless threat to that planet?"

"I wasn't sure what you thought of me afterwards," he admits. "You could only see me one of two ways: hero or villain, and I wasn't prepared to see disgust for me in your eyes because of my decision."

"You're so stupid!" I say, closing the distance between us and wrapping my arms around his neck. "Of course you're the hero of the story, Ethan. You don't know how to be anything else."

When Ethan wraps his arms around my back, I feel more complete than I ever have in my whole entire life. It's not just because I've found my soul mate. It's because I've found someone who is like me in so many ways that he doesn't even realize yet. Everyone has a light and a dark side, but it's the choices we make and the people we let into our lives that determines which side wins. I've let my dark side drag me down into a cesspool of misery, but now, I'm doing my best to reach for the light. I know Ethan can help me get there. All I need to do is have a little faith.

"What is that smell?" Ethan asks, sniffing my hair and neck.

"Uh, I'm not sure," I say, bemused by his sudden fascination with my aroma. "Is it a good or a bad smell?"

"Intoxicating," he practically moans, using his right hand to pull my hair away from my shoulder to give him better access to my bare skin. When he sniffs the crook between my neck and shoulder, I do something that I rarely ever do. I giggle.

"That tickles," I tell him.

Ethan kisses the tender flesh there and causes my whole body to tremble in excited anticipation. My body begins to ache in certain private places as they practically beg for more attention from him. It's been so long since I made love to a man, I barely remember how good it used to feel. In a way, I don't mind that loss of memory so much. I've only had one lover in my life: Timothy. I would rather not compare my experiences with him to the ones I'll have with Ethan.

As Ethan's lips make a warm trail down my shoulder, I can still hear him sniffing me like I'm a flower. It makes me ponder what it is he's actually smelling.

Reluctantly, I decide to take a step back from him.

"I think I need to take a shower," I tell him. "The woman who groomed me for the king may have put a lotion on me that I didn't know about. It could be what you're smelling."

"I'm not sure I understand what difference that makes," he replies, at a loss about my need to explain his reaction to me.

"What if she put some kind of magical pheromone on me to make me more attractive to the king?" I suggest. "Apparently, she didn't consider me beautiful enough to be marrying Manas. Lady Maya may have thought she was doing me a favor by sprinkling an attractant on my skin to make me more desirable to men. I would rather make sure that it's me that's getting you all hot and bothered and not something artificial."

"I can assure you it's you, Jules," Ethan says with certainty.

I look around the room and see a door that must lead to the bathroom.

"Do you have a shower I can use, and perhaps something I can wear afterwards?"

"If you want, I can take you back to your apartment to shower and change clothes," he offers.

Normally, I would accept that type of suggestion, but I have no way of knowing if Helena has gone back to my place. If she is there, I definitely don't want Ethan running into her. Neither of them seem ready to consider the other person's side of the argument, and I don't want to run the risk of an altercation between the two of them just because I want to bathe.

"I would rather stay here," I say, making my way toward the bathroom before Ethan starts asking too many questions. "Just leave whatever you find for me to wear by the sink."

I walk into the bathroom and quickly shed my clothes before hopping into the shower. I don't dare take too long, even though I'm thoroughly enjoying the soothing warmth of water cascading down my body. I make sure to wash the makeup Lady Maya applied off my face because I have no idea if it might be causing the effect. When I step out of the shower, I dry off and slip on the white, oversized robe Ethan left for me by the sink. Once I towel dry my hair, I step back into the bedroom to find Ethan. He's still shirtless, for which I am eternally grateful, but he changed out of his tight-fitting leather pants into a pair of loose-fitting ones. They almost look like pajama bottoms, but I think these are worn during physical combat training.

"Are you feeling any better?" he asks as he meets me in the center of the room. "I have to say, you look more beautiful without all that makeup on your face."

I pull the collar of the bathrobe away from the right side of my neck.

"Smell me," I order as I crane my neck to the left in order to give him ample access.

Ethan smiles at my odd sounding request, but complies without complaint.

He leans over, sniffs the crook of my neck, and lets out a pleased moan.

"Damn it," I say, turning around to head back into the bathroom. "Maybe I need to scrub harder."

Ethan phases to the doorway of his bathroom to prevent me from entering.

"Jules," he says with a small smile, "I'm just attracted to the way *you* smell. I don't think that Lady whatever-her-name-is put anything special on your skin to make you more attractive to the opposite sex." He walks up to me and asks, "Why is it so hard to believe that I'm attracted to you?"

Honestly, I'm at a loss for words. I don't know how to respond, so I say nothing at all and just shrug my shoulders helplessly.

"Come here," Ethan says, holding out one of his hands to me.

I walk the four steps it takes until I'm standing right in front of him.

"Don't get too excited," I warn him. "I don't go all the way on a second date."

Ethan smiles. "Is that what this is? Our second date?"

"I'm going to count it as the second date," I inform him. "Because tonight will be our third date, and I can assure you I expect a full on make-out session before the night is over."

Ethan pulls me in close and begins to nuzzle my neck again.

"And are these dating rules of yours hard and fast ones, or are they flexible?" he murmurs, just before he begins to tease the sensitive skin on the side of my neck with his lips.

"Right now," I say, closing my eyes and allowing myself to enjoy the multiple sensations Ethan's tiny kisses are having on my body, "I would have to say they're extremely flexible."

Ethan moves his mouth up to my ear and whispers, "Good, because I'm not sure I can wait for a fourth date to go beyond a make-out session. I would take you right this minute, if you would let me, and I can assure you that neither of us would be the same again afterwards."

The sensation of his warm breath and the urgency in his voice makes me want to throw caution to the wind and drag a willing Ethan to his bed. Would it be so wrong to make love to a man I've only known for a couple of days? He is my soul mate, after all. It's not like he's just some random stranger off the street. And he's an angel to boot; you can't get much purer than that.

At least I don't think you can ...

"How many women have you had sex with since you came to Earth?" I ask Ethan point blank.

He immediately stops kissing my neck in order to look into my eyes, and I feel like I've just dumped the verbal equivalent of a cold bucket of ice water on the situation.

"Why is that important?" he asks. "Especially right now."

"I don't know how it works here on Earth," I say, "but on my world, we have things known as sexually transmitted diseases. If you've been with a lot of women, you need to be tested before we go any further."

I can tell I have indeed broken the mood when Ethan takes a step back from me.

"I'm human," I say as an explanation for my caution. "There are some diseases that can kill me or, at the very least, make me sick."

"Don't take my pulling away as me not understanding your

concerns," he replies. "I just never considered it a possibility that I could have a disease. Angels don't normally get sick, but to be on the safe side, I can have Desmond run the necessary tests before tonight."

"I'm sorry if I completely destroyed the mood," I apologize, feeling like a dolt for being the STD patrol girl.

"Don't be sorry," Ethan tells me, bringing me back into his arms. "I should probably take you home now, though, so I can go see Desmond and get checked out."

"How long is it until the party?" I have to ask because I'm not sure how long I slept after I got home.

"It's in a couple of hours."

"A couple of hours!" I start to panic. "I haven't had time to go shopping to find something to wear!"

"I don't think Anna or Malcolm will care what you wear to it. They just want you there."

"But I care," I say, realizing Ethan still hasn't mastered the thought processes of females yet. We don't like to be under- or overdressed for a social function. Both are sins against fashion and good manners. "My mom probably has something I can borrow. We're about the same size. Taking me home is probably a good idea. I'll need some time to get ready."

Ethan touches me on the shoulder and phases me to the living room of my apartment.

"I've always wished I could phase," I say, feeling a tinge of envy. "Instant travel beats walking any day of the week."

Ethan leans over and kisses me on the cheek. "I'll come back here to get you in a couple of hours."

"Okay," I say, wondering something. "Why is it that you haven't kissed me on the lips yet?"

"I was hoping to share our first real kiss with you tonight, if that's all right."

"Yes. I would like that. I was just confused. I mean, it felt like you wanted to ravish me in your bedroom just a minute ago, but we haven't even had a mouth to mouth kiss yet. It just seemed odd is all."

Ethan smiles. "If we're going to follow your rules of dating, then I would like to make all the small steps we take in between as special for you as I can. Is that all right? Or do you want me to go faster?"

"Can we be flexible about it all?" I suggest. "And decide on things together as they happen?"

"I can be flexible," Ethan promises, but the statement sounds more sexual in nature by the deep timbre of his voice.

"Go get tested," I urge him. "I may want a demonstration of just how flexible you are sooner than you think."

Ethan begins to laugh but phases away before I can hear it end.

I quickly go to my bedroom, grab my phone off the nightstand, and call my mom.

All I'm able to get out is a quick, "Hey, Mom."

"Jules!" I hear her call out from the living room.

I end my call, and before I can even stand from the side of the bed, my mother phases into the room.

"Oh, thank goodness," she says, bringing me into her arms as soon as I stand.

"Mom, too tight," I squeak out as she continues to squeeze me. She loosens her grip, but doesn't let me go.

"Enis and I came over here earlier when Roan told us you were back home. We were surprised you didn't call us yourself to let us know, but I guess you were exhausted from everything because we found you sound asleep when we phased over here."

"I'm sorry," I apologize. "I should have called you before I fell asleep. I was just so tired I didn't even think about it."

"It's okay," she says, letting me go to take a step back and look at me.

I see her squint at the robe I'm wearing.

"Is that new?" she asks. "I don't remember you owning a bathrobe."

"I just came back from Cirrus," I tell her. "I had to see Ethan."

"Cirrus?" From the perplexed and surprised look on her face, I already know what her next question will be. "Who took you to Cirrus?"

I could lie and say Zane did, but I don't lie to my mother. It was one of the most important rules we had in our house when I was growing up because I knew either my mom or Uncle Enis would always know if I lied to them.

"Helena took me to see him," I admit.

My mother crosses her arms over her chest before asking, "And why, pray tell, was she even here?"

"To eat all of my peanut butter?" I say jokingly to lighten the mood.

"Jules ..." my mother replies in that voice that lets me know she's quickly losing patience with me.

"You're not going to like the real answer any more than that one," I tell her. "She told me that the baby has basically hijacked her powers and that he was the one who brought her here and wouldn't let her leave. Then she ate all my peanut butter and phased me to see Ethan so he and I could talk."

"Are you and Ethan having problems?" she asks before looking pointedly at my robe. "Or has your relationship progressed further than I thought?"

"A little bit of both, I guess," I say.

I go on to tell my mother everything about my time in King Manas' black fortress and Ethan's refusal to even look at me after the duel. I also tell her that against all odds, Ethan and I are soul mates.

"Enis and I already assumed that the two of you were," she reveals.

"And you didn't think I needed to know that kind of information?" I ask in surprise.

"For humans, being someone's soul mate doesn't automatically mean you'll fall in love with that person. And since you've gone through so much in the past few years, we weren't sure you would open yourself up to Ethan."

"I'm making him get tested for STDs," I tell her. "Saying it out loud like that makes it sound sort of stupid now that I think about it."

My mother smiles. "I seriously doubt he has a disease, unless War Angel biochemistry is different for some reason. But it's better to be overly cautious. I'm glad all of my talks about such things sunk into that thick skull of yours."

"That's all you and Uncle Enis talked about when I was a teenager. I don't know why though. Timothy was my only lover."

"Yes, that's true," my mother says, averting her gaze from mine like she's hiding something from me.

"Mom ..." This time it's my turn to use the warning voice. "What aren't you telling me? You have that guilty look you get when you don't want to tell someone bad news."

My mother looks back at me and seems to deliberate about whether or not to voice what's on her mind.

"Just let it go, Jules. What happened is in the past now, and you have a chance at a beautiful future with Ethan. At least, I assume you've decided to give him a chance."

"Yes. I'm giving him more than a chance, but you need to tell me what it is you're keeping from me. Spill it."

My mother sighs in resignation. "I'll tell you, but you have to promise me that you won't let it affect the happiness you're allowing yourself to experience right now."

"Just say it!" I yell, becoming upset with all of her delays.

"When you were teenagers, we discovered that Timothy had multiple partners."

I feel sure if I'd had anything inside my stomach, I would have thrown it all up with my mother's revelation.

"You knew he was cheating on me, but you didn't tell me?" I ask her, angry and confused that my mother and Uncle Enis kept this information from me for so long. "Why didn't you ever say anything?"

"Who were you going to believe at the time? Me and Enis, or your beloved Timothy? You were young and in love, and we knew that if we tried to tell you, we would run the risk of losing you. After we discovered what he was doing, we did the best we could. Enis threatened to kill him if he ever cheated on you again, and I made sure Timothy was tested for every known disease."

"Since Uncle Enis didn't kill him, I assume that means he stopped cheating on me."

"He did," she tells me, pausing because she has more to say but doesn't seem to want to say it. "But after the accident, he did seek out female companionship again."

"How could I have been so blind?" I ask. "How did I not see the type of person that he was until it was too late?"

"You loved him," she says by way of explanation. "In hindsight, we know we should have told you about his affairs while you were teenagers, but we acted selfishly because we didn't want to risk losing you."

I sit down on my bed, feeling as though my whole life has just been one long lie.

"Why didn't you tell me any of this after he committed suicide?" I have to ask. "Why did you let me mourn his death when you knew all of this about him?"

"Would it have helped if we had told you about his unfaithfulness, or would it have sent you even farther over the brink? We couldn't take the chance that it would do the latter. We couldn't lose you because of that bastard."

Now it all made sense. I never could understand the underlying hostility between my mom, Uncle Enis, and Timothy. Now, as I think back on it, I realize that the tension between them all started while he and I were teenagers. How could I have been so blind to the type of man he truly was?

My mother sits down beside me while I process the secret she just revealed to me about a man I once thought I knew better than anyone else in the world. Now, I realize I didn't know him at all. Perhaps I never did.

"Why did he stay with me?" I question. "If he wanted other women, he should have just left me."

"I think Timothy loved you, in his own way."

"No wonder Uncle Enis always hated him."

"Not always," she reminds me with a sad smile. "When you were children growing up, we both loved him a great deal. When we found out that he betrayed you, if felt like he betrayed us all."

"I was such a fool. I should have seen the type of man he was."

"I think a part of you did in the end, but by that time, you were so angry at him all we could hope for was that you would eventually let him go. We had no way of knowing things would end so tragically."

I feel numb. The man I thought I knew and wanted to build a life with was nothing more than a liar. I almost let my guilt over Timothy's suicide ruin what I might be able to have with Ethan. I'm being given the opportunity to experience real love now, and I get to do that with an angel who's my soul mate.

"Thank you for telling me, Mom," I say. "I guess I needed to hear the whole truth to make it easier to move on. I can't change what happened in the past, but I can affect what happens in my future."

"Ethan's a good man," my mom says, looking happy and excited that I'm finally ready to start thinking about my future again. "He will be loyal to you now and forever. I have no doubt about that."

"Me either," I say, finding a reason to smile.

I realize now that it's time for me to let my past remain there. Everything—good and bad—has forged me into the person I am today, but my future doesn't have to be a mirror of my past. I'm ready to move on. I'm ready to build a life that I want to live.

CHAPTER 18

"I don't think I've ever dressed up as much as I have these past few days," I declare to my mother as I sit on the stool in front of the vanity in her bedroom. Applying makeup has never really been my strong suit, but since we're running short on time, I do the best I can while my mom rummages around in her closet to find me something suitable to change into.

"Did they make you wear formal clothing while you were in King Manas' fortress?" my mother calls out from her walk-in closet.

"Yes, but the clothing wasn't the problem. The people were. I don't know what's wrong with them, but everyone I met who lived inside Manas' palace needed a good spanking."

My mother laughs. "I can't say I've ever been to Laed-i. In fact, I don't think any rebellion angel was ever stationed there."

"Probably because there wasn't any need. I'm sure the Manas family was already making it an intolerable planet to live on without any rebellion angel help."

Through the reflection in the vanity's mirror, I observe my mother walk out of her closet carrying a dress I've never seen her wear before. I turn around on the stool and watch as she lays it out on her bed. The dress is mauve and composed of alternating sheer lace and solid material panels. You can tell that it's a couture dress by the cut, style, and intricate detail work, especially along the left side where an expertly designed raised fabric detail curves up along one hip, arches between the breasts, and ends around the lower part of the left sleeve. A set of tiny rosettes cover the top of that particular sleeve while its match on the other side is left bare.

"That dress is gorgeous," I croon. "Why have I never seen you wear it?"

"Oh, I didn't buy this for me," she says. "I bought it for you a couple of years ago."

"For me?" I ask, perplexed by the notion that she's kept this gown hidden away in her closet all this time. "Why?"

My mom sighs and smiles wanly as she looks away from the dress to me.

"I was hoping that you would drag yourself out of your depression and find a suitable young man to go out with on a proper date. Plus, when I saw it at the shop, I knew it was made for you. I just pray that you haven't lost too much weight for it to fit properly."

"Only one way to find out," I state, standing up and walking over to try the dress on.

Luckily for me, the dress fits perfectly. My mother hands me a pair of matching shoes that can't even be seen until I walk because of the long mermaid style bottom of the dress.

"And you look as beautiful as I thought you would in it," my mother declares with a smile on her face as she gazes at me with a look of immense pride.

"You don't think this dress is too fancy to wear to a kids' party?" I ask.

"This isn't the type of event that will have cake and clowns, Jules," she tells me, walking back into her closet presumably to find herself something to wear. When she comes back out with a simple light blue chiffon dress, she continues. "This party is meant to introduce the people of Cirrus to their future rulers."

"Seems like a lot of responsibility to place on such young shoulders."

"It'll be years before they ascend to the throne. I believe Anna and Malcolm simply want to make sure their citizens feel connected to the children while they're still young. Having a close relationship with the people they govern will undoubtedly make them better rulers in the long run. And considering the fact that the next generation of War Angel-human hybrids are already being conceived, I'm afraid Liana and Liam won't have a quiet or easy life."

"I'm sure Anna and Malcolm will prepare them for their futures well. Neither of them seem to be weak minded."

"They're some of the strongest people I know. They've been through a lot—both together and individually—and I'm afraid they still have more to go through, especially since there are three princes of Hell still in control of their own cloud cities on Earth."

"Do you think I'll see any of them tonight?" I ask.

"Oh, I highly doubt they were invited. If they do show up, it's because they're crashing the party. Now, help me with my dress so we're not late arriving there."

"Ethan is supposed to be picking me up in a few minutes," I tell her as she sheds her clothes and I hold out her dress to make it easier for her to step into.

"Just zip me up and I'll take you right back," she says. "Enis and I will go ahead of you to make sure everything is clear."

"You make it sound like we're entering a war zone," I joke.

"It's hard to tell what kind of scene you might walk into on Earth," she replies in all seriousness. "Hale and the other rebellion angels who decided not to take God's offer of forgiveness are still out there. Even though I doubt they'll show their faces tonight, you never know. They're all a little unhinged, especially Hale. When you're dealing with people who have nothing left to lose, it's never a good idea to turn your back to them. You always have to be on your guard."

"That doesn't seem like any way to live your life, though. Always having to look behind you to make sure no one is sneaking up to stab you in the back? No thanks."

"Sometimes you just do what you have to, Jules, and make the best of a bad situation. I think Anna and Malcolm have figured out how to balance everything and still provide their children with a good life. You've met Lucas, haven't you? He's probably one of the most confident and well-adjusted young men I've ever met."

"I would have to agree with you there," I say, looking at the clock and seeing that it's almost time for Ethan to return to my apartment. "Okay, Mom, phase me back home. I don't want to keep him waiting."

My mother does as I say without question. Once we're standing in my living room, she leans over and gives me a small kiss on the cheek.

"I'll see you in Cirrus, and smile, Jules, you look lovely," she tells me.

After my mother phases away, I end up standing awkwardly in the center of my living room waiting for Ethan to arrive. One reason I don't sit down to wait is because I'm afraid it might wrinkle my dress, and secondly, I want Ethan to get the full effect of me when he phases into the room. Thankfully, I only have to wait about five minutes before he phases in a couple of feet away from me.

Ethan is wearing a simple black suit, but the way it fits his body so perfectly leaves me speechless. Even if he wasn't my soul mate, I know I would still consider him the most handsome man I'd ever met.

I watch as his eyes travel the length of me with a lingering gaze, as if he's making sure he notices every detail.

"Jules," he says, "you look gorgeous."

"Right back at ya," I reply, unable to prevent myself from smiling at him and doing my own ogling. "Do you think I'll fit in at the party?"

"No," Ethan answers, meeting my gaze, "you'll definitely stand out in that dress, but in a good way. I fear I may end up having to beat off a few would-be suitors this evening."

"You could be right about that," I say, looking down at myself. "I do look pretty hot in this dress."

"I think that might be the understatement of the century," Ethan states.

I smile so wide after hearing Ethan's words that my cheeks begin to ache.

He walks up to me and holds out his left arm, crooked at the elbow for me to take.

"Come on," he says. "We shouldn't deny the people of Cirrus an opportunity to see what true beauty looks like."

"If you keep flattering me like that, I may just have to kiss you for it," I tease.

"Then you can count on me flattering you all night long," he replies with a small grin. "Oh, and Desmond has given me a clean bill of health. So if you want to take advantage of me this evening, by all means, feel free."

I laugh. "I'm pleased to know that you're healthy, and I will certainly consider you a strong candidate for ravishment later tonight."

Ethan looks at me with raised eyebrows. "Only a strong candidate?"

"Okay," I relent, "the only candidate, but don't tell my other would-be suitors that. I would hate to break their hearts."

"I think my heart is the only one you'll have to worry about this evening," he murmurs.

I look him straight in the eyes and say, "You don't have to worry about that because breaking your heart would break mine too, and I've decided to make more of an effort not to do that anymore."

"I'm glad to hear it," he replies, looking more than pleased by my words. "And I promise to never do anything to make you change your mind about that."

"I'm glad to hear it," I tell him, using his own words to express how much what he just said means to me too.

"Do you need to grab anything before we go to Cirrus?" he asks.

I suddenly feel a well of panic rise inside my chest. "Was I supposed to bring a gift for the babies?"

"No, this isn't that kind of party," he reassures me. "You only need to bring yourself."

"Good. I'm not sure I would have known what to buy a prince and princess of a cloud city anyway. They probably have more than they need as it is."

"They do have what they need, but Malcolm and Anna are very cautious when it comes to spoiling them. They never want the children to feel like the world owes them anything. They want the kids to feel privileged to have what they're given, not entitled."

"Why isn't Lucas in line to inherit the throne?"

"He isn't related to either Malcolm or Anna by blood. Malcolm adopted him when he was just a baby, and according to the law in Cirrus, only a direct blood descendant can rule after Anna and Malcolm are gone."

"That's a shame. Lucas is so bright and considerate of others. I'm sure he would have made a great leader."

"You don't necessarily have to have a title to have power. I feel sure the twins will go to their big brother for advice when they need it."

I take in a deep breath before saying, "Okay, let's go before I lose my nerve."

"Why are you nervous?"

I look at Ethan and say, "I'm nervous because I feel like this is the first step I'm taking into a life I want, and I know how much Anna and the others mean to you. I guess I'm worried that I may not fit into your world, but I want you to know that I'll do my best to blend in."

"Jules," Ethan says, looking confused by my words, "you already are a part of my world. Anna loves you. Malcolm respects you, and my men think you're strong enough to put up with my moods."

"Your moods?" I ask, finding it hard not to smile uncertainly. "What exactly is there to put up with?"

"For one, I can be surly on occasion ..."

"Ah, like the time we first met?" I ask knowingly. "I've been meaning to ask you something about that since Anna explained a few things to me about soul mates. From what she said, you should have known the instant you saw me that I was your soul mate. Did you?"

"Yes."

"Then why were you so argumentative with me during that whole conversation? I thought for sure you hated me."

Ethan sighs heavily. "Can I answer that honestly without it hurting your feelings?"

"Sure," I say hesitantly, not liking where this conversation is going.

"Initially, I was disappointed that you were my soul mate."

I don't say anything because I feel sure he has more to tell me, and I want to hear it all first before I let his words affect me.

"All you seemed to be interested in was getting paid to find Helena," he goes on to explain, "and I couldn't understand how my soul mate could be concerned about money when there was so much more at stake. But it didn't take me long to figure out that you were exactly the type of person I needed in my life, and amassing a personal fortune wasn't your primary goal."

"I can understand that," I tell him, truly meaning it. "The part of my personality you met first was the bounty hunter part. I have to be ruthless and not budge when it comes to getting paid. It's just part of the job."

"I know that now, but during our first encounter, I didn't."

"There's a lot about me that you don't know yet, but I hope, given enough time, you'll become familiar with everything. Now, let's go to Cirrus before my mom and Uncle Enis come looking for us."

Ethan phases us to the ballroom of Anna's palace. I remember looking inside it from its veranda the first time I was brought to Cirrus. Back then, I could only imagine what kind of parties were held within its walls. Now, I'm a part of one. As I look at the people already present, I can see that my mother was right about my outfit blending in well among the other guests.

"Evelyn! She's here!" I hear my Uncle Enis shout.

My mind suddenly flashes back to a school dance where my mom and uncle were chaperons. I was uncomfortable the whole night because at least one of them always kept their eyes on me. Sometimes, I feel like they'll never stop watching over me, but in a way, I guess I hope they don't. You should always have someone watching your back, and who's better qualified to do that than the people who love you most in the world?

"Well, look at you all dressed up," I say to Uncle Enis as he and my mother walk over to us. "You clean up nicely, Uncle Enis. It's been a long time since I saw you in a tuxedo."

I remember the last time he wore one. It was at my wedding, but I don't particularly want to bring that occasion up with Ethan so close. Tonight is supposed to be about making a fresh start, and mentioning my marriage to another man just doesn't seem appropriate.

"I couldn't very well meet the future rulers of Cirrus and not at least make an effort with my appearance," my uncle tells me, straightening his bow tie to perfection.

"Besides," my mom says, "he's my escort this evening. I wasn't going to show up with someone who looked like a street urchin."

"I don't dress that badly," Uncle Enis protests.

"Eh," I say. "Sometimes you do, so I have to agree with Mom on this one."

Uncle Enis looks at Ethan. "Do you see how they treat me? Are you sure you want to be a part of this family, Ethan? Sometimes I feel like the two of them gang up on me unmercifully."

"Only because they love you," Ethan points out.

"True," my uncle says, looking straight into Ethan's eyes, "and I love them too. Just so we're clear on that. Jules may not be my daughter by blood, but I love her more than anyone in this universe."

It doesn't take a genius to read between the lines of Uncle Enis' words, and Ethan seems to readily pick up on the warning held within them.

"I understand" is all he says in response, but it seems to be enough to earn a nod of mutual understanding from my uncle.

"Ladies and gentlemen, may I have your attention please!"

With those words, everyone's eyes are drawn to the dais in the room where two gold throne chairs are situated. I see Jered standing there, waiting for everyone to stop talking and give him their undivided attention.

"First of all," he says with a congenial smile, "I would like to thank all of you for coming this evening to meet the future rulers of Cirrus, Princess Lillianna and Prince Liam. Empress Anna and Emperor Malcolm asked me to say a few words on their behalf before they and their children join us. Although we've all had a rather tumultuous year, peace and prosperity have blessed each of us since returning to Cirrus. In the next few years, the empress and emperor intend to continue their work in the down-world, which should greatly benefit us all in time. As their children grow stronger, so will Cirrus and its territories. If we all strive to work together, nothing can stop us from remaining the most powerful cloud city on Earth!"

People begin to cheer their support of Jered's words. Some do so with great gusto and some with reserved optimism. There are a few in the crowd who simply stand still and do nothing in order to show their doubts about Cirrus' future. I'm not really surprised by their pessimism. You can't please everyone, especially when politics are involved. Considering how many people do seem to support what

Anna and Malcolm are doing, I would call their reign a very successful one so far.

"Now, please help me welcome your future king and queen, Princess Lillianna and Prince Liam!"

As if they were listening for Jered's introduction, Anna and Malcolm phase onto the dais with their children while Jered quietly steps off to the side of the platform. The thunder of applause from the crowd is almost deafening. From what I understand, this is the first time anyone outside of the palace has been allowed to see the twins, and the picture the five of them make as they stand together on the dais is rather awe-inspiring.

Malcolm stands proudly in a white suit that is cut similarly to Ethan's outfit. He has Liam perched in the crook of his right arm while holding one of Lucas' hands. When Liam begins to squirm in his father's hold, Malcolm has to let go of Lucas in order to reposition his testy little prince.

Anna is wearing a beautiful lavender gown befitting an empress. The body of it is sheer lace with swaths of chiffon strategically placed along the front and down the skirt. The gown flows around her body as she moves, surrounding her like a cloud of pure elegance. Liam and Lucas are wearing suits that match their father's while Liana looks like an angel in a full-skirted white sleeveless dress that has lavender butterflies embroidered into the skirt.

As soon as the applause dies down, Anna speaks.

"Thank you all for coming here tonight and welcoming the latest additions to our family and to Cirrus. Our greatest hope is that you will all become an extended family to Liana and Liam. Each of us have suffered losses and hardships over this past year, but I, for one, only see a bright future ahead of us all."

"I'm glad to see that *someone* has a bright future ahead of them," a new voice says, interrupting what was supposed to be Anna's chance to speak to her citizens.

Everyone standing on the dais looks over the crowd gathered in front of them toward the grand staircase in the room. Most of us turn to discover the identity of the interloper of the celebration. Standing at the top of the stairs is a nice looking young man with brown hair and intense eyes. He's dressed in a severe military style black uniform.

"Silas," I hear Ethan whisper in surprise as he keeps his eyes fixed on the young man.

"Is that Jered's son?" I ask him, chancing a glance in Jered's direction and clearly seeing the answer to my question. The devastation and remorse Jered feels as he gazes upon the son he's been searching for is clearly written on his face. "Why is he here?"

"Whatever the reason, it can't be a good one," Ethan says as he turns his head to the right to look at Roan through the crowd. It's only then that I notice that both Roan and Gideon are looking toward Ethan, as if awaiting special orders.

Ethan looks at each of his men and then up to a particular vantage point on either side of the staircase on the second level.

"I'll be right back," Ethan whispers to me. "Stay close to your mom and Enis in case there's more to this than an awkwardly timed family reunion." Ethan looks at my mom, who is still standing beside me. "Take her back to Sierra if things get out of hand here. This may be meant to act as a distraction for a more coordinated attack by Hale and his followers. I need to go position more of my men around the area in case it is."

"I've got her," my mom tells Ethan, taking hold of one of my hands with her own. "Go do what needs to be done."

Ethan leans over and kisses me on the cheek before whispering in my ear, "Stay safe."

He phases before I'm able to make a reply or return his kiss. I sigh in disappointment because I don't want him to leave. Every time we part, there's an emptiness that forms inside my chest as though a piece of me is missing. I begin to wonder if this is how all soul mates feel when they're parted from one another.

A tense silence falls over the assemblage as we all wait for someone to break it.

"Hello, Father," Silas says, staring down at Jered with unbridled contempt. "I heard you were looking for me. Well, here I am!" he declares, spreading his arms wide as if daring his father to say what's on his mind in front of the whole crowd.

Jered phases up to his son and reaches out to take him by the arm, but Silas backs away, just out of his father's reach.

"I would rather discuss matters in private, Silas," Jered tells him. "And this is not the place or the time to make a spectacle of yourself."

"Perhaps you're right," Silas agrees, nodding his head as he makes a pretense of considering his father's words. "Then again, what if this is the only chance you ever get to ask me for my forgiveness? I could be yanked back home at a moment's notice, and then you would spend the rest of your miserable life always regretting that you didn't seize this opportunity when you had the chance. Are you ready to live with a lifetime of regrets, Father? If you want to speak your piece, say it now!" Silas yells angrily. "Otherwise, it will only fall on deaf ears and a closed heart later. I'm giving you this one chance to make things right with me. Don't waste it."

When I look back at Anna and Malcolm to see how this public display of family drama is affecting them, I notice something odd.

"Where did Lucas go?" I whisper to my mother.

She looks up to the dais, and I see her face go slack with shock. She quickly grabs ahold of Uncle Enis' arm and says, "She came for Lucas."

Uncle Enis follows my mother's gaze and his face instantly mirrors her surprise and worry.

"This isn't good, Evelyn," he says uneasily.

"Who came for him?" I ask just as I hear Anna shout out Lucas' name.

Anna's panic as she stares at the space where her oldest son was standing gives me all the answer I need even before my mother says, "It had to be Helena. Silas only follows her orders."

Helena used Silas as a distraction to grab Lucas right out from under everyone's noses. I just don't understand why she did it. What is it that she plans to use him for, and more importantly, what will it take to make her give him back?

CHAPTER 19

(Helena's Point of View)

Lucas looks up at me as I stand behind him with my hands still resting on his shoulders.

"Hi, Helena," he says in that sweet voice of his. Normally, his innocence would grate on my nerves, but for some reason, it doesn't today. I'm not sure if pregnancy has made me soft, or if it's because I know I have a child of my own on the way and can imagine him gazing at me the same way Lucas is right now: full of naive trust.

When I take my hands off his shoulders, he calmly turns around to face me.

"You don't look surprised that I snatched you away from your parents and brought you here," I say, briefly looking around the bedroom that he and his mother stayed in while they were my guests in Hell.

"I'm not surprised," he states with a nonchalant shrug. "I knew you were coming."

I almost ask how, but of course, I already know the answer to that question. His special gift of seeing into the future is the reason I brought him here in the first place.

"Why didn't you warn your parents that I would be coming for you?" I have to ask.

"Because I think Cade would want me to help you, if I can."

"Do you already know why I brought you here?" I question him, wondering just how far into the future he was able to see.

He shakes his head. "Nope, but I'm sure you'll tell me when you're ready."

"You're such an impertinent little man," I tell him, remembering that he dislikes it when I call him a "little angel." "Most people quake at the mere thought of me, and those unlucky enough to come face to face with me in my domain cower because they know what I will do to them."

"I'm not most people," he states confidently, lifting his chin up a notch higher to prove his bravado, "and I know you won't hurt me."

"Oh really?" I say, intrigued by his foolish deduction. "What makes you believe I won't?"

"You love Cade," he says, "and Cade loves me. I don't think you'll hurt me because you know how sad it would make him in Heaven. He's already hurting because he can't be with you, and I think you love him enough not to cause him any more pain."

Lucas has always been far wiser than his young years, but I suppose that's not exactly surprising. He is the reincarnation of Gabe Kinlan, the vessel of Archangel Gabriel. I wasn't sure if Gabriel would take over Lucas' body when I brought him to Hell, but I can see that Lucas is still in full control and holding his own quite well against me. His trust in my feelings for Cade are well-founded.

"I need you to do something for me," I tell him, knowing I don't have a great deal of time. I can feel Anna and her angels on Earth trying to phase into my domain, and although I enjoyed our fun and games the last time they were here, their presence would only be a distraction that I don't need right now.

"I kinda figured that already, Helena," he tells me. "Do you want me to look into your future again?"

I vigorously shake my head. "I would rather you didn't. I already know what my future holds, and I don't need to have it confirmed. No ..." I say, placing my hands protectively on my belly. "I would like for you to show me my son's future."

"Oh," Lucas replies, looking confused. "I don't know if I can do that, Helena. He's still inside you, so I can't touch him directly."

"Yes, I've thought about that," I tell him, unsure if my relationship with Lucas is strong enough to ask for what I need him to do. "If you can place a little bit of trust in me not to hurt you, I believe I can give your powers a boost of energy. That's one reason I brought you here instead of somewhere else. I can channel the power of Hell and hopefully feed some of its energy directly into you to strengthen your gift. Are you willing to at least try, Lucas? It would mean a great deal to me if you did."

I don't like practically begging a child to do something for me, but I need to know what my son's future is destined to be. Will I be a good enough mother for him? Will he ever be able to love me as I am, or will he hate me for the things I've done and will undoubtedly do in the future? I can't help the way I view the universe. Lucifer designed me to be a destroyer of worlds and to cause as much pain and suffering as possible to humanity. To go against those two ingrained principles is like asking a river to flow upstream against the laws of nature. I am who I am, and there's no way to change that.

"I can try," Lucas says hesitantly, appearing uncertain my plan will work, "but I can't promise you that I'll see anything besides your future."

"And if you do see my future, can you keep it to yourself instead of showing me as well?"

"I'm sorry," he says, truly apologetic, "I can't control that either. I don't know if it's because I'm still so young or what. Maybe when I get older, I'll learn how to handle what I do better, but I can't right now."

I nod. "I understand. Just do the best you can then, and we'll go from there."

I reach a hand out for Lucas to take. He stares at it for a moment, and I begin to wonder if he might be rethinking his bargain with me.

"If you want to know about the baby's future," he tells me, "I think I need to touch your belly, Helena. The closer I am to him, the better."

"I suppose that makes sense," I say, finding his request a reasonable one. "Go ahead and touch me. Then I'll place my hand over yours to give you a small burst of power."

Cautiously, Lucas lifts his left hand and gently places his palm against my stomach.

I feel my son move inside me as if he senses Lucas' touch. I quickly cover his little hand with mine to diminish the risk of him inadvertently channeling my own future with his gift.

Just like the time before when Lucas showed me the aftermath of Cade's death, I can see momentary flashes of my son's future. Tears begin to burn my eyes as I watch him grow from infancy to adulthood in only a few short seconds. Not all of the moments I see are happy ones though, and I know my son will have to find his own way in the universe and learn how to handle its many prejudices and preconceived notions about him. I should feel consoled that he will always have a loving mother to go to for advice, who will support him during the hardest parts of his life, but I don't. Instead, I feel sad and angered by what I'm being shown.

Lucas removes his hand from me when the montage of my son's future stops.

"That's as far as I can see," he tells me, looking uncertain about what my reaction will be to what he just showed me. "Are you all right, Helena?"

I feel twin trails of warm tears stream down my cheeks. In order to block out Lucas' concerned expression, I close my eyes and take in a deep breath to calm the churning of my raging emotions. I have to remind myself that what Lucas showed me is only one possible future. Nothing is ever set in stone because all sentient creatures have free will. I refuse to allow the future to play out the way Lucas foresees, and I know exactly what I need to do to change it.

I open my eyes and look at Lucas, filled with a new sense of determination and purpose.

"Thank you for showing me that," I tell Lucas as I quickly wipe away my tears. "I know what needs to be done now."

Lucas narrows his eyes on me with a great deal of suspicion. "That doesn't sound good. What are you planning to do?"

"Nothing you need to worry about," I calmly reassure him, not wanting to alarm him any more than he already is.

Since the moment I brought Lucas into my domain, I've felt multiple attempts by those on Earth to phase in and rescue him. I've basically been ignoring their pitiful efforts, but now I feel an intriguing and unlikely challenger attempt to phase into my realm. On a whim, I decide to allow this one entry to see where it will all lead.

My sister's daughter, Liana, phases into the room. I can only imagine the turmoil Anna and Malcolm are feeling right now considering I have two of their children at my mercy.

Liana sits on the floor between me and Lucas with her head tilted up as she stares at me with her bluer than blue eyes. Her white hair and unique eye color are all signs that she and I are still connected to one another through the seal I gave her. Unexpectedly, she lifts her arms up to me as if asking to be picked up. She smiles and makes a happy gurgling sound like she believes her cuteness will win me over and make me do her bidding.

Since leaning down isn't exactly an option for me right now, I snap my fingers, which instantly makes her rise into the air until she's hovering right in front of me.

"And what brings you here, little one?" I inquire, wishing she was old enough to answer the question. "Your mommy and daddy are going to be very cross with you for coming to see me."

"Put her down, Helena!" Lucas orders, brandishing a silver dagger he must have had hidden inside his jacket somewhere.

"You *do* realize that dagger has no effect on me, don't you?" I ask him, amused by his daring effort. "At most, it would only give me a little sting."

"A little sting is all I need," he says bravely. "Now, put my sister down before I come and get her from you."

"Fine," I tell him, "catch!"

I fling Liana backwards, forcing Lucas to drop his dagger in order to use both of his hands to grab ahold of his sister. As soon as Lucas has her, I notice a far-off look come into his eyes, and I know he's having a vision about Liana's future. He stays that way for a good five seconds before regaining his senses.

Lucas brings Liana in close until she's snuggled safely against his chest. She wraps her chubby baby arms around his neck and begins to giggle. Lucas simply continues to hold her tightly to him and looks up at me warily. I presume he saw me in his vision about Liana's future.

Before I can ask him what he glimpsed, she phases herself and Lucas back home.

I let them leave because I have a more pressing matter to attend to at the moment. I need to kill someone in order to change the future I saw for my son, and the sooner I do it, the better I'll feel.

Without warning, a searing jolt of pain erupts along the base of my abdomen as if the muscle and skin there is about to be split in two by my son. It's the same type of pain that I felt earlier, telling me that my child is impatient to be born. It was the main reason I risked going to Cirrus during the party and used Silas' daddy issues as a distraction. The first time I felt this pain, I knew I didn't have much time left and needed to hasten my timetable for asking Lucas for his help.

My son moves again, only this time it feels like he does a complete somersault inside my womb, and I fear I know exactly what it is he's preparing to do in there.

"Not yet," I beg him as the agony of him bearing down against my pelvic bone drops me to my knees.

Pain is not a new companion to me. I've felt it many times before, but the agony I'm suffering through now doesn't even compare to my past experiences. Desmond warned me that the birth of my son wouldn't be an ordinary one and that I would need his help to ensure we both survived the ordeal. He practically begged me to come to him when it was time for my baby to be born, but I don't know if Desmond is at home right now or if he is in Cirrus for the twins' coming out party. No matter where he is, I don't have time to seek him out for help. Right now, I need to follow through with my original plan and hope that the person I need to kill happens to be home. My son will just have to wait to be born until I can secure that his future is with me.

I phase to my victim's home only to find the space devoid of her presence.

"Where are you, Jules?" I ask the empty living room. Either Jules is still in Cirrus with the others, or she's with her mother, Evelyn, in Grace House. Since both Lucas and Liana are presumably back home by now, perhaps they decided to continue the party despite my short abduction of Lucas. If that's the case, it could be hours before Jules comes back home, and I simply don't have the luxury of waiting around that long.

Considering this delay a real possibility and knowing I'm in no condition to take on all of Anna's angels at once, I decide to phase to Desmond's home in the down-world of Stratus to seek his help. I attempt to phase there, but nothing happens.

"Don't do this to me right now," I beg my son. "Mommy needs to get help. Please let me go find Desmond so he can bring you into this world safely."

Again, I try to phase to Desmond's house, but my son continues to block my powers. He obviously wants me to stay right where I am.

"Are you that eager for me to kill her?" I ask him, not sure if I'm impressed or worried that my child could be so bloodthirsty. I feel him press down even farther, as if telling me he's preparing to be born whether I'm ready for him to be or not.

My legs begin to feel wobbly, and I know it's only a matter of time before I collapse onto the floor in a helpless heap. I stumble toward Jules' bedroom. Once there, I carefully lie back on her bed, which helps relieve a portion of the pressure I'm feeling as my son stubbornly tries to enter the world.

"I'm sorry our evening together has to end so abruptly," I suddenly hear Ethan say in the living room.

"It's all right," Jules replies graciously. "I understand. You know where to find me after you've secured things in Cirrus."

"I wish I didn't have to leave you," he moans in frustration.

"Then go do your job and hurry back to me," Jules urges.

"I'll return as soon as I can," he promises her. "Get some rest while I'm gone because you'll need your strength for what I have planned for us later."

Jules giggles. "Then go. The sooner you're through, the sooner you can share these big plans of yours with me."

I hear Jules sigh sadly, telling me that Ethan has followed through with her request and has gone back to Cirrus.

The rustle of material warns me of her imminent entry into the bedroom. As soon as she steps inside, I plan to use my telekinetic powers to snap her neck and end the threat she poses to my future with my son.

Suddenly, I feel a rush of fluids gush out between my legs, soaking Jules' bed beneath me. An involuntary scream escapes my mouth as I feel my baby move as if he intends to crawl out of me all on his own.

"Helena!" I hear Jules shout in panic as she rushes toward the bed.

"He's coming," I moan, knowing that I can't kill her yet. She's of more use to me alive than dead right now. "I need your help delivering him, Jules. He won't let me phase to Desmond."

"Okay," she says, quickly taking in the situation. "I need to check to see how far along your labor is to see how much time we have. Do you mind if I look?"

"Do it," I say, giving her my consent to look between my legs. Jules stands and lifts my wet skirt up to my thighs. After she removes my underwear, I hear her gasp in surprise at what she sees.

"His head is already crowning," she tells me in a calm voice, even though I can practically taste her fear and panic in the air.

I begin to shake my head violently. "He can't come out naturally. Desmond needs to cut him out of me."

Jules takes in a deep breath as she tries to steady her nerves and think of something to do.

"I need to call my mother," she decides. "She can find Desmond for us and bring him to help you."

"I don't care what you have to do! Just get him here!"

Jules grabs her phone off the nightstand beside the bed and makes a call. Evelyn doesn't take long to answer.

"Mom, I need for you to phase to Earth and find Desmond. Helena is in my apartment about to give birth."

Evelyn suddenly appears in the bedroom, quickly assessing the situation with a single glance.

"Why are you wasting time? Go get Desmond!" I scream at her, causing the walls of the bedroom to tremble with only the power of my voice.

"How far along is she?" Evelyn asks Jules, ignoring my plea.

"The baby's head is crowning," Jules replies, "but she says Desmond told her he would need to cut the baby out because he can't be born naturally."

Evelyn meets my gaze and asks, "Why is that, Helena?"

"What does it matter?" I scream in aggravation. "I need Desmond! Find him and bring him here now!"

"Desmond was in Cirrus before Ethan brought me home," Jules tells Evelyn. "He was checking Lucas and Liana for any ill effects from being in Hell."

"And where exactly in Cirrus was he?" Evelyn asks.

"Anna's quarters."

"Don't tell my sister what's happening," I order Evelyn harshly, lifting my upper body with my arms. "If you tell her, she'll tell Ethan, and they'll both come here to take my baby away from me."

"I don't think that's the worst thing that could happen to the child," Evelyn states. "Letting you raise him seems like a much worse fate."

Even though I feel as if I'll be split in two at any moment, I'm still able to muster up the strength to reach over and grab Jules by the front of her neck. She struggles and tries to pull my hand away, but I tighten my grasp until she starts making choking noises.

"Get Desmond and bring him here alone," I order Evelyn as I hold her daughter hostage. "If you don't do as I say, I swear I will break her neck without giving it a second thought. And don't get cute, Evelyn. Don't go home and tell Enis to come here to look after Jules, or I will end her life as soon as he phases into the room. Is that understood?"

There's nothing like placing the life of a loved one in danger to make people do exactly what you want them to do. Evelyn phases to Cirrus right away, and I loosen my grasp on Jules' throat just enough to let her breathe again. Killing her will have to wait until after the birth. Right now, I need everyone's cooperation, and placing her life in jeopardy just got me what I wanted from Evelyn.

A few minutes pass and I begin to wonder just how much Evelyn truly cherishes her daughter's life. I begin to get uncomfortable lying on top of Jules' now wet bed, and I attempt to phase us somewhere else, hoping that my son will let me go where I really want him to be born. Thankfully, he does, or perhaps he's too preoccupied at the moment to prevent me from phasing us all to the cabin in the mountains where he was conceived.

I end up losing my grasp on Jules when my son makes a rather aggressive attempt to enter the world on his own. I swallow a scream as the pressure becomes too much to bear. I suddenly hear what sounds like two twigs being snapped in half.

"Was that your bones breaking?" Jules says in a hoarse voice as she gently rubs the front of her neck with one hand and looks around the bedroom of the cabin. Surprisingly, she continues to sit next to me. I'm not sure if she's an idiot or allowing her compassion for my son's survival override her better judgment.

I shake my head against her pillow as warm tears stream out of the corners of my eyes. I know exactly what just happened to my son and feel helplessly alone as he endures unimaginable pain from being trapped inside me.

"I need Desmond!" I sob hysterically as I close my eyes, unable to bear the thought of my child suffering as he vainly attempts to be born.

"I'm here, Helena."

I open my eyes and see Desmond rush to the other side of me. I assumed Evelyn would have enough sense to follow my phase trail from Jules' apartment to the cabin.

"You were right," I tell him through my tears, "he needs help, Desmond. Tear me open if you have to. I don't care what you need to do, just save his life!"

"No one is dying today, lass," he vows. "I promise I won't let that happen. Now, let me take a look to see what's going on."

Desmond performs a quick examination before opening his black leather doctor bag to pull out a slim silver laser pen and what looks like a large translucent bandage.

"Pull her dress up over her stomach," Desmond instructs Jules, who quickly complies. He then places the bandage on the underside of my belly, and it immediately clings to the skin. "This will numb the area so you don't feel me cutting into you," he tells me before placing the tip of the silver pen in his hand a few inches below my belly button. "I'm going to use this laser to make my incision. Are you ready?"

"Just do it!" I scream, partially because I'm in pain but mostly because I don't want my son to die inside me.

Desmond quickly runs the laser from one side to the other across my belly, but I immediately see worry and confusion crease his forehead as he stares at his incision in surprise.

"What happened?" I ask, because I truly couldn't feel anything. "Why aren't you getting him out?"

Desmond looks up at me.

"The cut healed almost as fast as I made it," he tells me. "I didn't realize you can heal so quickly. I can't get him out this way."

"Then use something else to cut me open!"

"I'm afraid anything I use will have the same effect."

A moment from the past comes to mind, and I know exactly what Desmond needs to slice me open with.

"You need to get Anna's sword," I tell him. "She stabbed me with it once. It might be able to cut me deeply enough for the wound to stay open and give you time to get my son out."

Desmond stands from the bed. "I'll be right back."

I can see from his phase trail that he's gone directly to Cirrus. I simply hope he's able to speak with Anna alone and that she gives him the sword without any fuss.

Of course, when he phases in with Anna carrying her sword by her side, I want to curse him out for betraying me. He must see my thoughts about his actions in my expression.

"She wouldn't let me have the sword without coming with me," he quickly explains.

"No one knows that I'm here," Anna assures me. "Malcolm went to put Lucas to bed, so he'll be preoccupied for a while. I'm only here to help you and your son, Helena. You have my word."

"Then do it," I challenge her. "Help me save my son, and maybe we can finally put all of this bad blood between us to an end, Anna."

Anna nods in relief. Her sword bursts into orange flames as she holds it up to my belly.

"Are you ready?" Anna asks Desmond. "The last time I used it, she was still able to heal quickly from the wound. I'm not sure how long the cut will remain open."

"I'm ready," Desmond says, prepared to snatch my son out of my womb as soon as Anna makes the laceration.

With skilled hands, Anna quickly runs the tip of her sword across the underside of my belly. I see Desmond begin to move in to grab my son, but then he stops and shakes his head. The distressed look he gives Anna tells me everything I need to know.

"The healing was slower than with the laser, but it's still happening too quickly for me to get him out of her," he tells my sister. "Can you think of anything else that might work?"

"Yes," Anna replies as she looks up at me. "But you're not going to like it, Helena. I think we need to use the sword from alternate Earth."

"No!" I scream vehemently. "Ethan has that sword, and you know as well as I do that he'll try to take my baby away from me as soon as he's born, Anna!"

"It's the only thing we have left to try. If we don't use it, your son can't be born," she reasons. "Once he's out, I'll talk to Ethan on your behalf. I'll order him to stand down if it comes to that. You have my word."

"Why?" I have to ask, confused by her need to help me. "Why would you even want me to keep my baby?"

"I'm not sure that I do want you to keep your son," she admits, looking openly conflicted by the notion. "I'm scared of what you might do to him not only with your love, but also with your hate. Yet there's a part of me that wonders how much sooner Lucifer would have asked for forgiveness if he had been the one to raise me. Maybe if he had, you and I could have been brought up as true sisters, and you wouldn't be going through all of this right now."

"I probably would have just killed you when he wasn't looking," I say truthfully.

"Perhaps," Anna agrees. "But maybe not, Helena. I think all you've ever wanted was to feel accepted for who you are. Cade did that for you, and you were able to open yourself up to someone else for the very first time in your life. This baby could be the key to changing who you are."

"Why does everyone keep wanting to change me?" I ask angrily. "I like who I am!"

I feel my son struggle inside me, yearning to be born and causing me pain again. Then the pressure eases, and I no longer feel him moving. I don't feel anything.

"Get Ethan's sword, but don't you dare bring him here!" I scream in panic. "I don't care what you have to do to get it, just save my son!"

"I think you mean our son."

I look over to the doorway of the bedroom and assume I'm hallucinating because the miracle I see before me can't possibly be real. I'm not the kind of creature who is allowed to have happy endings.

"Cade?" I cry as I begin to realize he isn't just a figment of my imagination. He's real because I can feel his love for me reignite my soul and fill my cold heart with warmth. I hold my hand out to him, beckoning him closer so I can feel his skin against mine once again to prove he's real.

As he steps farther into the room, so does someone else: Ethan.

The instant I see the War Angel who has been hunting me from one corner of the universe to the other, I feel betrayed by the one person I thought I could count on. The one person I love. I let my hand drop to the bed, no longer wanting to feel Cade's touch, because he's brought my enemy with him.

"He wants to take our baby away from me!" I scream in anger at Cade, feeling the warmth of my love for him turn to rage. "How could you bring him here? How could you betray me like this?"

Cade sits down on the bed beside me. Before I can protest any further, he leans down and kisses me gently on the lips. Except, it isn't just a kiss. It's the sweet breath of life. As soon as I breathe it in, I feel our son begin to move again, giving me the answer to why Cade has been allowed to come back.

"You're his Guardian Angel?" I ask Cade as he pulls away far enough to look into my eyes. His love for me is so naked on his face that my anger with him has no chance of surviving. It withers away, retreating into the deepest recesses of my soul—for now.

"Yes, I am," he answers with a small smile as he gently glides the tips of his fingers along my forehead and down the right side of my face in a gentle caress. "I'll protect him, Helena. I'll watch over our son while you're unable to."

"I can protect him," I argue. "I would never let any harm come to him. Don't you trust me enough to know that?"

"I know you would," Cade says with a note of sadness, "but you know as well as I do that you won't be the one who raises him. Lucas has already shown you his future. You know what needs to happen next."

"But why?" I cry, unable to comprehend how letting a stranger raise my son is the best thing for him. "Why can't I be the one who raises him?"

"Once he's born," Cade begins, "you will lose your ability to cross the veil between Hell and Earth. I think you've suspected for a while now that his soul is a seal, just like Liana's and Liam's souls were created from their seals. When you lose the energy of his soul, you won't have enough to remain here any longer. You'll be trapped inside your domain again."

"Then I'll take him to Hell with me and raise him there," I contend.

Cade slowly begins to shake his head. "You know that isn't right, Helena. If you raise him there, he'll soak up all of the hate in your domain and become a monster. Is that the way you see our son? As a monster?"

"He doesn't have to stay there all the time," I argue, desperately trying to figure out a way for me to keep my child. "When he comes of age, he can use the Nexus to travel to wherever he wants to go in the universe."

"He won't be able to phase," Cade reveals. "None of the descendants of War Angels will be given that ability. God decided that they shouldn't inherit that power because it would make them too formidable."

"I can go get him," Anna volunteers unexpectedly. "I can phase to Hell and bring him home with me whenever he wants to visit."

"That would solve part of the problem," Cade agrees, "but it wouldn't solve the most important one."

"What problem?" I ask, wondering why Cade is so determined to keep me out of our son's life. "Tell me why you don't want me to raise our child."

"You've become even more powerful than when I last saw you," Cade tells me. "And even though I would give everything that I am to see you grow through loving our son, that same love would destroy him, just like it destroyed me. You won't mean to do it. Just like you didn't mean to kill me, but it will happen if you try to raise him in Hell, Helena, and deep down, I think you realize that too."

"But he's the only piece of you I have left," I sob, feeling as if Cade is asking me to rip my own heart to shreds by giving up our child. "I can't lose him. I refuse to let him go!"

"Then you will doom him to death by your hands. Even I can't bring ashes back to life."

"This isn't fair!" I scream as all of my hopes and dreams of a life with my son are snatched right out of my grasp. "Why does God hate me so much? First you, and now our son! Why does He insist on taking everyone that I love away and leaving me with nothing?"

"He isn't trying to punish you," Cade says. "If anything, He wants to see you grow and become more than Lucifer made you to be. You have so much potential, Helena. If you would only see that, maybe things could be better."

"I'll never have what I want," I tell him, feeling as if my whole world is meant to be nothing but a reminder of loss and missed opportunities. "If I can't have you or our son, there's nothing left for me here to care about."

I force myself to turn my head to look at Jules, who is still sitting beside me. In the visions of the future Lucas showed me, I saw her being the mother to my son that I can never be. They'll share moments of laughter and even tears. She'll be the one person in his world that he'll feel like he can always rely on. I suppose my son could have selected a worse mother. At least he didn't choose Anna.

"My son has chosen you to be his mother," I tell Jules, earning me a surprised look from her. "Don't treat him like a replacement for the one you lost. Treat him like the gift that he is."

"Why me?" she asks in shock.

"I've seen his future and I've seen the mother you will be to him. He'll love you with all of his heart," I sob, knowing I'll never be able to see him look at me like he will Jules. "And I need for you to promise me that you'll cherish his love for you because that's something I'll never be given the opportunity to do. Give me your word that you'll never take his love for you for granted."

Jules nods. "I promise you I won't, and I'll make sure he knows who his mother is and what she gave up for him."

"No," I say, letting go of even that small portion of my son's life. "Promise me you won't tell him about me. Make him believe that he's your son, Jules. I don't want him to ever feel like he was abandoned by his parents." I look over at Ethan because I know he and Jules will be the ones to raise my son. "And you need to be the father Cade would have been to him, Ethan. Show him how to protect himself because he'll get picked on because he's different. Never let him feel ashamed of who and what he is. Can you promise me that you'll do that?"

Ethan nods. "Yes. I promise I will, Helena."

"Then use your sword and help me bring my son into the world," I tell him before my own selfishness convinces me to change my mind.

Cade positions himself beside me on the bed so we can watch the birth of our son together.

The sword Ethan has been carrying around to try to kill me with bursts into blue flames. As delicately as Anna did, he uses the tip of the sword to make an incision on the underside of my belly. Desmond immediately reaches inside my womb. I feel a slight tug and pull as he maneuvers my son's head out first. I hear those around us gasp in surprise when they see what it is that makes my son unique in the universe.

As Desmond pulls the rest of his body out, a pair of white wings glisten on his back in the light of the room. I can tell they're broken by the way they lay awkwardly against his sides. Cade stands from his position on the bed and goes to our son, taking him out of Desmond's hands and cradling him in his arms. A soft golden glow surrounds them as I watch, and I feel as if I'm an observer to a miracle. Two beautiful things happen all at once. I hear my son's first cry as he fills his lungs with the universe, and I watch him spread his wings as he opens his eyes and looks into his father's face for the very first time.

"Would you like to cut the umbilical cord?" Desmond asks Cade.

"Give us a moment first," he tells Desmond, holding our son up for me to see. "Look at how beautiful he is, Helena. Look at what you made."

All I want to do is reach out and touch my son, but I know what is normally a small act for everyone else is an impossible one for me. I would go mad from torment and end up hating myself for an eternity if I destroyed the only physical proof of Cade's love for me. I refuse to destroy him like I obliterated his father's earthly form.

"Cut the cord," I say, knowing that once the final physical link we share is severed, I will be doomed to live in my domain alone for quite some time.

Cade looks down at our son and kisses him on the forehead.

He looks between Ethan and Jules before saying, "Could the two of you come over here please?"

Jules leaves my side and joins Ethan in front of Cade. Ethan places his hand on Jules' left shoulder as Cade hands her our son. I watch with envy as she's able to hold him in the safety of her arms, knowing that I will never be able to do something so simple.

"He's your son now," Cade tells them both. "Love him as much as his mother and I do, and he will love you just as fiercely in return. If he needs my help as his guardian, I will come back, but I hope he never requires the only type of help I can provide."

I know why Cade just said what he did. If our son needs his help, that will mean that he has died and has to be brought back by the breath of life. It makes me wonder why God believes my son requires a guardian angel in the first place. As far as I know, only the descendants from Caylin and Aiden's line were granted such protection. What is it that God wants my son to do for Him in the future? If I know Him, He has a plan of some sort, and it obviously includes my child in some way.

"I can promise you both that he will always feel loved," Jules says as she looks between me and Cade.

"No more drinking," I order her sternly. "You're a horrible drunk, and I won't have my son being raised by a lush."

Jules lets out an embarrassed laugh. "I promise. No more drinking. You have nothing to worry about where I'm concerned. I have too much to live for now."

"And you have to raise him someplace where no one can tell him the truth of his origins," I say.

Jules nods in total understanding.

Cade walks back over to the side of the bed, sits down beside me, and takes my hand once again.

"Cut the cord," he tells Ethan.

"Wait!" I say, frightened that this might be the last time I see both my son and Cade again. "Give me one last kiss before you have to leave me again."

Cade smiles and squeezes my hand. "I need for you to put a little trust in me right now, Helena." He looks over at Ethan and says again, "Cut the cord."

I know when the cord is severed by Ethan's blade because I find myself on my bed inside my own room in Hell, but I'm not alone.

"How are you still with me?" I ask Cade, clasping his hand even tighter just to make sure he's real.

"Did you honestly think my father would make me leave you now when you need me the most?" he asks.

I wrap my arms around his neck, bringing him in close, but I wince in agony because the cut on my abdomen is still open.

"Lie back," Cade orders me, having sensed my reaction to the pain. "I can mend the wound."

"I don't understand why it's not healing on its own," I say, dumbfounded. "I'm in my domain now. It should have healed as soon as I returned."

"Some wounds take longer to heal," he tells me, placing his hands on the laceration. I see a golden glow emanate from his hands, just like when he healed our son's wings. "There you go. All better."

Cade returns and lies down beside me to bring me into his arms. I soak in his warmth and inhale his scent, knowing this dream can't last forever.

"How long will He let you stay with me?" I ask.

"Until it's time for me to go," Cade replies cryptically.

"Will this be the last time I ever see you?" I have to know.

"No. My father told me that I would see you two more times before the end."

"Before the end of what?"

"Before the end of everything, I suppose. All things must have a beginning and an end. He must believe we're coming close to the end of something important."

"Or it could take a millennium or two to get there." I sigh.

"However long it takes, I know I'll be given the chance to see you at least two more times," Cade says, holding me close. "And I'll take those two times gladly. It's more than most people get to have."

"Yes, it is," I agree, just before I let the weight of everything that's happened finally sink into my soul. I begin to sob uncontrollably over the loss of my son and the brighter future I thought I would be able to have with him in my life. After his birth, I believed I would be granted at least one person in the world who could learn to love me just as I am, but God must deem me unworthy of such a privilege.

As I continue to cry and attempt to unburden my heart of its loss, Cade hugs me even tighter to him, as if he never plans to let me go, even though we both know he can't stay with me forever. I may be powerful, but God is still stronger.

I don't know what God is up to, but I feel sure He has an ulterior motive for allowing Cade to stay with me. Perhaps He knew how upset I would be after being sent back to my domain permanently without my son. This could be His way of ensuring my wrath stays contained for a little while. I can't say for sure. All I do know is that this is one of the happiest and saddest days of my life. I try to keep my thoughts centered on Cade, but an image of my son's beautiful face keeps intruding into my thoughts. I'm consoled by the fact that I know Jules will be a good mother to him. I've already seen it. I just wish I could be there to watch him grow into the man I only got a glimpse of.

Perhaps one day, I'll be able to meet my son in person. As his father continues to hold me in his arms, I feel like I have proof that miracles truly can happen, even for a creature like me.

CHAPTER 20

(Jules' Point of View)

As I look down at the baby whose health and happiness were entrusted to me and feel Ethan wrap his arm around the small of my waist, a sense of finally finding my place in the universe fills my soul, causing my heart to ache, but in a good way.

"Why do you think he was born with wings?" I ask Ethan, gently stroking one wing with my free hand and finding its feathers softer than velvet against the tips of my fingers.

"I don't know," he replies, sounding as mystified as me over the small miracle cradled in my arms. Ethan looks at Desmond and says, "Do you have any idea why, Desmond?"

"I have a theory, but that's about all it is at the moment," he tells us with a small shrug. "I don't believe there's any way for me to actually prove it."

"Tell us what your theory is," Anna urges, obviously as intrigued to hear the answer as we are.

"Well," Desmond begins thoughtfully, "Helena has always had the power to make all manner of creatures in Hell. Considering she made her own body and basically her own genetic material, my theory is that she was able to manipulate the baby's genetic code into what she imagined her and Cade's child should look like. I don't even think she was aware that she was doing it, because when she visited me and we looked at him with a prenatal hologram device, she seemed as surprised as I was by his wings."

"He's so gorgeous," Anna croons, unable to stop herself from smiling at the baby in my arms.

"What are the two of you going to name him?" my mom asks, joining our little group as we all stare in awe of Cade and Helena's child.

"I understand why she doesn't want him to know who his real parents are," I say, "but I think he should have something of her and Cade in his name." I pause for a moment before I settle on the perfect one. "I think we should call him Calen, Cal for short."

"Cal," Anna says, trying the name out. "I like that. Will it be Calen Grace or Calen Knight, though?"

"I think Calen Grace Knight has a nice ring to it," I reply, giving Ethan a sideways glance to see his reaction to the combination of our last names.

His response is a smile, so I take that as a good sign that he heartily approves.

As Cal snuggles in closer against my breasts and falls asleep, I begin to wonder about Helena's other request.

"But where are we going to raise him?" I ask the group. "Helena wants us to take him to a place where no one can tell him about his true origins. Does a place like that even exist in the universe?"

"I have a suggestion," Anna says, looking warily at me as if she's not sure how I will respond to her proposal. "I actually spoke with Ethan about my idea before the party, but he said he wanted to wait and think it through first. Ethan," she says, looking at him, "my suggestion seems like a fortuitous one considering the current circumstances. It might be the safest place for all of you to go."

"Go where?" I ask, looking between Ethan and Anna.

"Laed-i," Ethan tells me. "Apparently the people there want me to rule them since I killed Manas, at least that's what Zane reported back to us. But I know you hated it there ..."

"I just disliked the pompous aristocrats who were in the palace," I correct him. "If the regular people there are anything like Verati, I think we would be happy on Laed-i. Besides," I look over at my mom, "didn't you tell me that none of the rebellion angels were ever sent to that planet?"

"Yes, that's true," she replies, looking thoughtful. "And because of that, it might be one of the most secure planets for you to raise Cal on. If we can keep the rebellion angels ignorant of his whereabouts, he'll be a lot safer. I would hate to know what Hale would do to Helena's baby if he found him. I'm sure he would try to blackmail her in some way, and I think we can all agree *that* scenario would not play out well for any of us."

"Agreed," we all unintentionally say in unison.

"So what do you think, Cal?" I ask him. "Does Laed-i sound like a good place to make our home?"

Cal smiles in his sleep. I'm sure he didn't understand a word I said. It was probably just the soft timbre of my voice that caused him to smile. Whatever the reason, I know now that he has officially captured my heart.

"Would you all mind excusing us for a moment?" Ethan says like a question when it's really more of a statement. "I would like to speak with Jules alone."

"I need to perform a thorough examination on Cal today," Desmond tells us. "Do you plan to come back here afterwards?"

"Let's meet up at Zane's house on Laed-i," Ethan replies. "I promise we'll be there in a few minutes."

Without waiting to see if anyone else has something to say or has a request to make, Ethan phases Cal and me to the planet with the magenta ocean. As we stand inside the white gazebo together, I naturally lean back into Ethan with Cal still slumbering comfortably in my arms. Ethan kisses the top of my head and hugs me close.

"I just thought we could use a few minutes alone," he tells me. "I don't think either of us were planning to become parents on our third date."

I have to smile at that. "No. Definitely not, but look at him, Ethan. He's absolute perfection."

"And he's ours," Ethan says proudly. "Cade talked to me before he brought me to your cabin. When he told me what his intentions were —that he wanted you and me to become his son's parents—I couldn't believe our luck. I knew how much you wanted to have children, and this little one was like an unexpected gift for us."

"Tomorrow is my birthday," I tell Ethan. "And I don't think I could have ever asked for a better gift."

"We'll need to move to Laed-i right away," he tells me. "It will be safer for Cal if we keep him off of either of our home worlds."

"Where will we live there?"

"I know one of Manas' castles is on the mainland, not too far away from where Zane and Verati live. If you want, we can make it our home."

"Well, I hate to tell you, King Ethan of Laed-i, but you still have to court me if you expect me to marry you one day," I state firmly. "But I'm okay with us living together under the same roof for the time being. We just have to have separate quarters."

I think we both know exactly where our relationship is headed, but even knowing that, I don't want to rush things with Ethan. I want to take all the little steps in between with him and enjoy those moments to the fullest. I never really dated. Timothy and I were just always together. So getting married was simply a natural progression of our relationship. Now, I have a man who seems to want to make me happy, and we've been given the most unique and precious child in all existence to love and protect.

"I fully intend to court you, Jules Grace," Ethan promises, dropping his hands away from me so he can turn to stand directly in front of me and Cal. "Not only do I plan to court you, but I also plan to marry you, make you my queen on Laed-i, and raise our son in a happy home just like Anna and Malcolm are doing for their children. I pledge to make our life together one that you will never regret living, and that our son will feel lucky to be a part of. The only family I've ever had are my brothers, but now I want to share the rest of my life with you and Cal. The two of you are my world now, and I want you to know that there is nothing that you can ask of me that I won't do."

"Then kiss me, Ethan Knight," I say, unable to suppress a happy smile after hearing his words, "and let our first kiss mark the beginning of our life as a family."

Ethan grins before leaning down to kiss Cal on the forehead first.

"I know I can never fill Cade's shoes, and I would never try to replace him," he whispers to Cal. "But I want you to know that I love you and will take care of you and your mother until the day I die. The two of you are my everything, and that will never change no matter what the future throws at us."

Ethan lifts his head and raises his right hand to caress the side of my face.

"I've never considered myself a lucky man, but in the last few days, I've met my soul mate, earned the right to rule a world that desperately needs a strong leader, and been given the unexpected gift of a beautiful son. If those aren't sure signs that my luck is changing, I don't know what is, Jules. And now, I get to kiss the most gorgeous woman I've ever seen and possibly share my life with her, if she'll have me."

"Hm," I say with my lips pursed, like I'm considering his request thoughtfully. "I just don't know. It really all depends on how this first kiss goes, so you better make it a good one."

Ethan's smile broadens, and I know he's beginning to understand my sense of humor.

"It'll be so good you'll never want me to stop," he murmurs with the promise of love and happiness dancing in his eyes as he comes as close to me as he can without crowding Cal.

"Bold words," I say, feeling my whole body ignite with breathless anticipation.

"True words," he replies back confidently before pressing his lips against mine and making good on his promise.

My life has never been this sweet and perfect before, and I thank Helena for entrusting me with her most precious gift to the universe. I know the life Ethan, Cal, and I will have together may not be free of hardships (almost no one is blessed with such a fairy tale ending), but I do know that Ethan and I will make sure our son feels safe, happy, and, above all else, loved.

EPILOGUE

PART 1. JULES

"What do you think?" I ask Cal as I twirl before him in my wedding gown. "Do you think your daddy will approve?"

Cal gurgles at me from his posh white silk pillow seat on the floor of the castle's living room and smiles like I'm the prettiest thing he's ever seen. I'm sure it's the way the diamonds on the gown sparkle when I move that's causing him to smile, but I also like to believe that he's just a happy baby who loves his life and his mommy.

"You know you look gorgeous," my mom says as she walks over to me with the veiled crown that goes along with the dress.

"It should considering how much this dress must have cost Anna," I tell her as she sets the small diamond and pearl crown on my head.

"Are you sure you don't want to wear your hair up?" my mother asks, studying me with her critical eyes. "I think the veil would work better if you did."

"I like wearing my hair down," I tell her for what feels like the hundredth time. "Ethan likes to tug on it, especially when we ..."

"Please stop there," my mother begs, holding up both of her hands in front of her face as if such an action will stop my next words.

"Kiss, Mom. What did you think I was going to say?" I chastise her. "Cal is sitting in the room. I'm not about to describe my incredibly wonderful S-E-X life with Ethan in front of him."

"I'm still shocked you only made Ethan wait three months before you agreed to marry him," my mom says as she fans out the back of my dress to prevent the silk from forming any wrinkles before I walk down the aisle. "You're normally not one to rush into things that are so important."

"Honestly, I would have married him the day we were given Cal, but then I thought better of it. This way, he can't claim a present is my birthday *and* my wedding gift. I'm sure to get two surprises now."

My mother chuckles. "Like you lack for anything."

I shrug. "It doesn't have to be a physical item. I'm just hoping for special day trips together when he doesn't have to worry about the state of this planet. Manas left it in more of a shambles than any of us realized. It's going to take us years to straighten things out."

"Do you think Ethan understood how much time tending to the needs of this world would take when he accepted the position?"

"I really don't." I sigh. "But Zane and Xander will be taking on more responsibilities soon, and Gideon asked to be stationed here as well."

"It seems like Anna is sending more and more of her War Angels out into the universe," my mother says, looking troubled by that development.

"Then I guess it's a good thing you and Uncle Enis will be moving to Cirrus to help keep an eye on her and her family."

"Are you sure you don't need us here? You know we would move to Laed-i instead, if you do."

I hold my hand out to my mother and she accepts it.

"Listen, Mom. I know you've been wanting to help protect Anna and her children for a long time now. This is your chance, and you need to take it! Besides, it's not like you can't phase over here every day, if you wanted to."

"I'm sure Ethan would love us interrupting his married life so frequently," she jokes.

"He knows how much you and Uncle Enis mean to me. Besides, you're family, and we will always make time for family no matter how busy our lives get."

Cal gurgles, drawing our attention back to him.

"Your mother may be marrying a handsome War Angel today," my mother tells Cal as she walks over to lift him up out of his seat, "but I get to have the most handsome angel as my escort."

"I can't even argue with that," I say, smiling at the picture my mother makes holding my son.

"I've been meaning to ask," she begins hesitantly, "has Cal shown any signs of having special abilities yet?"

I shake my head. "Not yet. We keep expecting something to happen at any time, but so far, he's just a happy little baby."

"How did you explain the wings on his back to the people on this planet?"

"That was fairly easy, actually. Since the people here don't know that much about Earth, we just told them that only the most blessed babies are born with wings. No one questioned the explanation when Ethan said it. I think Manas has everyone on this planet conditioned to accept anything the king tells them without even thinking about questioning him. It's not ideal to have such drones as citizens, but in this instance, it worked in our favor."

There's a light knock on the door, and I tell the two lovely ladies I'm expecting to come in.

Anna and Verati walk into the room dressed in their sleeveless coral bridesmaid dresses.

"You are beyond gorgeous!" a pleasantly pregnant Verati squeals with delight when she sees me.

"I owe it all to the dress," I tell her. "I can't thank you enough for having it designed for me, Anna. I've never owned anything this extravagant."

"You're becoming a wife and a queen today," she tells me. "If ever there was an occasion to wear something elaborate, this is the day. Besides, buying it allowed me to help a whole town in my down-world because they wouldn't take a handout from me."

Anna's eyes travel from me to Cal, and I see a look of sadness pass over her features.

"Can I hold him?" she asks my mom.

My mom looks to me for permission first, and of course, I nod my head.

Anna hesitates before accepting him into her arms, and I realize this is the first time she's ever asked to hold my son. I'm not sure why. She and her family have visited us on Laed-i a few times now over the past few months, but now that I think back on it, only Malcolm and Lucas have ever held Cal. It makes me wonder why she hasn't asked before this moment.

As soon as Anna touches Cal, he begins to clap his little hands together and gurgle with delight. I see a relieved smile grace Anna's face as she cradles him in her arms, being extra careful with the wings on his back.

"Hello, Cal," she says to him. "I'm your Aunt Anna. I want you to know you can count on me to always look out for you. I love both of your fathers very much, and I promise that you will never want for anything."

Cal gurgles in response to Anna's words. I have no idea what he thinks he's saying. Perhaps he's telling us all of God's plans for the universe. All I do know is that my son is happy, healthy, and wise beyond his years.

"Anna," I say, having considered the question I want to ask her multiple times but uncertain I want to hear the answer, "do you think I should abide by Helena's rule about telling Cal who his real parents are? Or do you think I should tell him?"

"That's really not for me to say," she replies, "but I believe there may come a time when you will have to tell him the truth."

"What makes you say that?"

Anna looks down at Cal. "Because he is his mother's son, and being born from Helena more than likely means he'll develop powers beyond anything we've seen before. I don't know what those powers will be, but he'll want to know where they came from. Since you're human, he'll know they didn't come from you. So, yes, I do believe you'll end up having to tell him about the woman who gave birth to him, but make no mistake about it, Jules, you will always be his mother. He will rely on your love for him as he grows and faces the hardships of the world."

"So, your advice is to wait to tell him?" I ask, just to clarify.

"You'll know when the time is right," she tells me. "And don't fear that he'll hate you for keeping such a secret from him. I was raised by a man who loved me so much that he became human for me. He never told me that Lucifer was my biological father, and I never resented him for keeping it a secret from me. Parents do what they have to do to protect their children, and Cal will understand that when the time comes."

"I hope so," I say, dreading that future day. Odds are it will be many years before that happens, but just knowing that it will scares me.

"Don't think about all of that right now," Anna urges me. "Today is a celebration of the love you, Ethan, and Cal have for one another. Focus on that and not something that will more than likely happen years from now. Enjoy happiness when it's offered to you, Jules, and let tomorrow sort itself out on its own."

Cal gurgles as if he agrees with Anna's advice to me.

There's another knock on the door right before Uncle Enis pokes his head inside the room.

"Are you ready?" he asks me. "I think the king is getting a little antsy standing up on the altar without you. And, just so you know, it's not nice to keep God waiting."

"What?" I practically yell. "Do you mean *the* God is here?"

"The one and only," Uncle Enis answers with a smile. "Ethan wanted to keep it a surprise. He said you've been hounding him to get our father to come here for a while now. So, surprise! God's officiating your wedding."

"I don't hound," I retort, walking toward the door and Uncle Enis, whose job today is to make sure I don't trip down the aisle. "I just asked if I could meet Him one day. That's all."

"Asking multiple times counts as hounding, Jules," he tells me with a congenial smile as he opens the door wider so I can walk through it and into the hallway of the castle.

"Well, it worked," I say giddily. "I'm just not sure I can take this day getting any better. Come on, ladies!" I say over my shoulder. I watch as Anna hands Cal back over to my mom while she and Verati take their positions in front of me. "We better not keep God waiting."

When I walk down the red carpeted aisle of the small chapel in the castle, I smile when I see Ethan standing before God, waiting for me to come to him. I was already told about the form God likes to use when He visits. Apparently, He chose the handsome body of a bald black man eons ago when He first met an ancestor of Anna's named Lilly. What I wasn't prepared for is the feeling of love He seems to be emanating. It fills the whole chapel, bringing me a sense of calm certainty.

I no longer feel unsure that I'll be a good enough wife to Ethan and mother to Cal. All of the doubts that I've been harboring over the past few months instantly fade away, and I know now that it was only my own fear that was feeding them.

Helena gave me her son to love and cherish. She trusts me to be the mother she can't be right now, and I have no intention of ever making her regret placing so much of her faith in me.

PART 2. GOD

Unsurprisingly, I'm met by Lucifer and Cade the instant I return to Heaven from the wedding.

"How is my son?" Cade immediately asks, looking anxious about any news I can provide about the welfare of his child.

"Happy," I tell him. "You and Helena chose his parents well, my son."

"And do you still believe our plan will work?" Lucifer asks, not sounding as certain as he once did. "How long will it take before we know for sure?"

"I have hope that everyone's paths will still converge," I reply. "But you know as well as I how unpredictable free will can be. The only thing I can be certain of is that everything hinges on her."

"I believe she's strong enough to do what must be done in the end," Cade says, full of confidence. "I refuse to believe otherwise."

"All we can do is wait and see how things play out," I tell them both. "Only time will be able to reveal the answer to us."

I see a flicker of doubt enter Cade's eyes, but I do nothing to snuff it out. Doubt can be a good thing sometimes. It can make a person strive harder for what he really wants, and that may be exactly what we need to succeed.

PART 3. HELENA

As I walk through the halls of my dark palace, I let my mind drift back to the stolen moments God gave me with Cade here. Why He decided to be so kind is still a mystery to me, but I dare not question His true motivation. In the end, it doesn't matter why He did it, or why He felt it was important for me to not feel so alone. Perhaps He was trying to give me hope, but I don't know what it is He believes I hope for. I know I can never be truly reunited with Cade, and according to what he told me, we will only be given two more chances to see one another. I have no idea when they will happen, but just knowing that they will gives me a sense of peace.

I abruptly come to a stop just as I pass the door to the room where Anna and Lucas stayed. Apparently someone has decided to come for another visit. I phase into the room and find my unexpected guest.

Liana has phased herself into my domain again and is playing on top of the bed with one of the pillows. When she sees me, she lets go of the pillow and holds her arms out to me.

I walk over to the side of the bed and just stare down at her as she continues to hold her arms up.

"You are a strange child," I tell her, dumbfounded by her presence. "Why do you keep coming here to me?"

With a huff of frustration—presumably because I refuse to pick her up—Liana takes matters into her own hands and crawls across the bed until she reaches the side I'm standing next to. She stretches her hands out and grabs ahold of my dress' red skirt in order to pull herself up until she can wrap her arms around me.

I instantly freeze, unsure what it is she expects me to do next.

"Au-hel, hug," she practically orders.

For someone so young, she sure is bossy. Was "Au-hel" supposed to be "Aunt Helena"? How does she even know who I am? I feel her squeeze me hard as she repeats her words, practically demanding that I comply with her wishes.

Cautiously, I wrap my arms around her, which seems to satisfy her needs, but it doesn't exactly help me decipher why she's here. After a few more seconds, she lets me go, plops herself back down on the bed, and looks up at me expectantly.

"I have no idea what it is you want from me," I confess.

Liana huffs again, as if I'm frustrating her by my lack of cooperation. She phases, and I can see that she's gone back to Cirrus. I feel relieved that she's gone, but my relief is short lived, because she returns within a few seconds holding a small red ball with white stars painted on it. I watch as she rolls it across the bed to me.

"P-ay, Au-Hel," she says, looking pointedly between me and the ball.

"You *are* just a one-year-old, right?" I ask her, wondering how someone so young can be so self-possessed.

Liana huffs again and looks at me disappointedly.

"All right, all right," I say, relenting to her wishes and leaning over to roll the ball back to her across the bed.

This seems to satisfy her because she giggles in glee and rolls the ball back to me.

I'm not sure what's going on with Anna's child, but I see her need to bond with me as fortuitous. I only slightly regret giving her one of the seals when she was born. That decision inadvertently doomed me to a forever life in my domain. Since I can no longer leave Hell, I wasn't sure how I would be able to continue with my plans. If these little visits with Liana end up happening on a regular basis, I may still be able to succeed. Yet, do I really want to now? I've still been granted two more visits with Cade, and I don't want to act too soon and waste those chances to see him again.

I suppose I will just have to bide my time and wait. For now, I'll play Liana's little game with her. If she decides to keep visiting her Aunt Helena as she grows up, perhaps I can slowly convince her to play one of my games and win me the universe once and for all.

I'm in no rush.

Time is the one thing I have plenty of ...

THE END...

A NOTE FROM THE AUTHOR

Thank you so much for reading *War Angel Contingent*, the first book in *The Everlasting Fire* **Series.**

If you have enjoyed this book please take a moment to leave a review to show your support. To leave a review please visit:

War Angel Contingent
http://bit.ly/WarAngelContingent-US

Thank you in advance for leaving a review for the book and I hope you enjoyed the first installment of the *Everlasting Fire Series*. The next book will be entitled *Between Cirrus and Laed-i*. This story will follow the lives of Liana and Cal from infancy into young adulthood.

The next book that I will write that takes place within the Watcher universe will be *Sweet Devotion: Mae and Tristan's Story.* I know many of you have been patiently waiting for this story since *Devoted.*

I plan to have it completed this autumn before the holiday season.

Sincerely,
S.J. West.

NEXT FROM S.J. WEST

THE VAMPIRE CONCLAVE SERIES

Moonshade, book1 of **The Vampire Conclave Series.**

"Find me, Sarah..."

When a handsome stranger whispers these three little words to Sarah Marcel, she knows her life is forever changed.

For two weeks straight, Sarah's been unable to eat, sleep, or even form a coherent thought properly. She fears she's losing her mind until a chance encounter brings a man into her life who seems to hold the key to solving her problems. With a single touch, he's able to ease her troubled soul and bring her some much-needed peace. Yet, just as Sarah believes she's found the solution to her dilemma, he disappears.

As Sarah begins to unravel a mystery surrounding her family's past, she quickly discovers her role in a world that's hidden from most humans. Being a Marcel comes with certain responsibilities, and there are some things that you can't hide from forever.

Exclusively on Amazon! FREE on KU!
Amazon US http://bit.ly/Moonshade1-US
Amazon UK http://bit.ly/Mooshade1-UK

ABOUT THE AUTHOR

Once upon a time, a little girl was born on a cold winter morning in the heart of Seoul, Korea. She was brought to America by her parents and raised in the Deep South where the words ma'am and y'all became an integrated part of her lexicon. She wrote her first novel at the age of eight and continued writing on and off during her teenage years. In college she studied biology and chemistry and finally combined the two by earning a master's degree in biochemistry.

After that she moved to Yankee land where she lived for four years working in a laboratory at Cornell University. Homesickness and snow aversion forced her back South where she lives in the land, which spawned Jim Henson, Elvis Presley, Oprah Winfrey, John Grisham and B.B. King.

After finding her Prince Charming, she gave birth to a wondrous baby girl and they all lived happily ever after.

As always, you can learn about the progress on my books, get news about new releases, new projects and participate on amazing giveaways by signing up for my newsletter:

FB Book Page: @ReadTheWatchersTrilogy
FB Author Page:
https://www.facebook.com/sandra.west.585112

Website: www.sjwest.com
Amazon: http://bit.ly/SJWest-Amazon
Newsletter Sign-up: http://bit.ly/SJWest-NewsletterSignUp
Instagram: @authorsjwest
Twitter: @SJWest2013

If you'd like to contact the author, you can email her to:
sandrawest481@gmail.com

THE EVERLASTING FIRE SERIES

Made in the USA
Columbia, SC
08 July 2017